THE RT HON. LORD HURD OF WESTWELL, CH, CBE enjoyed a distinguished career in government spanning sixteen years. He was educated at Eton and Trinity College, Cambridge, where he obtained a first-class degree in history. After joining the Diplomatic Service, he went on to serve at the Foreign Office before running Edward Heath's private office from 1968 to 1970 and acting as his Political Secretary at 10 Downing Street from 1970 to 1974. Following terms as Minister of State in the Foreign Office and the Home Office, he became Secretary of State for Northern Ireland, then Home Secretary before his appointment as Foreign Secretary in 1989. He was MP for Mid-Oxfordshire (later Witney) from 1974 until 1997. He is now the Chairman of the Prison Reform Trust charity.

Douglas Hurd, who is the author of ten books, lives in Oxfordshire with his wife Judy and their son and daughter. He has three grown-up sons from his first marriage.

THE SHAPE OF ICE

Douglas Hurd

A *Warner* Book

First published in Great Britain in 1998 by
Little, Brown and Company
This edition published by Warner Books in 1999

A CIP catalogue record for this book is
available from the British Library.

ISBN 0 7515 2363 1

Typeset in Goudy by M Rules
Printed and bound in Great Britain by
Clays Ltd, St Ives plc

Warner Books
A Division of
Little, Brown and Company (UK)
Brettenham House
Lancaster Place
London WC2E 7EN

For

Philip and Jessica

7.xii.02

U3A

Witney.

The Convergence of the Twain
(Lines on the loss of the *Titanic*)

In a solitude of the sea
Deep from human vanity,
And the Pride of Life that planned her, stilly
couches she.

Jewels in joy designed
To ravish the sensuous mind
Lie lightless, all their sparkles bleared and black and
blind.

Dim moon-eyed fishes near
Gaze at the gilded gear
And query: 'What does this vaingloriousness down
here?' . . .

Well: while was fashioning
This creature of cleaving wing,
The Immanent Will that stirs and urges everything

Prepared a sinister mate
For her – so gaily great –
A Shape of Ice, for the time far and dissociate.

And as the smart ship grew
In stature, grace and hue,
In shadowy silent distance grew the Iceberg too.

Alien they seemed to be:
No mortal eye could see
The intimate welding of their later history.
Or sign that they were bent
By paths coincident
On being anon twin halves of one august event,

Till the Spinner of the Years
Said 'Now!' And each one hears,

And consummation comes, and jars two
hemispheres.

Thomas Hardy

Chapter One

Sunday August 31

Perhaps she was right. Because he was still angry with his wife, the thought that she might be right depressed him. He was striding, fast to show fury, up through the neat olive trees. There was no path and he had to scramble up on to each terrace in turn, which was undignified. He paused to look back down at Louise by the swimming pool. She had levered her blue canvas beach chair to a sitting position. Her smooth, grey hair was entirely orderly. There was no agitation in her next move, which was to take up the two-day-old *Daily Mail*. She was calm; he usually fussed at the beginning of their arguments. That, and the fact that she was five years his senior, gave her the first, though not always the last, advantage.

'You talk about service, you mean giving orders. That's what you enjoy. It's not helping others, it's your own superiority, that's what you won't give up.'

Those had been her last, most wounding words. Simon pushed on up the olive grove until it narrowed to a point. A hedge fringed with ripe blackberries separated the olives from a deep country lane. He knew where the thorns were thinnest and how to pick his way down the slope to the road. Then up past the cemetery and the beehives to the big church of San Leonardo on the ridge.

They were arguing about whether he should retire as Prime Minister of Britain. He was only fifty-five. He felt fine and everything the doctors now said about that heart attack in the spring was reassuring. At least, everything they said to him. Simon had known some years back a man who had been touched by death and recovered. That man, an Arab, had thereafter changed his whole cast of thought and way of life. The crisis past, he handled each day as if it was an uncovenanted gift to be spent with meticulous care. Simon did not feel that way in August, after his deep stabs of pain and fifteen minutes of unconsciousness in March; but Louise did. She carried on her shoulders the fear of his death, or so she said. Only rest, rest, rest, the lifting of burdens, the banishing of red boxes, would keep him alive. She had calmly argued with an authority surpassing that of doctors. As his compromise, they were resting here for a fortnight, in this Tuscan farmhouse, friendly from many past summers, lent to them by old friends. But Louise had so far refused to accept the holiday as a compromise. This afternoon she had reopened the barrage for his immediate resignation and retirement.

Simon knew the church at the top of the hill would be shut. Anyway it was unappealing, a gaunt yellow and brown product of the late 1920s. But beyond the campanile, right on the edge of the spur of hillside looking north to the Arno, lay a small scruffy garden. He had often come here to empty his mind of holiday trivia and force it towards the future. These olives were older and thinner than those in the grove he had just left, gnarled and unproductive. At the foot of each tree was a small inscribed grey stone, one or two of them split by the roots of the tree. '*Giovanni Alghieri, Caporetto 1917*', then '*Georgio Alghieri, Isonzo 1917*', then '*Patrizio Fulci, Vittorio Veneto 1918*', and so on for twenty trees. Then a few more with larger, newer stones, still grey and local, but these with photographs of young men. '*Franco e Bernardo Antonelli, vilmente uccisi dalla soldataglia tedesca 8 maggio 1944*'. Wars had fortunately stopped (for the time being) just as the space available in the garden was exhausted. The left-wing municipality had sought, unsuccessfully, to sum up the matter with an abstract sculpture in alien white soapstone in the centre of the path, 'A *tutte le vittime delle guerre*'. Simon felt that the olive trees did it better.

'Service'. Those conscripts of the Great War no doubt had some vague notion of service as they were driven against the Austrian positions on the costly mountains and rivers of the north.

Later on, in the Second War, did Francis and Bernard join the partisans in order to serve their country or to give orders to others? Did their wives, like Louise, tell them not to be silly, to stay at home and harvest the olives? Of course the stakes that Simon Russell put on the table were different, and smaller. To be vilely killed by the German soldiers was harsher than any penalty to be endured by the Prime Minister of Britain.

The sun was in the west now, beginning to hover over the jagged mountains of Carrara across the broad valley beneath him. All that marble had come from those mountains for all those monuments, to popes, princes, poets and the more successful politicians. They were attempts to persuade an ignorant posterity shuffling by that their rulers had also been servants, of God and man.

He wondered if his colleagues in the Cabinet ever thought of these matters. Rather than force his mind back to Louise's question and his own future, he let it stray to speculation about Peter Makewell. The Foreign Secretary pretended to dislike foreign food and foreign travel, though he had managed to survive plenty of both during four years in his present post. Whether through genuine choice or to preserve this austere reputation, he would be taking his holiday in Scotland, in a lodge of creaking dark brown wood, tepid rust-coloured bathwater and enormous breakfasts. Simon and Louise Russell had gone stalking there one autumn. It had been Louise who shot the stag.

By contrast the Chancellor of the Exchequer would be taking no holiday. Simon was not at all sure where Joan Freetown was spending that August, but it did not signify.

Whether in Switzerland or Long Island or her own rectory in the Cotswolds, she would be at work. For her a holiday comprised a switch from the company of Treasury officials and red boxes to that of professors and directors of think-tanks. She would be working by now on the third draft at least of her speech for the Blackpool Party Conference in October. Before long his fax would rattle with some proposal of great rigour and complexity that she wished to include. Simon's thoughts turned more happily to the last of his significant colleagues. Roger Courtauld, Home Secretary, would simply be enjoying himself with family, bat, bucket and spade. His Conference speech would be the most difficult of all. The prisons were overflowing and the police cells bulged expensively with prisoners on remand. Army camps had been commandeered. On the other side of the coin, the burglars locked up five or six years back had, to a large extent, served their sentences. They were now romping out to resume their chosen profession, pushing up the crime figures all over again.

But Roger Courtauld down in Devon would not be bothering himself with any of this. His Conference speech would be scribbled in a Blackpool hotel at around two o'clock in the morning after several receptions and a party dinner. A few hours later it would be booed and cheered in equal measure. Roger would survive because he appeared not to mind whether he survived or not.

The Prime Minister was diverted by a lizard, which darted irregularly among the stones at the edge of the memorial garden. He enjoyed analysing his colleagues. His feel for people was famous; but this was of no help in taking his own decision.

He would stay. That was what he wanted. That was what he would do. To hell with analysis of motives and reasons. It had been a mistake to come and brood in this garden. To hell with justification. He was Prime Minister of Britain. He liked the job. He was good at it. No one could shove him out. He would stay. He looked at the lizard, and asked it to applaud. He turned away from the garden, afraid of second thoughts.

As he walked down the steep lane his mind turned to what he would say to Louise. He could not meet her main objection, which was that he would kill himself if he continued. That stab of pain would come again, she said, and this time prove mortal. He knew that this was a real fear, not a cloak. But other worries relating to herself and the family helped to explain her persistence. She disliked the long hours and the uncertainty, not knowing when a weekend or a holiday would be ruined. He could do nothing about that. She disliked a good many of his colleagues. He could not turn them into amusing, unselfish companions for her. Above all, she disliked the publicity, the hard light that beat incessantly on each corner of their lives. She feared it, particularly for Julia, their seventeen-year-old daughter, as she grew toward the inevitable limelight.

Simon paused before the half-gap in the hedge, but instead of taking it moved on down the lane. It was not for a Prime Minister to scramble through blackberry bushes. The lane would eventually bring him round to the start of the modest chestnut avenue that was the proper approach to their farmhouse. He needed a few more minutes to complete his thoughts. He had to find a way to win his wife round. First, he must cut the workload. He had discovered some time before one of the best kept secrets of his office, that a Prime Minister did not have to be as busy as his colleagues. They carried a daily load of departmental paper from which he was free. It was not necessary to intervene as often as most Prime Ministers did. He could also liberate several evenings a week by clamping down on the public dinners that he had once enjoyed but which now wearied him almost as much as they did Louise. But Louise would not be softened by such good intentions. More was needed. He cast around for a new thought and found it. He would get rid of his Chief Press Secretary. An unfair idea, certainly, but politics was an unfair trade. Louise thought the man was useless. In fact, Joe Bredon was a grey, competent Whitehall veteran, mild and thorough. But he had been in the job two years. No one would think it remarkable if he moved on. Or was moved on. A new spokesman, full of flair and magic, who would ensure either silence or (less good) favourable publicity.

No, he must not overegg the argument. Louise would see through any prospectus that glowed too brightly. A lighter schedule and a less irritating Press Secretary did not add up to a new life. But it might work.

Chapter Two

Monday September 1

TORY MP SUED FOR ASSAULT

'I trusted him', says mauled starlet.

PM TO QUIT IN SEPTEMBER

Simon heeds wife's health urgings.

RUSSELL TO STAY ON

'Louise keeps him there', says friend.

CAUGHT WITH HOSE IN HAND

Yorkshire water chief held in dawn raid.
'Roses were dying', pleads tearful girlfriend

BULLFIGHT PLANNED ON PLYMOUTH HOE

Devon girls fête Spanish fishermen

TORIES IN POLL SURGE

Eight-point lead over Labour

THE TIMES

Too good to last

PETER RIDDELL

As he strides through the Tuscan countryside or lazes by the pool, the Prime Minister has no police protection. Neither has the Foreign Secretary among the grouse in Invernesshire, the Chancellor of the Exchequer in the Cotswolds or the Home Secretary on his Devon beach. Since this spring's relaxation of security the gates at the entrance of Downing Street stand open, and we can walk freely past the Prime Minister's house and down the Foreign Office steps to the Park, as our grandparents did before us. There can be no more striking symbol of the calm that has descended on British politics. My colleagues do their best to stir things up in the best tradition of the silly season. But in vain. The Opposition has not recovered from Tony Blair's defeat last year, and his surprise move to Trinity College, Cambridge. The final passage last month of the bill privatising the Post Office has virtually brought to an end the Government's manifesto commitments, though we are not yet halfway through the Parliament. The Prime Minister seems to have recovered fully from his heart attack. Under his soothing guidance politics have gone to sleep. The battles of Thatcher and Foot seem a generation away. Even the battles of Hague and Blair were fierce by comparison. Inflation at 4.5 per cent, unemployment tolerable, Ireland peaceful. The Europe of Twenty pausing under a tranquil Austrian Presidency, the weather hot and dry. Only the prisons are troublesome, and even they have simmered down. I can never remember such a general tranquillity.

And yet, and yet . . . It cannot last. History cannot really have come to an end. Nor should it. Politics do not work well without controversy. Somewhere in the distance some new discord, even some new disaster must be preparing. Thomas Hardy wrote a poem called 'Convergence of the Twain' about the slow and unseen growth of the iceberg that sank the *Titanic*. We commentators scan the horizon with a mixture of eagerness and anxiety.

One cloud is already forming. I predict a traditional but fierce row on public spending. The problems there have been managed by strong economic growth, but not solved. The Chancellor is the least naturally peaceful member of the Cabinet. She . . .

'Good poll in the *Times* this morning,' said Clive Wilson, an eager young backbencher. His black hair was brushed back sleekly over his small head.

His host frowned into his soup. Wilson was a good shot, which was why he had been invited to Craigarran. But a Royal Duke was present, who could not be expected to do more than grunt if party politics were discussed. In any case Peter Makewell, Foreign Secretary, increasingly discouraged political chatter in his house. There had been a time . . . but now he preferred to talk of the shortage of grouse, the spread of bracken up the hill, the plight of the distillery and, if pressed, the choice of Inverness as European City of Culture.

Life was more complicated at Craigarran than when he had first bought the estate of 18,000 acres. The new Scottish Parliament in Edinburgh had borne down hard on the Highland lairds, whether English or Scots – though more by bureaucracy than from the added taxes they had feared. Peter Makewell had to negotiate every year a written agreement to allow hikers and even youths on mountain bikes access to substantial parts of the estate in return for continuing to exercise his sporting rights. They eroded and despoiled the very environment their spokesmen pretended to champion. But this was a minor nuisance compared to the countervailing pleasures that suited him exactly – bare majestic glens and mountains, a climate autumnal from early July to end November, soft rain almost constant on blackberries and heather, the line of friends walking up the grouse, while platoons of deer watched from the higher slopes just below the mist, waiting their turn.

The soup was tepid, but that was his own fault. Three red boxes had arrived in locked security sacks from Euston. He had decided to tackle one before dinner. He had snoozed over it, sitting in his study overlooking the slope that fell away to the burn. The box had been carefully packed as usual. There was nothing haphazard about the geological strata of the papers it contained. On top was an attractive folder of telegrams to be flipped through for the latest news. Then a submission about a loan for the Ukraine, solid but not impenetrable. Then the Private Secretary in London had encouraged him to further work by inserting a draft guest-list for a dinner next month – an easy choice. Then, coming towards the heart of the box, a thick minute from the Chancellor of the Exchequer about the Foreign Office budget in the public spending round now under way. The minute was long and turgid. The cuts proposed were absurd. There was a tough battle ahead before the Budget in November. The intricate figures and the thought of all the wearisome autumn arguments had turned drowsiness to sleep until the dinner gong jerked him awake.

His guests were mostly old friends in both senses of the adjective. Wilson the backbencher and his own nephew Rupert were the exceptions. Rupert had taken the shepherd's cottage near the top of the glen to write the definitive Elizabethan prose poem in the style of Spenser.

His uncle supposed that he was crossed in love. The others had been out on the hill all day, on each drive hoping for the onrush of grouse which never came. But it had been a good day, and all felt the pleasure of stretched muscles, windbeaten face and sound sleep to come. The wives were content, including Peter's sister, who carried a gun herself, was always placed in the next butt to her husband, and was now a little noisy with her soup.

Young Wilson, out of tune with everyone else, pursued his political conversation.

'Do you think, sir, that Simon will be fit to carry on?'

The Foreign Secretary did not mind being called sir, but disapproved of the use of the Prime Minister's first name by a young man who could hardly know him.

'The Prime Minister is robust and has a strong sense of service,' he replied, with deliberate pomposity. Then, heading away from politics, he asked Rupert about the progress of the prose poem. On past form Rupert, fresh from hours of silence in the shepherd's cottage, would talk for at least ten minutes about Spenser and Sidney. And so it proved. Clive Wilson, unable to continue, signed off by saying to himself, but audibly: 'Politics is the only really fascinating subject.'

Later, in bed, surrounded by the solitude created by his wife's death the previous year, Peter Makewell thoroughly disagreed. He recognised the change in himself. Many other interests and affections had fallen away, and in particular party politics. He was seventy, his wife was dead, his children self-sufficient and scattered. The only two things he cared about now were the work of the Foreign Office and Scotland. The first fascinated him, and he knew he would hang on to it as long as he could. Edward Grey, after all, had done ten years. The second, Scotland, simply bewitched him, a Sussex man born and bred. If he lay very still, though the water was low in August, he could hear the conversation of the stream.

. . . She sat in the hard chair behind her desk looking out past the oak tree to the parched field. In that field once upon a time her three children had kept their ponies. The children were now grown up, and dispensing financial services in the world's emerging markets. She was waiting for the courier from Advanced Transport to bring her evening fix of work. The Prime Minister had declined to privatise the Government Messenger Service but the Chancellor of the Exchequer had long stopped using it. The courier allocated to her by AT was called Henry. He was short, with an open smile and brown curly hair. Sometimes if he arrived punctually on his motorbike she spent five minutes improving his political education, which was primitive. But there would be no time for that today. Her personal organiser had flashed that he had left London at five pm as usual. It usually took ninety minutes to reach the Cotswolds, but it was now nearly seven pm. She was expecting in her box tonight the report of the seminar in Zürich to which she had sent her chief planner. She ought to have gone herself. Instead she had agreed to take two weeks' holiday with her husband in their house at Little Stourton. The Treaty stipulated two weeks' holiday for the two of them together. It had seemed sensible to take it in August. But this had clearly been a mistake. The seminar had put forward challenging ideas about the fiscal consequences of compulsory private saving for old age. She should have been there. She needed ideas for her Conference speech. She needed ideas for her future. More important, the country needed new ideas to jerk itself out of torpor. There was no merit in an 8 per cent lead in the polls if you didn't know what to do with it.

Tapping her silver pencil on the flat-topped desk, Joan Freetown brooded for a few moments on the Treaty she had negotiated last year with her husband. She and Guy had been at cross purposes ever since she had become Chancellor of the Exchequer after the election. Within hours she had sold the ponies, given away her Labrador, resigned as Church Warden, cancelled most of their social engagements in the country, and started to convert part of the stables into a separate study for herself. Guy, confronted with these decisions which she felt were well within her sphere, had been furious. A Treaty had been necessary to keep their marriage going. The Labrador had been retrieved, Guy and the Labrador's right to shooting weekends acknowledged, and among a number of minor provisions the two weeks' holiday was ring-fenced. Joan knew what her husband had failed to recognise. She admitted privately to herself that she had acted selfishly, in exaltation at her new life. She was fond of her husband and wished him well. But their shared world had gone for good. The swing still hung from the apple tree, but there were no children to use it. They had played ping pong in the barn, camped on summer nights under the oak, parents in one tent, children in the other. The children had trotted and jumped, tobogganed on the slope by the copse, bowled and batted erratically on the uneven turf. Guy had joined in all this as an enthusiast. She had done her bit, but he had been the splendid indispensable parent. That was all past. Now she saw him on a stepladder cutting dead heads off the lilac by the front gate. A useless task, and the stepladder wobbled dangerously. The two of them talked easily enough on trivia. They shared a room though not a bed. He was the only person with whom she did not discuss politics or the finance of the nation. But despite the Treaty between them and the chit chat, they did not really communicate any more.

Here was Henry at last on his bike, with his open smile and tight jeans. He had been held up by a police roadblock between Oxford and Witney. They were looking for three prisoners escaped from Bullingdon prison nearby. There was something slack in the Prison Service, she thought, just as there was something slack in the minister who presided over it. Even the thought of the Home Secretary irritated her. She ripped open a packet of confidential work with a silver paper knife presented to her after a fierce lecture in Chicago. Roger Courtauld would certainly not be working. His convicts were escaping, and even worse his departmental budget was overspent. But somewhere he would be enjoying himself, putting on weight, laughing. It was the laughter which she, humourless from birth, found particularly inept. She felt that he laughed to vex her.

She had to choose among the various offerings now on her desk from the big envelope of confidential work whose throat she had just slit. Most tasty would be the record of the Zürich seminar, but to choose that first would be like taking the chocolate first from a Christmas stocking.

In a separate folder was the fourth draft of her Party Conference speech. The thickest package contained the latest correspondence about the public spending round. Out of boredom she had taken this over from the Chief Secretary, her second in command, who normally handled it. Annoyingly Joan had always found her own mind empty when she approached this file or chaired the necessary meetings. Public spending was like a bad play. It numbed actor and audience with tedium. The spending departments and the Treasury both overplayed their part, overstated their case, then moved with stale arguments towards a predictable conclusion. Fight as she might against it, Joan felt a compromise coming on.

She decided to try what a little malice would do. She looked for the flagged Home Office file inside the bundle. There it was, just as she remembered. In reply to the Chief Secretary's circular letter asking for reductions, Roger Courtauld had sent a jaunty three pages, much the shortest submission from any of the major spending departments, offering no reduction, bidding for an *increase* of 5 per cent. Prisons, police, probation, drug prevention – there they all were, figures plucked from the air and commended on broad political grounds. 'I could not possibly justify smaller figures for any of these main categories. We have promised the public to strengthen these services, and we must do so. We have called the tune and now we must pay the piper.' No hint of efficiency savings, no hint of performance indicators. Intolerable. A neat ephemeral note from her own Private Secretary was pinned to the first page. 'I understand privately that the Home Secretary dictated this minute himself, discarding a rather longer draft from his officials, which proposed a standstill in Home Office spending rather than the increases indicated here.' Quite so. She could imagine him, late at night, cigar in hand, whisky glass on the mantelpiece, unloosing this extravagant nonsense into his dictating machine, chuckling as he spoke.

Very well. She flipped through the rest of the pile of replies to her demand for savings. Something dry and unforthcoming from the Foreign Secretary, reams of course from Social Security, defiance from Scotland, meagre morsels of sacrifice from the right-wingers at Agriculture and the Environment, total silence from Defence. Very well. She had had enough of this blinkered insolence. They had collectively agreed at Cabinet in July on a total of £390 billion. Their individual bids, as the covering Treasury note showed, added up to £415 billion. This was the usual ritual. But she, Joan Freetown, was not going to dance the usual dance. She selected an old-fashioned plump fountain pen and began to write fast. The thought and the ink flowed freely for half an hour. Then she moved quickly down the little spiral staircase into the library, out on to the lawn. Guy saw her walk through the gate at the top of the ha ha into the field that separated the copse from the dried-up bed of the stream. It was a quiet and beautiful evening. Still hot, but with the beginnings of a breeze. The shadow of the oak lengthened up the slope towards the grey drystone wall that marked their boundary. It was not at all usual for his wife to leave her work before dinner. A fresh surprise followed.

'Make me a vodka martini,' she said when within earshot. 'Strong please, Guy. For both of us. And find the cigarettes in the drawer of my dressing table.'

There had been no mention of vodka martini in the Treaty. There was affection in her voice. She seemed happier than he had seen her for months. She rarely smoked, and that too was a good sign. But he was not entirely happy himself. His wife's contentment was always greatest on the eve of battle.

*

A grey hot mist smothered the harbour. Though only twenty-nine, Zhou was Deputy Chairman of the Board of Financial Control of the Special Autonomous Region of Hong Kong. Because it was Saturday morning, the open-plan office on the nineteenth floor was empty. On the desk of his own office, behind a small forest of spiky plants, his secretary had, as instructed, placed his incoming mail. He wondered whether she wondered why. Members of the Party were meant to be zealous, but how was the cause of the People's Hong Kong helped by his coming in to pick up a ragbag of business letters and circulars on a Saturday morning? There was one cause, however, that was certainly served. The weekly magazine advertising holiday tours was there as usual. So was the slim envelope, slipped in between its leaves, five pages from the end. He opened it to check the amount. He felt exhilarated. This could go on for ever. The mist was coming down more thickly, obscuring the higher blocks of flats on the Peak behind him. He imagined that President Jiang Ze Min winked at him from the coloured photograph on the wall. He winked back.

*

Sean could have sworn there was still a chalk mark on the paving stone at the edge of the car park. That must be wrong. It was fifteen years since anyone had needed to unload a lorry and place its lethal contents so precisely in relation to Newry police station. The bushes had grown since then, giving good shelter for the mortar. He finished his calculation. The date of the Chief Constable's visit was still a fortnight away. Plenty of time for pleasant anticipation. A phrase half learned in class at St Teresa's down the road

given no paper to eat. Roger Courtauld got his children to answer the phone, and returned no calls. At the Home Office irritation mounted. True, there was no crisis, rather an accumulation of worries. The graph of prison admissions was soaring. Hardly anyone seemed to get bail. In this heat, prisons and inner cities simmered. Acting chief constables, in charge through August, were suspect. Acting prison governors were no better. The Chancellor of the Exchequer would certainly not take that minute about Home Office expenditure lying down. John Upchurch, who had worked in the Finance Department, knew that its statistical basis was unsound. It was one thing for the Home Secretary to declare that he must not be disturbed for two weeks. It was another thing for the two to lengthen into three, and this on the pretext of a village cricket match. The Minister of State theoretically in charge was a ninny. Roger Courtauld often gave officials hell and rejected their advice. He enjoyed life to the full and could hardly, they thought, be described as a safe pair of hands. But he provided spice for their lives, and did not shirk decisions. When he was away they missed him. John Upchurch would never quite admit this, even to himself. That would amount to admitting that a politician was an essential part of the machine. John believed in the machine pure and simple. The cogs and wheels of the Home Office and Whitehall were his inspiration, and he prided himself on his skill in manipulating them. It had not always been thus. Tall, slim, dark-eyed, he had dabbled at Newcastle University with left-wing politics and a teenage girl poet, with whom he had shared a student flat on a grey street winding up from the Tyne. But once he entered the Civil Service the door clanged behind him, and he quickly purged himself of all eccentricity. Working with Roger Courtauld was a penance and a challenge. Roger's absence on holiday was for the first few days a sheer pleasure to his Private Secretary. But as the anxieties multiplied in the department, the machine began to strain and clank and emit weird noises. John knew his duty. He took a first-class ticket to Plymouth and a taxi eastward ten miles to Holbeton and the South Devon coast.

His prayer was answered. A drizzle, which in itself might be ignored by any self-respecting cricket match, converted suddenly to a downpour. Within ten minutes Upchurch was conscious of a hubbub coming towards him. Bicycles swishing through muddy grass, a yelping of dogs with tangled leads, children shouting in recrimination, a great voice bellowing cheerful orders – the Home Secretary and his family were returning to their holiday cottage.

'Ah, John, safe journey? Got a crisis, have we? I'll get you a beer.' Roger Courtauld seemed larger than the doorway through which he had passed. His white trousers were stained with green. His stomach pushed forward in segments between the buttons of a thick white shirt. His bald forehead glistened with a mixture of sweat and rain. 'Richard here ran me out, little bastard.' With a great paw he shoved a can of lager into Upchurch's hand, then passed to the more urgent task of organising lunch and the afternoon. It was too wet for the usual barbecue. Soon children sprawled over the comfortable dilapidated armchairs and sofa of the cottage sitting room, squabbling over sausage rolls, Kit Kats and highly coloured ice-creams.

'The wet weather programme will now go to the vote,' said the big voice. 'Those in favour of dam-digging on the beach signify in the usual manner . . . Those in favour of the Dartmoor hike . . . The dam-digging has it. Next, orderly queue for the loo. We set out in five minutes.'

John Upchurch had not voted. Surreptitiously he consulted the timetable for trains back to Paddington. Another wasted day.

Artemis Palmer lay in bed and resented the young man's naked back. They had slept together for nearly a year now. She had been attracted by the straight fair hair, straight nose, straight blue eyes, straight spine. Frank, of excellent family and schooling which had petered out, was a PR man. He had no fixed job, but did not fret. After he had made love he always slept without stirring. By contrast, she had a marvellous job, and fretted incessantly. This morning she fretted about Joe Bredon, her immediate superior. He really was not up to the job of the Prime Minister's Press Secretary. He dithered and delayed. It was high time he moved on. No wonder Louise Russell despised him. She was right. For a moment, closing her eyes, waiting for the alarm clock to confirm the start of the working day, Artemis wondered if the Prime Minister dared to turn his naked back on Louise.

Chapter Three

Sunday September 7

Louise was trying to argue down the price of what she was discussing across the counter, silver-wrapped balls of amalgamated chocolate and nut in a blue box. No one had recognised her yet at Pisa airport, but she was in danger of attracting attention as she brandished her mixture of Euros and Italian lire. You could not bargain effectively in an airport lounge. The Prime Minister moved further away from her, embarrassed like an Englishman.

He had put on a tie for the first time in a fortnight, and carried a light linen jacket. He looked exactly like the other holidaymakers now pouring in through customs from the British Airways Airbus that would soon carry him on its return journey to England. A police dog was sniffing for drugs on the carousel, leaping nimbly from one suitcase to another as they revolved. Only in Italy,

Simon thought, could there have been such a display. Everywhere else the suitcases were sniffed at quietly behind some curtain. Turning to his own countrymen and women, he decided that they were distinctly plain – indeed plainer than usual today in their combination of holiday gear and pale skins. Some of them recognised him as they came past the passport counter pushing trolleys, others knew only that they had seen him somehow on television. They whispered briefly among themselves before dispersing to the car hire or the hotel buses. His recognition factor had never been high, and he did not mind any more.

'Had a good holiday then, Prime Minister?' said a tall man with glasses and thin bare legs, just as Louise rejoined him.

'Yes, indeed, thank you.'

And indeed he had, but of a different kind from the holiday waiting for the tall thin man. The man no doubt was heading from an ordinary life of commuting, desk work, television into an exceptional fortnight of shorts and pasta, swimming pool and a picture gallery or two, maybe even the opera. For Simon the ordinary life was the exception. He had just carved out a fortnight of ordinary life and was heading back to the tragicomedy that filled the other fifty weeks of the year. Most strangely, he had just decided to continue the monstrous existence.

There it was, his odd life, ready for him, out on the tarmac, through the doors of the terminal, concealed in the waiting Airbus. He had by superhuman effort, and with Louise's strong help, kept at bay for that fortnight all or almost all manifestations of office – private secretary, government car, official hospitality and, above all, paper. The fax machine in the farmhouse had dribbled once or twice. The prefect of the province could not be prevented from coming on the first day to present his compliments and take coffee on the lawn. But otherwise the fence round the holiday had held. Did he feel better for the rest? It was still too hot to be sure. There had been no more spasms of pain in his chest. He had eaten well. His bowels had worked. He had stopped taking the tiny pink painkillers at night. Touch wood, touch wood. The real test lay up the steps in the Airbus. The tarmac shimmered in the intensity of the afternoon. From Downing Street via Her Majesty's Embassy in Rome had come three red boxes of work for him to tackle on the flight home. They would be waiting for him, on the seat or perhaps in the small luggage compartment in the cabin, guarded by a secretary. Everything, health or sickness, political success or failure, would depend on how he felt when he saw those boxes on the aircraft. He shied away from the test.

'Time to be boarding, Excellency,' said the airport manager.

Simon pecked Louise on the cheek to signify the end of the holiday and thanks for her help. Then, clutching his hand case, he marched with her to the aircraft steps.

Tuesday September 9

Two days later Simon Russell hid the newspapers under the bedclothes as his daughter came into the room.

'Mum says you want to ask me something.'

Julia was seventeen. She moved fast to the bedside as if her body under the nightdress was a limbless whole. She had washed her face free of make-up, but not her dark blue eyes, now surrounded by extra dark blue and black. Simon, looking at a girl, knew that he was being looked at by a woman.

He was not prepared with the necessary questions.

'What happened last night?'

'You know. I went to that dance with Alex. You said I could.'

'What happened when you got home?'

'Nothing. Nothing at all. He brought me in a taxi. They let me in as usual. Not late, either. Well before two.'

'I'm told you were in a bad state.'

'Who said that?'

Simon lay still so that the *Sun* and *Daily Mail* did not crackle under the sheet.

'There were several people around downstairs. I hear your dress was torn and your face a terrible mess. Not good.'

Julia stepped back from the bed. She swept black hair away from her face and looked straight at him.

'That's nonsense.'

'So what did happen?'

Julia paused. She had good practice in translating the happenings of teenagers into the language of parents. Simon thought he knew that the translation was almost always faithful to the original. But it took time to emerge.

'Well, there was some fooling around at the end. At the swing door in the hotel as we all came out. We tried to see how many could squeeze in the same space. I was last in. The dress got caught when the door began to swing. It's badly torn. In fact it's a wreck. I wasn't hurt.' A pause. 'That's all.'

'Then why did your face look like people had been throwing paint at it?'

Julia looked taken aback. Then she remembered.

'It wasn't that bad, Dad. That was more fooling about, in the loo. There's a game about putting on different faces at midnight. We experimented on each other. It wasn't a big success. In fact it got a bit out of hand.'

'The whole thing was completely out of hand.' Louise had returned to the room. The fact that she was fully dressed gave her a clear advantage over her husband and daughter. So did the fact that she had already lost her temper. She pulled back the sheet from the double bed, revealing Simon's white chest and the two tabloid newspapers, which she seized and thrust at Julia.

They were late editions. There had been no time to concoct more than a headline on the front page of each paper. As sometimes happens, they had both come up with the same one.

WHAT WILL DADDY SAY?

and in small type beneath the picture one added

Julia home at dawn.

The coloured photographs were the story. Julia leaned against a famous door, hair dishevelled, lipstick, powder and mascara smeared in confusion across her face. Her long pink dress was badly torn; one knee showed through the ruins. Worst was the inane smile and the slender arm fondly waving at the camera.

'I never trusted that Alex,' said Louise savagely. 'Were you too drunk to see the flash?'

Julia gasped, turned and ran from the room.

'Was that necessary,' said Simon, without a question mark.

His wife was in full flight. 'She can't live in a cocoon. She's the Prime Minister's daughter. She has to face that. She has the fun, she has to learn to pay the price – just as I do. Someone would have shown her those papers anyway before the day's out. I promised her once I'd always tell her the truth, and I'll damn well keep that promise.'

'A foolish promise, I'd say.'

'Not at all. I gave it when you had your heart attack. That fool Bredon tried to keep the papers out of this flat so that she wouldn't read how bad you were.'

'He was right. The papers exaggerated.'

'Of course they did. They did again this morning. I believe

the story about the revolving door. It's too silly for her to invent. But everyone will look at her for a month as if she'd been raped. She has to realise that. If you live at this address the world sees you through a distorted magnifying glass.'

'I'd better talk to Bredon.'

The remark was meant to pacify, but failed. His wife laughed.

'What can he do except bleat?'

'Leave that to me.'

In the privacy of the bathroom, the Prime Minister tried to think. Here in 10 Downing Street activity smothered thought. Yet thought was badly needed – thought about his wife, his daughter, his health, as well as the disorderly band of political problems that always danced around him, sometimes merrily, more often close and threatening.

Before the official day began he asked Bredon to come up to the flat. Grey-haired, competent, without imagination, Joe Bredon had done well at the Treasury. He had been strongly recommended as (of course) a safe pair of hands, after a somewhat raffish interlude when the Press Office had been run by a red-haired enthusiast from the Foreign Office. There was nothing raffish about Joe. Once the Prime Minister, passing near the Bredon home on his way west to Chequers, had on an impulse dropped in to consult Joe about an impending press article. It had been Saturday afternoon. He had discovered Joe watching television, wearing his blue office suit.

'A bad story,' said Russell, pointing at the two tabloids.

'Yes, indeed, Prime Minister. I was sorry to see it. As to the photograph, I can't think how a professional could have got past the security gate. So . . .'

'It was taken by a friend. A former friend.

'Can you stop it getting into the *Evening Standard*? The girl's dress was torn in a revolving door.'

Bredon pondered this. 'Not easy, Prime Minister . . .'

'You should simply put out a statement to that effect.'

'All the mornings would carry the statement tomorrow as an excuse for printing the original story. Together with the picture, if as seems likely it is generally available. Probably the evening television as well.'

'So what do you propose to do?'

Bredon paused again. 'I can quite see how upsetting this must be to you, and Mrs Russell. And of course to Julia. But the truth is that these stories are not widely credited. They fade away rather faster than perhaps at the time one would anticipate.'

Unusually, Simon Russell's patience snapped. 'Ring the Editor of the *Standard* straight away.'

'The first edition is probably already . . .'

But being a safe pair of hands involved having more sense than to finish that particular sentence. With a final 'Yes, Prime Minister' Bredon shambled from the room.

'Well, what is he going to do?' asked Louise, entering from the breakfast room, coffee cup in hand.

'You've been listening.'

'I never do.' He knew she didn't.

'In effect, nothing. Nothing to be done.'

'"In effect, nothing",' she mimicked. 'Nothing, nothing, nothing. Have you sacked him yet?'

'I must choose the right time.'

She seemed about to explode. Then, 'I'll see you this evening. Have a good day.' And she was gone.

*

Anatoly Dobrinsky drove down the Lenin Prospekt in the Mayor's car. In all serious Russian cities the main street had been given back its pre-revolutionary name. But Murmansk was not a serious city. The street had never been called anything except Lenin Prospekt. Women wearing kerchiefs were sweeping the dusty public garden as he passed. Lenin was still there, chipped and stained in white marble, above a fountain choked with rubbish. Kiosks selling soft drinks and cheap clothes lined the street in front of peeling apartment blocks. The shops at the base of each block were shuttered, bankrupt. A solitary sparse lilac bloomed in front of the Mayor's office. In Murmansk the lilacs bloomed only in August.

Dobrinsky felt the anger rising, as usual, within him. They had voted for him because he was new and handsome, and had promised to close the nuclear power station. But he had been reading about 1917 and about 1991, about the storming of the Winter Palace and about Yeltsin on the tank outside the White House in Moscow. Murmansk was his fief, but Murmansk was not enough, because it was not serious.

But there was something serious down the road, something of which Moscow and the world would take notice. His driver pointed to the signpost where the street forked and lifted his shoulders. Thirty kilometres away that road reached Severomorsk, the base of the Northern Fleet. The driver knew the road well, for Dobrinsky had spent many days electioneering with the sailors. But that chapter, that small event was over. The next chapter was not ready. Dobrinsky told the driver to return down the Lenin Prospekt back to the hotel which he had commandeered, as the Mayor's office, and as the headquarters of his future.

*

In the first months of the Russell premiership the Principal Private Secretary had brought the daily diary up to the flat and discussed it with the Prime Minister over coffee. Louise had stopped the practice. In most weeks this was her only time alone with her husband. She erected an invisible barrier at the top of the stairs and at the exit of the slow, creaking lift. Only in an emergency were officials allowed to climb to the private flat on the second floor. Ministers occasionally called late at night for a reflective whisky, and this Louise encouraged. But as regards the mornings she was absolute.

So Patrick Vaughan, Principal Private Secretary, was waiting below the flat in the study on the first floor. Simon Russell appeared at eight thirty, punctual as usual.

'Good morning, Prime Minister.'

'Good morning, Patrick.'

'The holiday went well, I gather.'

'Very well, Patrick. And yours? Excavations in good order?'

Patrick was an amateur archaeologist. Aged forty, in the office he was neat and deeply conventional, dressed always in dark blue or dark grey. In August he left his wife and children, whom he hardly saw at other times, and dug with Oxford students round an unpromising prehistoric fort on the Berkshire downs not far from the Uffington White Horse. The Prime Minister had seen once in a local paper a photograph of Patrick, lightly bearded, emerging in jeans from a dripping tent, carrying a mess tin apparently full of porridge. It contradicted everything he knew and saw of the man. But life was like that.

'Thank you, the excavations were particularly interesting this year.'

'You must tell me about them.'

There would never be time to hear about Patrick's excavations.

'Now, back to the grindstone, I suppose.' There was something about Patrick, and the return to office routine, that led Simon Russell into cliché. He would never have used the phrase with Louise.

Patrick Vaughan produced the white oblong card that each day for fifty weeks governed the Prime Minister's life. Simon sometimes imagined it as a smart card invisibly loaded with energy, which he would draw on until eternity. Since his heart attack he wondered whether one day he would suddenly run into debit beyond the agreed overdraft and in an instant lose the card for ever.

Tuesday September 9

9.00 am	Chairman of the Party, Chief Whip
9.45 am	Premier of St Kitts/Nevis
10.00 am	Economic Policy Committee (EPC)
12 noon	Constituency Secretary
1.00 pm	Lunch in flat – private meeting
3.00 pm	Foreign Secretary
4.00 pm	Lord Cross
5.00 pm	US Ambassador

'Quite a light day,' said Simon without irony. And so it was. Parliament was still in recess, so no Commons duties. No big meals to sit through. A free evening. Until recently there had been only four or five such each year. But he had carried through his decision in the lane in Tuscany. His staff had already been instructed to cancel evening engagements unless they were absolutely necessary. 'What's the private meeting at lunch?'

Patrick went slightly pink. This was a slot that Louise had captured. He himself would have liked the Prime

Minister to spend lunchtime catching up on his paperwork. Not all the red boxes had been dealt with on the flight back from Pisa. But he had known better than to push the point. 'I believe Julia's headmistress is coming in . . .'

'Of course.' Change the subject quickly. 'What's the agenda for EPC?'

'A general review of the economic scene, Prime Minister. You will remember we usually have one immediately after the holiday. Actually, I understand that the Home Secretary is still away, in Devon I believe, and decided not to return for the meeting.' An inaudible sniff. 'The Chancellor is keen to hold it none the less. I am not sure, but I think she wants to make an interim report on the public expenditure exercise.'

'Going well?'

'Not entirely smoothly. There was a summary in your box yesterday . . .'

'Yes, indeed.'

So life began again, not entirely to Simon's satisfaction. He liked Patrick Vaughan but he needed someone to whom he could talk about everything. Louise cut him off if he tried to engage her on politics, so he no longer tried. He had no close friend with the necessary range of interests, political and personal. So his life was divided into several segments, and this amounted to loneliness. Patrick Vaughan had the intelligence, and perhaps lurking somewhere the sympathy to act as a confidant and companion in arms. But before that could happen Patrick would need teasing to penetrate his formal Whitehall vocabulary and rescue the human being behind it. Simon had chosen Patrick with care from a good list submitted to him by the Cabinet Secretary. But a Prime Minister could not go round Whitehall saying, 'I need a friend.' Friendship was not a matter of paper qualifications or formal interviews.

The two men got on smoothly enough together, but in many conversations they never came anywhere near the crossing point to friendship.

The official day opened easily. Simon Russell had taken the deliberate decision that the heavyweights in his Party should hold the great offices of State. He had in the past seen powerful political figures with time on their hands poking from outside into the affairs of big departments for which they had no responsibility. In the Russell Government the Chancellor of the Exchequer, the Foreign Secretary and the Home Secretary carried the political clout because they carried the responsibility. Getting them to work together was difficult, but he accepted that as his job. It followed that the Chairman of the Party and the Chief Whip were subordinate figures, competent and a bit colourless. They came to see him together every week. This Tuesday, after a flat August, they had very little to report. Sir Rupert Cranleigh had died after a long illness and they fixed on a date for the by-election. With a lead of 8 per cent in the polls they did not worry too much about the result in a safe Sussex seat. They spent ten minutes looking ahead to the Blackpool Party Conference in six weeks' time. The PR men had suggested alternative slogans for the publicity. The Party Chairman was not surprised to find that the Prime Minister disliked them all. It was always one of the most difficult and least important decisions of the year. He pointed out that time was getting on, and they would really have to make a choice next Tuesday. Next they discussed how to ensure that the Cabinet heavy-weights took the same line on public spending. It was always awkward that the Party Conference was held just as the argument between departments was at its height.

The two men were given coffee in the study towards the end of the meeting, and were sipping when Patrick Vaughan's deputy, who handled foreign affairs, slipped his long nose around the door. The Premier of St Kitts/Nevis was downstairs. That was easy. Sir Joshua had come to have his photograph taken with the Prime Minister in front of the fireplace in the outer hall, where there was space for a crowd of Caribbean journalists. Decency required that before this climax the two Prime Ministers converse for a quarter of an hour in the Cabinet Room (Russell's second cup of coffee). They discussed the banana trade and measures against drug-running. If only every appointment was so smooth running.

The Ministerial Economic Policy Committee met in the Cabinet Room when the Prime Minister took the chair. His was of course the only chair with arms to it. His gaze slipped across the long coffin-shaped table to the door leading on to the small terrace with steps down to the garden.

He could see the wisteria on the wall that separated the garden from the Horse Guards, but at that distance could not be sure whether it was getting ready for an autumn flowering. The garden, the sun, the outdoor world were receding as he entered a winter of work. This particular meeting was taking exactly the form Russell had predicted to himself. It seemed as if he had spent half his premiership sitting at that table under the portrait of Walpole listening to Joan Freetown analyse the economy. She had circulated a paper in advance, most of which she had as usual written herself, so that it was largely free of the jargon of economists. But she was not content with this. She now added emphasis by speaking in a manner all her own, pitched at average halfway between conversation and oratory, but rarely staying at that average. Sometimes her voice sank low and husky, but that was a prelude to a burst of loud, intense sentences accompanied by the clash of bracelets as her right wrist and forearm struck the table. She was a plump, handsome woman of medium height, always sharply dressed, her immaculate black hair now fronted by a wave of silver, softer in colour than the bracelets, but apparently of the same metal. Russell had trained himself to listen to her with half his mind. Less than half was dangerous. He could not, for example, have written love letters as Asquith did at meetings of the War Cabinet. The Chancellor might suddenly appeal to him for help. But he thought he could work out her tactic. She emphasised those passages of her paper that described the danger of inflation and the need to restrain public spending. There were four ministers present who ran departments with large budgets, but Roger Courtauld their usual leader was absent. Without Roger Courtauld the Home Secretary to protect them the spending ministers were like bleating sheep, chivvied this way and that by the wolves of the Treasury. Peter Makewell, the only other heavyweight present, had his own Foreign Office budget to defend, but he would do that separately. He intervened less and less often on domestic matters. Indeed Russell could see that the Foreign Secretary was dipping surreptitiously into the latest folder of overseas telegrams. Russell sensed that the Chancellor still had a good deal to say. She would not be able to force a decision on departmental budgets today because it was not on the agenda, but she was hardening her approach to intimidate those colleagues who had not yet settled with her.

The other half of Russell's mind wandered to the matter of Joe Bredon. He had promised Louise to get rid of him. It would be better to do it before the Downing Street team, Bredon included, resumed the habits of working together, which the August holiday had interrupted. The act of dismissal would be awkward, but not in the top range of embarrassment. Bredon had three years to go before retirement. Even after years of delaying, downsizing, contractorisation and similar convulsions, there were still a few green pastures in Whitehall for exhausted workhorses. Lord Downbrook, Leader for the Government in the House of Lords, could certainly be induced to take him. There would be a whisper or two, but no drama or disgrace. The real problem was the choice of Joe's successor.

There would be no shortage of applicants. The job of Chief Press Officer at Number 10 was much sought after. He or she exercised an undefined sovereignty over all the information offices in Whitehall, had the right of entry into any meeting, knew everybody and everything. He? Or she? That was the point. The Prime Minister knew half a dozen seasoned men in other departments who would come if he called. Or more dangerously he could loot some bright young political warrior from a newspaper or one of the right-wing think-tanks. Or he could promote Artemis Palmer from second to top position in the Press Office. There was always a passing political advantage in choosing a woman, any woman. There was a personal advantage in that he knew Artemis, and so need not go through the penance of educating a stranger into his ways of doing things. Russell believed himself to be a thoroughly sane, balanced and reasonable man, but knew this could not be entirely true, of him or anyone else in politics. Politicians were by definition eccentric. His ups and downs, what he preferred to eat and drink, how he showed tiredness or distaste, the words he liked and disliked, his hours of work, his wife, his daughter, sudden small bursts of irritation, the kind of wit he relished or rejected – the three or four closest members of his team had to know about these things if they were to be useful. He could not teach these puzzles to others because he hardly knew them himself. Artemis

Palmer, as Bredon's deputy, had grasped the basic elements already. Then, she was not particularly beautiful. As the Chancellor of the Exchequer paused in her exposition and turned a page, the Prime Minister set himself to think of the face and body of Artemis Palmer. Her first name was absurd, as if her parents had tried to compensate in advance at the font for what she was to become – a tall, rather thin girl, with a pleasant English face, slightly hunched shoulders, fuzzy brown hair.

Joan Freetown increased in volume. Long study of the body language of his colleagues told the Prime Minister that this was not another false peroration. She was actually coming to an end.

'The facts I have set out in this paper lead to an unmistakable conclusion.' The bracelets clanked in agreement. 'The total we agreed for public expenditure in July is too high. Unless we can reduce it substantially the dangers of inflation will press upon us. I may be compelled in the November Budget to raise taxes instead of cutting them. It may be technically irregular, Prime Minister, but time is short and I propose that we decide at this meeting this morning to reduce the July total by just over 5 per cent to £370 billion.'

It was a try-on, an ambush. The spending ministers moved uneasily in their seats, knowing that one of them would have to enter the fray against this Boadicea, and blunt the scythes fitted to her chariot wheels. Peter Makewell, sitting next to the Chancellor almost opposite the Prime Minister, raised a pencil above his open folder of Foreign Office telegrams. Experience had taught him, as well as the Prime Minister, to listen to a colleague and read papers at the same time. A further 5 per cent off the Foreign Office budget would cause a lot of harm to the British Council and the BBC World Service, as well as to embassies. But the Prime Minister forestalled him.

'Thank you very much, Chancellor. That was as usual enlightening and forceful. As you imply, we cannot take a decision today on your final proposal which is new to us. It would be a big step. I think that if you want to proceed in this way you will need to put a paper setting out the argument you propose for the main spending programmes, and the consequences, to the Committee. Then it will need to go to full Cabinet.'

Maybe that had been a shade too abrupt. He watched the Chancellor weigh in her mind whether to challenge him. But he was procedurally correct and she would have few, if any, allies. She grumbled something about urgency but let it be. He moved quickly to close the meeting, summing up for the benefit of the Minutes, which the Cabinet Secretary would circulate next day.

'The Cabinet noted with approval the Chancellor's summary of the economic situation and invited her to circulate any proposals which as a consequence she believed necessary.'

He added a warning familiar to them all, and in this Cabinet reasonably well respected.

'It's obviously imperative that nothing be said outside this meeting about any new proposals. Any leak would raise questions we cannot at this stage answer.'

The meeting was over. The Prime Minister glanced to his right at the cluster of officials seated at the end of the table just in front of the two white pillars. Joe Bredon was putting his papers together before he went to his daily briefing of political correspondents. Bredon would handle this well enough. There was nothing to say, and he would say it adequately. No one had ever complained of his skill as a stone wall. It was when an idea or an initiative was needed that doubts arose. For a second Simon Russell, quite independently of Louise, itched to be rid of this grey, sound man and place his own and the Government's reputation in more adventurous hands.

The next forty-five minutes with his Constituency Secretary Martha Johnson passed quickly. She had dealt skilfully with the correspondence from Harrow North in his absence. She had kept for his return some difficult letters. There were three or four from seven-year-olds in the same school, passionate against fox hunting; a complicated complaint about a proposed housing development in which the Chairman of his local Conservative Association was involved; two letters criticising Peter Makewell and the Foreign Office for being too friendly to the Arabs in their latest spat with Israel over Jerusalem; and a handful of tax, pension and child maintenance cases. He spent most of the time topping and tailing answers already typed out, but he always read the incoming letter before signing the reply. A year earlier management consultants had produced a report on the efficient use of the Prime Minister's time. They had recommended that the Prime Minister delegate to his Political Secretary the answering of constituency letters. He had rejected the recommendation.

He knew that neither the American, French or Russian Presidents nor the German Chancellor had such a chore. But he relished the unique personal relationship between himself and a not particularly beautiful or distinguished cluster of suburban streets. Sometimes he envied colleagues with distant rural seats who received half as many letters as he did. Often he lamented that many of the incoming letters were nowadays drafted by some pressure group, not by the individual who signed them. But on the whole he enjoyed this part of his job.

Lunch upstairs with Julia's headmistress was another matter. He admitted to himself that the woman's main fault was to know his daughter too well. A handsome woman with tightly coiled grey hair, she sat thin-lipped and upright in her chair, pecking at her lamb cutlet. She described an intelligent, lazy girl whose A levels would not quite get her to university and whose behaviour out of class set a poor example to others. As she mentioned the half-empty bottle of Pimms found at the bottom of Julia's work box her eyes lighted meaningfully on the open drinks cabinet in the corner of the room. She appeared to show no interest, let alone gratitude, at being invited to share lunch with the

Prime Minister of Britain. Her conversation never strayed from the affairs of St Clare's School for Girls, conveniently placed between Ascot and Sunningdale, Sunningdale being the nearest railway station. Louise, who was in private much the more severe parent, reacted to the cool analysis of her daughter by springing to her defence. As the two strong-minded women wrangled in detail over this episode and that, just remaining polite, Simon realised the futility of the occasion. Julia had bolted, not from home, but from the controls of home and school. She would now have to be treated as an adult. The two rival racehorse trainers were disputing the best means of closing the door of an empty stable. He rose to go as soon as was decent.

Patrick Vaughan was waiting for him in the study, wearing his tentative intermediate look, neither relaxed nor irredeemably gloomy. He carried as usual the second edition of the *Evening Standard*. The Prime Minister glanced at it and threw it aside.

'Nothing about this morning,' said Patrick, meaning the EPC meeting, 'and the lunchtime TV said simply there had been an economic discussion.'

'Good. Was the Chancellor much vexed?'

'I don't think so. Her proposal took Treasury officials by surprise. She can't have expected to carry it today. If I may say so, you handled it skilfully, Prime Minister.'

Patrick was too professional to scatter compliments. He knew the difference between a civil servant and a courtier. So the Prime Minister was pleased. As a result he made a mistake. On the spur of the moment he told Patrick that he intended to replace Joe Bredon with Artemis Palmer. Until he spoke he had not finally decided on Artemis. He had meant to say nothing to Patrick until the deed was done. Now he was committed. Patrick retreated at once into his shell.

'You disapprove?' after a moment's silence.

'No,' said Patrick slowly. 'There are no rules for the position. It's too close to you. You have to be satisfied.'

'So does the press. Will Artemis satisfy me and them?'

Another pause. 'Yes, I think so.' Simon could tell there were doubts lurking behind the spectacles, but not articulated. Patrick never blurted. Every thought was fully prepared before it passed the gateway.

'So I'll see Joe at the end of the day.' Change the subject. 'No need for anyone to sit in with Lord Cross.'

'Right. I thought I'd cover the Foreign Secretary and ask Henry to do the American Ambassador.' Henry Plunket, the one with the long nose, was the private secretary specialising in foreign affairs.

'Fine.'

'There's one more thing.' The two men were still standing. Patrick took a paper out of the folder he was carrying. 'This is the latest JIC report from Northern Ireland. I'm afraid they have upgraded the likelihood of a return to violence. There is some quite firm evidence of detailed planning of terrorist attempts by the Breakaways, both in the province and on the mainland.' Patrick spoke in grammatical sentences with occasional subordinate clauses, not pompous but rounded, indistinguishable from the minutes he wrote.

Russell took the report, topped with a red Top Secret warning. His mood changed for the worse. He crossed the room and sat at the chair behind his desk. One night in Italy he had woken abruptly, after dreaming that the Irish Troubles had started again . . . A man had been shouting and running, blood pouring from his mouth, in a street of neat two-storey redbrick houses. It had never been unlikely. They had known for a year that the Breakaway faction of the IRA who rejected the Blair Settlement was still in business. They had gone to ground after the assassination of Gerry Adams. They were mostly young men, previously unknown to the RUC and the Garda, immensely secretive. The Prime Minister and the British and Irish peoples had just hoped that no news was good news. But this was rarely true.

The report estimated that there were now two hundred Breakaways, concentrated in West Belfast and County Armagh. In Londonderry and the Catholic areas west of the Bann there was as yet no sign of them. But two hundred was four times as many as in the last report.

'Dublin will have seen this?'

'Yes, Prime Minister. Police on both sides of the border and of course the Army have moved up to full alert. You will see that there is no precision about a target. But I believe that every reasonable precaution has been taken.' A pause. 'Except one.'

The Prime Minister glanced sharply at Patrick, who had inflected his voice as if to suggest something unwelcome.

'Well?'

'The professional advice from the Security Service and Metropolitan Police is clear, Prime Minister. You ought to be given full protection at home and abroad. Together with five other ministers particularly close to Irish policy, and all the former Secretaries of State.'

'That's not acceptable,' Russell snapped.

'There will be a detailed submission in your box tonight.' Patrick spoke as if the Prime Minister had not spoken. Simon Russell had never had police protection. His ministerial experience had begun before the Troubles in Ireland had been brought to an end by the ceasefire, and the involvement of Sinn Fein in constitutional talks, but he had never had a job close enough to that struggle to make him a possible target. He knew enough from friends about the status of a protected person to know that he would detest it. Some ministers, senior officials and judges had liked it, particularly lonely widowers or bored couples. They relished having a companion. Even if that companion had to obey rules by drinking orange juice on a pub crawl, he could book theatre tickets, move suitcases in and out of a car or even, at a pinch, help prune the roses. Simon Russell knew only that he would hate to see the last rags of his solitude torn away. He would hate to lose occasional breaks of real privacy such as he had just enjoyed in Italy. Protection would be a courteous prison house, moving to envelop him wherever he went.

But there was no time to argue this thought, nor was Patrick the right antagonist.

The afternoon began to pass briskly. The Italian holiday became a speck of blue sky, disappearing fast as clouds built up.

He was glad to see Makewell. The two had little in common. They never met in each other's or other people's houses. But he and the Foreign Secretary trusted each other. Partly for that reason, and partly because the world was unusually quiet, Simon had not had to concern himself greatly with foreign or European affairs. They took up a good deal of his time, because of obligatory summits and visitors to London, but a much smaller share of his energy. Nevertheless he found it useful to see the Foreign Secretary for half an hour every week, two sane men comparing notes in an occasionally mindless world.

'Sorry to cut you off in EPC this morning.'

Sir Peter smiled. He wore a tweed suit rather too heavy for September in London. 'No matter. You were right. I would only have started her going again.'

The Prime Minister was not going to gossip against his Chancellor of the Exchequer. They started on the scanty agenda. Henry Plunket sat in a corner, almost unseen as befitted his station, recording only the conclusions, not the discussion. The Ruler of Qatar wanted to insist that the

Prime Minister should host a lunch for him during his impending State Visit. Out of the question. This would be to re-impose a chore that John Major had managed to be rid of. Makewell suggested new Ambassadorial appointments for Moscow, Bonn and Tel Aviv. The names had already been canvassed between the Foreign Office and Henry Plunket. One candidate had already been discarded because Plunket knew that the Prime Minister regarded him as too vehement. So no problem there. The heads of SIS and GCHQ had asked the Foreign Secretary to ask the Prime Minister whether their budgets could be excluded from the full rigours of the public expenditure round. Makewell pursued this for two minutes. It was an important point for the agencies. They were constantly having to switch resources at short notice from one subject or part of the world to another. They might now, for example, have to put men and technology back into Ireland. It was hard to do this and at the same time run each year the gauntlet of the Treasury's insistence on efficiency savings. The Prime Minister said this was not the time to press the request. Makewell, having been at the meeting that morning, saw the point and desisted.

Anything else? This was the time when they could range informally across the world, dealing in guesses, hunches and uncertainties, neither afraid of seeming foolish to the other. Henry Plunket closed his notebook but stayed in the room. Ten years earlier they would have had to hold an anguished discussion about the latest dilemmas in the

European Union. Since the decay of the single currency, the compromise at the Intergovernmental Conference and agreement on a timetable for enlargement to the East, a welcome lull had descended. But somewhere there was always something.

'Russia,' said the Foreign Secretary.

'Russia?'

'This man Dobrinsky in the north.'

Russell looked blank.

Henry Plunket, on the lookout for any suggestion that he might not have kept the Prime Minister properly informed, chipped in. 'You saw the reporting telegram, from Moscow, Prime Minister. In the box waiting for you at Pisa.'

'Yes, indeed. And there was a piece in the *Financial Times*. But he's a long way away, up in Murmansk.'

'Two things about him.' Makewell was always to the point. 'He's got strong personal appeal. And he may soon get control of the Northern Fleet. It's based up there. It's their best.'

'Nuclear weapons?'

'Exactly.'

'But Moscow has the key.'

'I hope so.'

'Hope?'

'I believe so. You may want the JIC to report. But he'll move south. He looks like a young god. Plenty of patriotic eloquence – we may have a civil war on our hands.'

'Our hands?' It seemed to the Prime Minister much less

serious than Ireland and much much further away. The Foreign Office still instinctively thought of itself as the world's judge and policeman.

'A civil war in Russia will stir everything up. The Americans. Eastern Europe. Perhaps China.'

Maybe. 'You'd better say something about Russia in Cabinet next week.'

'Right.' Patrick had closed the discussion on the Prime Minister's security by promising a submission in the box; the Prime Minister used a similar device to close the discussion on Russia. Procedure could be a great help in avoiding untimely decisions on substance.

Next, Lord Cross. He owned a morning and London evening newspaper as well as a batch of provincials. Though ageing now, he still showed commercial flair and skill in choosing editors. This was the only gift required of a proprietor. Unfortunately, Lord Cross also had political opinions. They had varied during his life, and the present batch had formed during the spasm of anti-foreign prejudice that had dominated the Tory press in the mid-nineties. Knowing that these opinions were out of date, he did not impose them on his editors. But there was an unwritten understanding that in return for a general and somewhat vague support for the Government in his papers, he could inflict them on the Prime Minister about once every three months. Russell had learned that, since Lord Cross no longer listened to anyone, the best technique was to nod and from time to time mutter 'Very interesting'. Nothing more was required, and in that way he could be out of the room in a little over thirty minutes.

The American Ambassador had been a professor at Princeton, until summoned to diplomacy by the second Clinton Administration. Having spent his working life up to that point in general discussion without decisions, he had gone through a change of a hundred and eighty degrees. He specialised now in abstruse points of policy detail, almost always unfamiliar to the Prime Minister. For that reason he managed only rarely to cross the threshold of 10 Downing Street. This evening he came clutching a long CIA intelligence report from Hong Kong. Russell could make little sense of it from the Ambassador's long elaboration. It seemed that the CIA had discovered a network of corruption in the Hong Kong Chinese administration and worried that the British and Americans would be blamed for it when the Chinese unearthed it themselves. Drugs came into it, as they usually did. Contrary to the reason he had given three days before when requesting the call, the Ambassador carried no message from the President. Russell promised several times to read the CIA report diligently. Eventually the Ambassador realised he would get no further, and took his leave.

Now, of course, Bredon. He could put it off. Most things could be put off. Sometimes this was not cowardice but sense. A problem often postponed could disappear, or take a completely different shape. But getting rid of Bredon could not wait. Louise would soon tax him on the matter, perhaps tonight. Patrick Vaughan now knew his intention. Patrick was thoroughly discreet, but Russell had a rule of thumb that a secret known to two people as well as himself was no longer a secret.

Bredon looked the same evening as morning, Friday as Monday, September as January. Louise had described him as a car always driven at 45 mph, dangerous in a crowded town, a different kind of dangerous on a motorway. Russell supposed that Joe Bredon guarded himself against pessimism by never feeling enthusiasm. In a crisis, when others were in disguised panic, this genuine calm could be reassuring. In normal times it caused the irritation that Russell had felt earlier.

Russell offered an armchair, which was taken. He offered a whisky, gesturing to the cabinet in the corner, but it was refused. Having thus signalled that this was an exceptional conversation, Russell saw only embarrassment in any further preliminaries. Joe Bredon wore a light grey suit and plain blue shirt, with a surprising tie, long formless splashes of brighter red, blue and yellow. The tie would have shed a surprising light on the man's character had the Prime Minister not recognised it as the insignia of the Sydney Olympics.

'Joe, I think it's time you moved on.'

Silence, no reaction on the face. Russell also watched body language. There was no shift in the chair, no movement of hands.

'You've looked after me well. I've no criticisms. But

we're moving into a new phase now, a more difficult phase. I can see trouble ahead on public spending and the Budget, on Ireland, abroad in Russia, perhaps Hong Kong. Rightly or wrongly I've decided to carry on myself, but I feel that I need fresh ideas round me, and that means fresh faces.'

'I understand, Prime Minister.' Bredon sat still in his chair, but there was a little more blood in his face. 'And of course you have to consider your own domestic angle.'

For a second, Russell stared. Bredon was almost certainly referring to troubles past and future with Julia, perhaps Louise. It was at such moments that his mind moved quickest. He decided to interpret it differently.

'Yes, of course, my health. The doctors give a good report, no reason why I should have another heart attack. It's in the hands of God, rather than my Chief Press Officer.'

Not a flicker. Silence continued.

Russell leaned forward in his chair.

'I don't know if you want to continue in this particular line of business, Joe. Of course the Treasury would be glad to have you back as part of their policy team. If you wanted another top press job with a senior minister, I know Lord Downbrook is looking for a steady pair of hands.' The Prime Minister would not have used the cliché, if he had been fully at his ease.

'That would be kind.' Bredon did not pause to consider the offer. He was not a car at all, Russell thought, he was a tram, and someone else always pulled the lever that decided his direction. The interview was at an end. The decision had been communicated and received. Russell saw no need to tell Bredon today the name of his successor. It remained only to bring the discussion politely to a close and to organise a farewell party. But a feeling from Simon's earlier, less calculating life asserted itself. He wanted to break through the crust of Joe Bredon's self-possession and sympathise with whatever was inside.

'You'll be glad, Joe, really, won't you? You've had a long slog. I've driven you hard. A bit more time won't come amiss for proper holidays, your family, the theatre.' Once, only once, Joe had asked to absent himself from an official dinner to take his wife to the theatre on her birthday. It was the sort of thing Russell remembered.

'I've greatly enjoyed working with you, Prime Minister.' No waver. 'And I would be grateful if you could speak to the Lord Privy Seal as you suggested.'

The crust remained intact.

Chapter Four

Tuesday September 16

The Prime Minister waited for the lift and wished he had taken the stairs up to the flat. It was said that the lift had been made inordinately slow to suit Lady Dorothy Macmillan's heart condition. Simon Russell felt that, in his case, waiting for the lift was much more likely to be lethal.

It was a week since he had sacked Joe Bredon and told Patrick and then Louise that Artemis Palmer would be his next Chief Press Officer. But Joe was still at his desk, nothing had been announced and, despite Patrick's nudges, he had not yet spoken to Artemis. He was not sure why. If he found himself postponing an action on which he had decided it usually meant that some irrational reluctance had taken charge. But the matter could not be allowed to drift any longer. It was surprising that there had been no press leaks. He must clear his mind before tomorrow.

There she was, walking briskly past the lift on her way to the front door out on to Downing Street. When she saw Simon Russell she disentangled her arm from the young man by her side. He was exactly her height, fair, blue-eyed and well brushed. After the moment's shyness she found her natural boldness.

'Prime Minister, let me introduce Frank; Frank, this is my boss, Simon Russell. Frank is in PR, Prime Minister.'

'So you're flying together.'

Frank looked nonplussed.

The Prime Minister had to explain. 'Birds of a feather.'

Artemis had caught it at once. They talked for twenty seconds about Frank's PR firm. The lad looked like a guards officer and talked like a plumber. The lift grunted to show that it had arrived. As the two left the Prime Minister, Artemis leaned her head over on to Frank's shoulder and put her arm round his waist.

In the lift, Russell decided finally to appoint her. She was emotionally committed elsewhere. He found that his hesitation had disappeared.

A light whisky in his favourite chair, and a good Corona. His doctor knew nothing about the cigars. A compromise on the point with Louise became possible after the discovery that it was only *cheap* cigars that left an unacceptable reminder in the curtains and cushions next morning. She knew the importance of these rare moments when he could work at ease. Usually he came back from an official dinner or meeting just before eleven pm to face the day's paperwork. Then he would sit at his desk upstairs, hunched and disciplined, not skimping the work, but getting through it as quickly as possible. But this had been a rare light day. At its close he did not have to move into overdrive. Three red boxes and a black one were neatly stacked alongside the armchair. It was only eight thirty and the Prime Minister had already dined with Louise on scrambled egg and a hunk of cheddar cheese on an oatcake. He should be through in a couple of hours, if he could retain the necessary combination of physical ease and intellectual stimulation.

For at their best the boxes could stimulate. The black box came from his Political Secretary and he opened it first with a separate key. The constituency letters that he had dictated or approved that morning, then the latest private poll from Conservative Central Office measuring the previous month. This was reasonably satisfactory. August was always a tricky month. Neither Opposition nor Government was able to make real waves during the holiday. Only events could do that. August was famous for crises, but this year there had been none. The Government's lead remained steady – 42 per cent voting intention compared to 34 per cent for Labour. Then a letter in an unfamiliar hand – a woman's hand. Simon Russell turned to the signature on the sixth page. Who was Charlotte Wilson of Tedworth Square, London SW3? As he read the letter, surprise deepened into distaste. After all these years in politics Simon Russell could still be taken aback by effrontery. He had not needed it himself to rise to the top, and he despised it in others, particularly when it was inept. He vaguely remembered Clive Wilson's wife, small, dark and pretty, with just too much make-up. Clive Wilson was attentive, even effusive, in support on Wednesday afternoons in the Commons at Prime Minister's questions. He was also, so the Foreign Secretary had told him, an excellent shot. Neither fact entitled him to office, yet this was what his wife urged.

> As you know, Clive is one of your <u>staunchest</u> supporters, and will never hear a word spoken against you. He is <u>longing</u> to be of real service to you, and with his marginal seat, promotion would be a real <u>boon</u>. He would kill me if he knew I was writing to let you know. He feels, and I feel even more strongly, that others less talented have been promoted ahead of him. You must forgive me for this, Prime Minister, but sometimes I do wonder whether loyalty really pays . . .

Simon sat back, trying to imagine Mrs Wilson as she wrote these words. Alone in the room? Her own idea?

On the whole, he thought not. He tore the letter into shreds, dropped it into the wastepaper basket, crossed the room to his desk and took a sheet of 10 Downing Street paper from the rack.

> Dear Mrs Wilson,
> I am most grateful for your note about Clive, and will remember what you say.
> With all good wishes.
> Yours,

Ambition was no crime but this was not the right tool to service it.

At the bottom of the black box he found the first draft of his speech for the Party Conference. He put it back immediately, unread. The Political Secretary, Jeff Scott, could not seriously expect him to focus on a speech, however important, a full month before it was due. This was just Scott's way of reminding his master that the Conference and his least favourite speech of the year were looming.

The whisky and the cigar began their benevolent work. The Prime Minister relished the red boxes and sped through them in top gear. A detailed commentary on the report from Hong Kong that had alarmed the American Ambassador, the latest round of correspondence between ministers on the public expenditure round (growing in asperity as the deadline approached), a new study by the Chief Inspector of Prisons on the implications of overcrowding – his mind leaped easily from one subject to another, his fountain pen ticked, annotated and recorded decisions as required. A contented hour passed. This was his trade, and on rare occasions such as this he felt master of it. The Prime Minister knew that he had two political gifts. His mind was educated and orderly, able to test and follow through an argument. He had a knack of seeing with some sympathy into the minds of others, which made him a good colleague and an excellent chairman. Other more heroic gifts such as a subtle intellect, a soaring imagination or resounding eloquence he left to others.

An hour passed, then another. The cigar abdicated. The whisky glass asked to be refilled but its request was ignored. The Prime Minister got up to wind the thirty-hour grandfather clock, the final ritual of his day. The clock, given by a wealthy patient to his grandfather the surgeon, was large but delicate. No one wound it when the Prime Minister was away.

He passed into the next room. Louise was asleep, tidily on her side of their double bed. An old-fashioned hardbacked novel lay sprawled open on its front beside her. *The Heart of Midlothian* – among her unexpected tastes was Sir Walter Scott. He carefully closed the book, and put it on her bedside table. Louise liked reading but had no respect for books.

In his pyjamas on his way to bed Simon visited Julia's empty room. It was impeccable now, as never during the school holidays. When Julia was at home he and Louise grumbled incessantly about a slum ankle-deep in clothes and all kinds of fashionable litter. But it was a sweet disorder. He resented now the impersonal tidiness that meant his daughter was away. He remembered earlier, noisier, happier childhood days in a house that was their own and with a daughter who still belonged to them.

A few minutes after the bulb by his desk had gone out, signifying that upstairs the Prime Minister had turned off his bedside light, the Duty Clerk received the message by secret fax from Stormont. 'Terrorist attack by Breakaways believed imminent, County Down.' The Duty Clerk looked at it carefully. There were no details of target or timing. There was no action the Prime Minister could take. The message would have been seen by all who needed to know. The Secretary of State for Northern Ireland was there on the spot, at Hillsborough Castle. He would have been woken by now. The Duty Clerk logged the message and let the Prime Minister sleep. He himself conjured up in his imagination a mortar concealed in the woods below Stormont manned by Breakaways in RUC uniform, aimed at that white overwhelming palace on the hill, symbol of Unionist rule.

Wednesday September 17

Allied to his political gifts Simon Russell had two physical attributes, hardly less important to a Prime Minister. Food and drink suited him, and he slept well. The alarm by his bed was regularly set at six fifty-five am. He was always half awake through the weather forecast, fully alert for the news. During his early career, the first morning news bulletin had been a friend to be eagerly welcomed and embraced, harbinger of another exciting day in the history of Britain and his own upward climb. Now the bulletin was an enemy, often bringing unwanted surprises to overload a full life. But that morning he expected nothing in particular.

'A mortar exploded two hours ago in Newry police station in Northern Ireland. Five police officers were killed and fifteen others, including the Chief Constable of the Royal Ulster Constabulary, seriously injured. The full list of casualties is not yet known. No organisation has yet claimed responsibility but police sources say that a warning signal was received, in vague terms, using a code known to the Breakaway Group of the IRA. This was the first terrorist attack in Northern Ireland or anywhere else for five years. It has been strongly condemned by church and political leaders. The Cardinal . . .'

Simon fumbled in the bedclothes for the television commander and switched on the set. He was just in time to catch the photograph. It was a still, taken at first light by a local newspaperman before the TV cameras arrived from Belfast. Already the photograph was hurtling round the world. Within hours hundreds of millions of people who could not find Northern Ireland on a map would know what had happened. A girl of about eight stood barefoot on the ledge of an upper-floor window in pyjamas, her face twisted with terror, clutching a small blue woolly rabbit with one ear. Behind her swelled a cloud of smoke, thick, white and threatening, so palpable that it appeared to pursue the girl towards the edge.

'It is now known that among the casualties was a little girl who jumped to her death a few seconds after this picture was taken. It is understood that she was the granddaughter of the Chief Constable, and that she was staying in the police station in advance of its re-opening by her grandfather at a ceremony planned for this morning . . .'

'Not again,' said Louise, and briefly wept.

The plans for the day disintegrated. The neat little diary card was torn up, the routine engagements cancelled, the haircut postponed. The Prime Minister dressed quickly and joined his Private Secretaries and Joe Bredon in the study on the first floor. Cabinet would have to meet. How soon could the Northern Ireland Secretary fly back from Belfast? He was on his way south to Newry now, of course. An hour there at the police station, an RAF plane to bring him back direct, say twelve thirty pm Cabinet. Sandwiches. Wine this time, not beer. Recall Parliament? Probably. Best done quickly. When did the Labour Party Conference start? Get in just before that, quick debate next Monday. Chief Whip to be sounded before Cabinet. Don't forget the Lords. Oh yes, tell the Home Secretary he really must come back for Cabinet. Plenty of time to get from Devon. Yes, it was essential as there would be a question of emergency legislation. An existing report on this? Yes, Lord Lloyd, 1996. Get it out, include in briefing for Cabinet. Meet backbenchers? Necessary, not necessary? Most would still be on holiday. Consult Chief Whip. Someone else should do it if it was done at all. Northern Ireland backbenchers would need special attention, of course. Press? Yes, press. TV cameras already outside in the street. PM would go out now and speak to them. No text needed. He would find own words. Interviews after Cabinet? No, too soon. Leader of Opposition? Right to brief him. Turnbull was usually sound in a crisis if he could be briefed before he was required to give his first comment. Ask him round here at one thirty. More sandwiches. What else? The substance, of course. Internment, troop reinforcements, appointment of someone to assume temporary command of RUC. Etc. etc. Cabinet Office to draft concise paper of options for Cabinet, clear with Defence, Foreign Office, Home Office, Number 10 – if possible with Secretary of State himself in Newry. Try to get him here by twelve for private word with PM before Cabinet. What else? The telephone rang.

'The Irish Prime Minister on the telephone, Prime Minister.'

'Ah Taoiseach, good of you to ring. Yes, evil is the word . . . I had hoped . . . yes, the little girl . . . terrible . . .'

All this was done with brisk competence. Everyone there was genuinely shocked and grieved. But there was no time now to express the emotions that hovered in the room. In the room was also a professional satisfaction, inevitable not callous, at being part of an effective machine of government, showing its capability at a terrible moment.

The Secretary of State for Northern Ireland was late in reaching Downing Street. This was understandable. He had had difficulty in extricating himself from the carnage and media interrogation at Newry. With a police escort he was weaving his way through the traffic on the Hammersmith flyover. The Prime Minister spent the time wondering how the man would carry the new weight thrust upon him. James Whitman was solid, dependable, English. The Irish of all persuasions believed that the English were too selfish and stupid to understand the complexities of Ireland. But the English politicians whom they most disliked were precisely those who did understand. Simon Russell had decided to promote from the backbenches this Dorset squire, almost the last of his kind in the House of Commons, and it had worked well. All the Irish politicians North and South criticised him, trusted him, and were glad to dine with him. Of course he had achieved no *solutions*, but then Russell had long concluded from his own reading that in Ireland the process was more important, because more credible, than a solution. The process meant interminable talks. Unionists of both Unionist parties, Nationalists of both Nationalist parties in the North met and argued and quarrelled and parted, and quarrelled again and argued and met in an everlasting country dance under the genial and sometimes uncomprehending supervision of successive Secretaries of State. So long as the country dance continued, and there was no bombing and killing, the absence of a final answer hardly seemed to matter. Until now.

But there was Patrick Vaughan at his elbow.

'Prime Minister, since you have a few minutes . . .'

'Well?'

'Would you like to speak to Artemis now? I happen to know that she is downstairs.'

'Artemis?' For a moment Simon Russell could not think what his Private Secretary was talking about, though a few hours before it had been at the top of his mind.

'Oh that. It can wait. Joe Bredon will do a perfectly competent job today. There's no hurry.'

'As you wish, Prime Minister. But I worry that the story will leak. I'm not sure whether Joe Bredon . . .' He paused.

'You think he'll tell tales?'

'Let's put it this way. If he's asked a direct question about his future, I suspect he may tell the truth.'

The Prime Minister thought for five seconds.

'Right, ask her to come up.'

Artemis came. There was no time for preliminaries. He hardly looked at her.

'Artemis, sit down. How long have you been working here?'

'Ten months, Prime Minister.'

'Right. You've done well. I want you to take over from

Joe Bredon as Chief Press Officer. Not at once. He must handle this commotion in Ireland. But in a week or so.'

Silence. So now he did look at her. Artemis was perched opposite him, her long body looking uncomfortable against the voluptuous contours of the armchair. She wore an old-fashioned flowered blouse with a frilly collar and large floppy bow at the throat. Then a pleasant tweed skirt, quite expensive, but not able to redeem the blouse.

'Well?'

'I'm surprised, Prime Minister. I never—'

'I thought you'd be pleased. Flattered, even.'

'I *am* pleased. But—'

'But what?' He sharpened his tone.

'But I'm not sure I'd fit. I'm not sure I have the right qualities.'

'I think that's for me to say.' The Prime Minister glanced at his watch. Damn the girl. James Whitman would be here any minute, Cabinet would start in twenty minutes, and he still hadn't read the Cabinet options paper. 'You'll do well. You're intelligent and steady, and most important, you know my ways.'

'And Joe?'

'That's my business too. But of course he'll go on to a good job. He needs a change, and I need a change. There's nothing against him.'

'But what will the press make of it?'

'Artemis, I don't have time for all this. I'm offering you a job at the top of your profession. Patrick Vaughan and I are clear that you will do it well. I ask you to agree. Do you agree?'

Another pause.

'Prime Minister, can I have twenty-four hours to think about it?'

She was flushed now, and for a dreadful second he wondered if she was about to cry or load on him some personal worry of her own. She had seemed happy enough last night with the boy on her arm. Why did everything become complicated once one thing went astray? It had been a mistake to ask her.

Cabinet went smoothly. Simon Russell knew that for a day or two Members of Parliament and the press would behave well. In the immediate aftermath of a disaster colleagues in the Government and the Commons, even the press, spoke and wrote with genuine feeling and restraint. It would not last. Within twenty-four hours, certainly as soon as the dead were buried, there would be awkward questions. He had gone over some of them with James Whitman in the upstairs flat a few minutes ago. Security had obviously grown lax after the short years of peace. Had anyone inspected the car park from the edge of which the mortar had been fixed? Was it really sensible to hold a publicised opening ceremony for the new police station? And, above all, how come that the little girl was sleeping in the station the night before the event? Arabella was her name. Bella, as the newspapers were already calling her, Bella because it fitted into a headline, screaming before her death against the fire about to destroy her, was piling up a ghostly fame as the hours passed. Children across the world would lie sleepless that night thinking of the fearful photograph they had seen on the news bulletin. She had been lost twice to her parents, once in the fire, now again when a girl with a name they had never used became the possession of the world, giving all subscribers an inexpensive moment of grief.

But none of this surfaced at Cabinet. James Whitman might not by himself have been able to give a sufficiently strong steer to his colleagues. They all liked him, but he had not been in the front rank of politics long. So the Prime Minister, contrary to his usual style, led from the front. He had spoken to Kingerlees at Defence immediately before the meeting, while the rest were clinking coffee cups in the hall outside the Cabinet Room. So he was able to propose the immediate despatch of an extra battalion to the Province. The Deputy Commissioner of the Metropolitan Police in London would fly over at once to Belfast to assume temporary command of the Royal Ulster Constabulary. Whitman had resisted this upstairs but the Prime Minister had swept him aside. The RUC themselves had no obvious candidate, and needed someone without a political or sectarian background to grip security without delay.

The Commons should be recalled from the summer recess for a two-day debate on Monday next. On a motion for the adjournment, Prime Minister would open. He went on to propose that the Foreign Secretary should fly at once to Dublin for discussion with the Irish Government. He would offer in confidence financial help to the Garda, maybe even to the Irish Army, so that they could be rapidly brought up to strength. He would discuss internment without trial and for the moment that possibility would be kept open, though it was only conceivable if carried out on both sides of the border, and the Irish were most unlikely to agree.

Whitman should see Doyle, the Sinn Fein Leader, and urge him to act in public and private against the Breakaways. An Ireland Committee of Ministers should be set up under the Home Secretary's chairmanship. Their first task was to consider before the Commons debate whether extra legal powers were needed against terrorism, either in Northern Ireland or in the United Kingdom as a whole.

The Prime Minister presented his proposals boldly, without elaboration, as if experienced people would know that they were the fitting response to the disaster in Newry. It worked. There was little discussion. Joan Freetown thought there was a case for introducing internment at once in the North, whatever the Irish reaction. She pointed out that if they waited, any chance of sweeping up any important Breakaways would vanish. The Home Secretary descended on her from a great height, analysing at some length the operational difficulties of internment without trial, stressing its short-lived popularity, and finally arguing against it as in principle unjust. Roger Courtauld had put some extra flesh on his big frame during his holiday. His face was red and rough, from wind and rain rather than sun. It was not clear that he had shaved that morning before leaving Devon. He was overdoing it, storing up trouble. The Prime Minister for a moment regretted asking him to chair the Ministerial Committee rather than chairing it himself. He had made the choice partly because Courtauld had experience in Northern Ireland, partly to tie down a loose cannon. Joan Freetown subsided, but from her expression and the movement of her wrists, the Prime Minister sensed her annoyance. The personal dislike between one important colleague and another in a Cabinet was the equivalent of lightning. You knew from the atmosphere that it was up there, stored in the sky, but you never knew where or when it would strike. At that moment the Prime Minister in his mind heard a faint rumble of still distant thunder. But he was able to wind up the meeting quickly.

'Notice anything odd?' he asked Patrick, who as usual stayed behind in the Cabinet Room after the ministers had left.

'Odd, Prime Minister?'

'A dog that didn't bark? Or rather, barked in the wrong place?'

'You mean . . .?'

'I mean the Chancellor. Here she is, locked into a fierce

public expenditure round, arguing bitterly about a million or two here and there – and she swallows without a murmur a big reinforcement of the Army in Northern Ireland, plus an offer of help to Dublin that is almost open-ended.'

Patrick paused.

'It's often like that.'

'Quite right. There are dozens of departments at the Treasury with the task of straining at gnats. Swallowing camels is a function reserved for the Chancellor herself. Strangest of all, she does it without noticing . . . Nothing fixed for lunch?'

'No, Prime Minister. You remember, we've cut right back on lunch-time commitments since—'

'Right, I'll go to the Beefsteak.'

Simon felt the political weather closing in on him. Forty minutes over sausages and mash with an amusing mix of non-political people would help the sun to dodge the clouds for a little longer. He misinterpreted as disapproval Patrick's fleeting look of concern. He soon realised its cause. Outside Number 10 Downing Street, between him and a lingering group of photographers, stood a sleek black Jaguar. Behind it was another, identical. Neither was his usual car. Nor did he know the stout bald man in the driver's seat of the front car.

'Protection,' murmured Patrick, 'I thought it best not to wait.'

Simon had put aside for further thought the submission on his personal protection in the box last night. But that was before Newry. He checked his irritation. Patrick had been right to bounce him.

'Beefsteak Club, please.'

The car was warm inside, and the driver had recently smoked a cigarette, though not in the car itself.

'How do I open the windows?'

'You don't, I'm afraid, sir. The car's completely sealed. But I'll adjust the ventilator.'

The moving prison moved up Whitehall, the prisoner sitting upright against the cushions, mourning for liberty and fresh air.

*

Dobrinsky was always amazed at the luxury of the Northern Fleet. He regarded Murmansk as the least attractive place of human habitation that he had ever seen. Nowhere except in the Soviet Union would large numbers of men and women have been compelled to live so close to the Arctic Circle. They had taken their revenge. A lack of paint, an abundance of rubbish, total absence of any elegance, no pride of past, no hope of future, every artefact rectangular and brutal, the people themselves ugly and humourless. Their only merit was that they had elected him Mayor which, properly seen, was a merit of his not theirs.

By contrast thirty miles away, the Northern Fleet at their base at Severomorsk glowed with tradition, efficiency, even luxury. The marquetry of four woods in the panelling of the Admiral's cabin reminded Dobrinsky of a room in the museum at Novgorod, where he had grown up. This was not, or not entirely, a matter of rank. One deck below in the petty officers' mess, even a deck lower among the ratings there was still space, style and a profusion of chess-boards. Dobrinsky had once heard the Admiral ask the commander of a visiting British frigate, only partly as a tease, how he managed to induce British sailors to live in such cramped conditions. In Russia the problem was the opposite: how to persuade sailors that their services were no longer needed, and they must leave their cocoon of discipline and security for the muddle of crime and corruption that symbolised post-Yeltsin Russia.

It was this dilemma that gave Dobrinsky and Admiral Volkarov a shared opportunity. The Admiral was stout, with a rough, red complexion and a thatch of white hair. He looked the part of naval hero, but all his manoeuvres had been on the stormy waters of Russian politics.

'Let us be clear,' said Volkarov, filling his guest's glass. 'Your proclamation will say specifically and without equivocation that all redundancies are to end forthwith through the Russian fleets.'

'Correct.'

'Northern, Black Sea, Far Eastern.'

'All three.'

'Army and Air Force?'

'That would go too far. At present, I have no idea what that would cost.'

'You have no idea what the Navy would cost.'

Dobrinsky smiled.

'But I need the Navy.'

'You will need the others to get you to the Kremlin.'

'Maybe. One step at a time.'

The Admiral paused. He had considered getting in touch with the Chiefs of Staff in Moscow. They were as troubled as he by the cuts in the services ordered by President Andreyev, the plump bearded economist who now ruled from the Kremlin. One quarter a Jew, they said, and it showed. But the Admiral knew the caution of his three service colleagues, which had earned them survival in the turbulence of Russian politics. They had not met this Dobrinsky, a politician with the bearing of a soldier, the passion of a preacher, the looks of a poet, a natural leader of Russians, so the Admiral thought. Knowing himself well, he wondered for a moment whether his high regard for Dobrinsky owed something to the young man's broad shoulders, slim waist and ready smile. The Admiral knew that his own life, spent overwhelmingly among sailors, had slowly reshaped his sexual tastes. But not, he thought, obscured his judgement or his own natural caution.

It was early days yet. But four of his warships, three frigates and a submarine, were already on their way round Norway, and would enter the Baltic next week.

*

'I don't understand you.' Frank shifted irritably on the hard bench. 'You've always wanted the job. Five thousand pounds extra a year is not to be sneezed at.'

Frank always seemed to talk in clichés nowadays. They were only a few yards away from the place where they had first made love. Artemis had been physically reluctant. She had also been vaguely conscious that a sophisticated government information officer with a degree, recently transferred to the Prime Minister's Office, ought not to give herself to a fair-haired young PR man with no degree, on the ground in Richmond Park during a heatwave in August, without even a rug. Frank had disappeared for a moment and returned, having taken the only bold decision of their relationship. It was a working day, and there were few people around. Anyone seeing Frank pushing his way back through the high bracken to the clearing where they had picnicked would have assumed that he wore at least trunks under his torso. Artemis guessed that he was naked and as he approached felt a new shiver, never evoked during earlier encounters with intelligent mates on university beds and sofas. Her excited surrender had been quick and total. Even that first time Frank had turned his head away afterwards and slept in her arms among the green fronds.

Now it was autumn, they were a year older, sitting in sedate clothes side by side on the bench overlooking Pen Ponds. In front of them were dogs, a kite, perambulators and a total absence of romance. They had shared a chocolate bar.

'It's a big decision,' she said.

'It's not a big decision at all. It's not even changing jobs.' Frank had changed several, each time moving sideways. 'It's a simple case of promotion. You've always liked old Simon. You've always said you'd cope better than that dimwit Joe Bredon. And . . .'

'And, what?'

'Well, sweetheart, it'd be a help to both of us.' He touched her long fingers with his own, and she saw the nails bitten to the quick. Frank wanted, but they could not afford, to move from Hammersmith to Chelsea or at least Fulham. He made the second bold move of their relationship. 'We could get married.' She knew it was spontaneous because he at once retreated. 'That is, if my own job works out well.'

So there it was. Or rather, quite clearly, there it wasn't. Frank had taken off his coat and slung it on the back of the bench. Through a gap between shirt buttons below the ribs she could see a ridge of flesh still brown from their holiday in Brittany. She found that glimpse of skin entirely sexless. His stomach was thickening as his hair thinned. Nowadays she was fondest of Frank when he lay helpless in sleep beside her. It was part of her life to protect him in a world where his asset, fresh good looks, was dwindling fast. But this was not, emphatically not, a basis for marriage. That was the easy decision. She turned her mind back to the difficult one.

'It's a pity I have to decide so soon.'

Frank did not entirely succeed in keeping the relief out of his voice that his proposal of marriage had been shunted into a siding. 'You don't,' he said. 'I can wait.'

She laughed, and touched his cheek with her hand.

'Silly Frank, I was thinking of the job, not marriage. You know perfectly well that being married would not suit us.'

Frank knew it. He was humble at heart. He realised that he could not keep up with Artemis as year succeeded year, as he spent more and more time on the racecourse, and his sideways movements began to tilt downhill. He returned to the argument on which he was certainly right.

'You mustn't keep him waiting. He's probably on the rebound already, thinking who else he should ask. You'll be busy. You'll enjoy the work, you'll be better off. And there's absolutely no downside.'

He was right. There was no downside. Except . . .

'I'll have to see such a lot of them.' It was the closest she came to telling Frank, or herself, her vague but real worry. He mistook it.

'Oh, you mean Louise. That old battleaxe. Yes, you'll have to keep out of her way.'

'I didn't . . .' Well, no point in pursuing that. Frank was right. All the arguments were on his side. No one would understand any other decision.

'You're right, Frank. I'll do it. But unless you get a raise too, we can't manage even Fulham.'

'Good girl.' He had won.

A breeze had begun to blow from the lake. Whistles and houts summoned dogs. Prams pointed homewards. They valked hand in hand towards Roehampton Gate. She varmed to him. He whistled without a tune.

'I'm glad you're happy,' she said.

'Because you've done well. Because we're happy ogether.'

Happy Frank, foolish Frank, she thought, not quite nowing why.

Chapter Five

Friday September 19

This was a non-meeting. They had the evidence. Zhou had been remarkably careless. The three old men in the upper room of the Bank of China regarded Zhou as a typical product of Hong Kong – promoted too soon, too greedy, for himself, careless even in self-preservation. The bank account into which the bribes flowed had been in his girlfriend's name, easily traced. They would have no difficulty in getting the story from her. But what story? Who had corrupted this senior official? Neither Zhou nor she had made confessions yet, though both, it seemed, were ready once they knew what they were expected to confess. They were both young, were used to comfort and had plenty to lose.

There was no need to spend time deciding what was the truth. The story, like all such stories, was complex. Some pieces of evidence contradicted each other. Supplementary questions would be needed to produce a coherent account for Peking. For there was no doubt that the matter went beyond the jurisdiction of the Hong Kong Special Autonomous Region. The decision about a political follow-up would have to be taken at the top level in the Forbidden City. But the three men no longer believed, as they had once believed, that the top level would necessarily take the right decision. The disciplined definite days of democratic centralism under Chairman Mao or even General Secretary Deng were long gone. Peking would need help. The account that they received must help them to the right decision. But what was the right decision? The confessions of Zhou and his girlfriend were a powerful weapon. Against whom should it be pointed? They needed to decide this before any supplementary questioning was authorised in the Kowloon prison where the two were held.

They had never met of course, the Deputy Chief of Police of Hong Kong, the Deputy Chief Executive of the Special Autonomous Region (SAR), the Deputy Chairman of the New China News Agency. This meeting never took place. Neither their superiors nor their juniors would know, nor would anything be written down. It was not nearly as easy now as in the old days in the old Party to organise these matters. Absolute discretion was needed. All three in the room were over seventy. Each trusted the others, bound together by age and too much knowledge of each others' past.

It was soon settled. The preliminary questioning suggested strongly that Zhou had been bribed by and given intelligence to a gang of heroin dealers based in Manila, with some impressive connection in the past with the CIA. Left to themselves the authorities in Peking would probably build this up into a conspiracy by the United States administration to subvert Hong Kong. Ever since the Chinese walk-out from the World Trade Organisation and the latest deployment of the US Seventh Fleet in the Straits of Taiwan, Chinese relations with America were bitter, each side leaping, even beyond reason, to pick quarrels with the other. But this did not suit the three old men in the top room of the Bank of China in Hong Kong. The quarrel with America harmed Hong Kong, and made their tasks much more difficult. There was a fatter target immediately below them, around them, in the container terminals, in the new airport, in the rival banks with Scottish and English names, whose palaces glittered in the autumn sunshine – the British presence in Hong Kong. It was true that the British appeared to have no part in the story of Zhou and his girlfriend. But that must be because the questioning had been patchy, inadequate, preliminary in character. They would need to change the responsible cadres, insist on correct procedures and a more rigorous examination of the evidence. This was now urgent. A satisfactory account should reach Peking within a fortnight.

'Quite like the old days,' murmured one of them as they waited for the lift.

It was not sensible to comment, even in the lift. Instead they looked without affection at the pervasive photograph of President Jiang Ze Min. His predecessors would not have attempted to smile like that. The man looked like a Western politician – almost as if he was running for election.

*

Simon and Louise were both back at Number 10 by half past nine – she from chairing a leukaemia appeal committee, he from a reception at Conservative Central Office to encourage the Area Treasurers of the Party. He had nibbled at the weary and inexpensive canapés that the Chairman of the Party had thought appropriate for this occasion, and was not hungry. He picked his way through the salad Louise had prepared before going out, and wondered how the two of them were going to get on. Louise at the other end of the table was reading the last edition of the *Evening Standard*. Under the new policy of freeing his diary there were going to be a lot more suppers like this.

On the surface their marriage had been almost without disturbance. She had shared his eager interest in politics and in the early days they had gossiped and debated and given little dinner parties in Cheyne Row. His friends were fascinated by this handsome older woman whom Simon had produced from nowhere. Louise had been forty-three when Julia was born, which made it for her an almost miraculous event. The birth had roughly coincided with his first ministerial office, at Transport. There had been no money for a nanny on top of the Chelsea mortgage. Louise had proved a strenuously conscientious mother. Neither had noticed, he supposed, how they had diverged, and let the shine pass from their marriage. She thought about Julia and their social life and money, he worried about work. She became authoritative and somewhat short of temper. He began to keep out of her way, preferring the company of his boxes and men-only dinners. They no longer made love. When he entered the Cabinet and later became Prime Minister this divergence fitted neatly into the nature of the job. Louise performed equably and in style her duties as a Prime Minister's wife. Luckily she discovered a gift for sculpting, and nowadays spent contented hours either with her professor in a studio in Wandsworth or following up his instruction by herself at Chequers. There was no time for a private existence together. Neither seemed to feel the loss of something that had never been strong. Their short holidays were spent enjoying sun, wine, unpolitical friends, music and pictures, none of those in abundance, none with passion. They were only awkward in each other's company after Louise had lost her temper after a disagreement.

His heart attack had brought them together. For the first time Simon had thought about their relationship. He realised that the mainspring of Louise's life was her wish that he should live, and be happy. He had been touched. If in Tuscany she had really pressed hard that he should resign, he would in the end have agreed. But she had realised that in that case, though he might live longer, he would not be happy. He saw that, and was again grateful. Now they were back in the routine, and he saw that the routine would drive them apart again. It was happening already, Louise was rustling the paper, and he was wondering whether to ring the Duty Clerk for his evening boxes. For a moment he thought of defying routine, of going to kiss Louise, of taking her through these thoughts and seeing what happened.

But she broke the moment.

'Joe Bredon is still here.' The tone was as yet even, unchallenging. He hoped it could stay that way.

'He'll be off in a day or two. He'll go to Downbrook in the Lords.'

'Who comes in his place?'

'I've asked Artemis Palmer.'

Louise lowered the paper and thought.

'I'm surprised.'

'Why?'

'She's an intellectual. You need a showman. Her intelligence will hold her back. And she's plain. The hacks won't like that.'

Simon relaxed. This was not too bad.

'She hasn't accepted yet.'

'Really? I'm glad she's got a bit of coquette in her. But she will, she will.'

Monday September 22

Her father, the Chief Constable of the Royal Ulster Constabulary, had taken a turn for the worse. She had been called to the hospital. The multiple fracture of his leg was sorting itself out, but the injury to his head where the roof beam had struck was not yielding to treatment. He was running a high temperature. His life was in danger.

Arabella's mother did not spend long by her father's bedside. She spent all of it thinking of her daughter. He was sedated and barely conscious, his outdoor face tossing this way and that on the pillow. They had never been close. As she watched him she could think only of him insisting that Arabella come with him for the ceremony at Newry. It would be his sixtieth birthday, and he had promised to give her a good time. 'A cracker of a time,' he had said. 'As my birthday present, please,' he had said, the last time she had seen him. She, thinking it was a small thing and that she owed him that much, had relented. Arabella, of course, had been keen. Arabella quite liked her grandfather. Arabella adored, or rather had adored salutes, uniforms and a brass band. There were plenty of these in Northern Ireland.

That was then. Now the flowers, wilting on Arabella's grave, had to be protected by a police guard. Outside in the corridor of the Royal Victoria Hospital were eight or nine police officers with submachine-guns. The Breakaways might well try to finish what they had begun. Several hospital porters with addresses in Nationalist areas of Belfast had been given paid leave for the duration of the Chief Constable's stay in the private room alongside Ward 8.

For herself she did not greatly care if her father lived or died. If he died there would be speeches and a memorial service, many more flowers and a new round of sympathy for herself. It would be a sympathy as routine as the setting of the sun. On the other hand if he lived there would be awkward questions and criticism and his final setting would not be happy.

The television was blaring in the waiting room among the magazines. As the news bulletin began she turned the sound right down. The Prime Minister was speaking in the House of Commons. It must be the special debate on Ireland for which Parliament had been recalled.

She could see that the benches were full, and members wore a serious, even sad expression. Politics, she supposed, drove Simon Russell as he stood tall and dignified at the dispatch box. Politics had driven the Breakaways to fire that mortar. She had no desire to hear what the Prime Minister was saying. She watched Russell finish his speech, collect his notes and sit down. From the mere opening and shutting of mouths she could not tell how he had been received. The camera switched to the Speaker who would call the Leader of the Opposition. Politics had emptied her own life of meaning by killing Arabella. She did not understand, or wish to understand what politics was about.

Chapter Six

Tuesday October 7

Since the Conservative Conference had last been held in Blackpool four years earlier the Cosmopolitan Hotel had changed its owner and its name. For veterans of the Conference this was normal. No entrepreneur seemed able either to make a profit out of a five-star hotel in Blackpool or to resist the temptation to try. Each change involved redecoration and each redecoration carried the hotel a little further from the honest reality of tower, sand, trams and outrageous illuminations that gave the town its natural character of a jolly grandmother. This latest change in the hotel from Cosmopolitan to Colosseum had imported pillars for the small downstairs swimming pool, a job lot of marble busts for the entrance hall and, most awkward of all, Roman numerals for the bedroom doors. Neither staff nor guests were at home with these, though neither found the difficulty easy to admit. The only comfort, as the porters and maids constantly observed throughout the week, was that the chaos had been even greater at the Labour Conference a fortnight earlier.

James Whitman sat alone in Suite I. At least that had been easy to find – though disappointing when found, being tucked away in a corner overlooking the main parking space at the side of the hotel. The debate on Northern Ireland was scheduled for the first afternoon of the Conference – during the period immediately after lunch when it was reasonable to hope that the audience would be sparse and a shade lethargic. His speech lay on the small shiny desk in the narrow cubicle that adjoined his bedroom and justified the title of suite. In the hotel's more spacious days the cubicle had served as a broom cupboard and his bedroom as the table-tennis room.

James Whitman had attended party conferences before, though only when held at Bournemouth in his own county of Dorset. Blackpool was alien to him. More important, there was no resemblance between his role then – a popular county Member of Parliament saluting acquaintances, saluted by Cabinet Ministers as he gave tea to his constituents in the public rooms – and the ordeal that faced him now. The Home Secretary had advised him, jokingly but not in jest, simply to read out the speech before him at a steady pace, not using the teleprompter, not attempting to reply to specific points in the debate that would precede it. He envied Roger Courtauld, heavy in body, heavy indeed in political weight, but light in spirit, always in good humour – a fat man always on his toes. The speech before Whitman was the work of a group of able civil servants now far away in London and Belfast, except for one who had temporarily vanished into the recesses of the hotel.

Whitman's main contribution had been to cross out a number of complicated words, substitute plain ones, and slice up the longer sentences with full stops. Though all his advisers knew more about Ireland than he did, they did not know the difference between a written essay and a speech that had to be delivered. They had drummed into him, as had the Prime Minister, that in Ireland every political phrase carried a load of controversial history. This meant that verbal changes which ordinarily could be made to improve the rhythm or logic of a speech without danger, were dangerous when the speech was about Ireland. This made him nervous. The telephone rang, white and square on the fussy brass and mahogany of the reproduction desk.

'Is that the Secretary of State for Northern Ireland? This is the Number 10 Office. I'd hoped to find your Private Secretary. Patrick Vaughan would like a word with you.'

He was on jovial uneasy terms with Vaughan, as fitted dealings between a second-rate minister and a first-class civil servant working for the Prime Minister.

'Secretary of State?' Patrick was having a rough time and had a hundred things to do, but did not betray it. 'The Prime Minister asked me to say that he would be coming to the Winter Gardens this afternoon to support you.'

'Ah . . .' Pause. 'Thank you. Will you thank him for me? Much appreciated.'

This was a new blow. 'To support' was a ludicrous phrase. Many of the new relationships thrust on Whitman in the last few weeks were worrying, but none more so than that with Simon Russell. He was not ambitious and had not particularly wanted promotion to the Cabinet. Now he was keen to keep it. The Prime Minister had been understanding and helpful that terrible day after Newry, but there was no intimacy between them. Because they were all roped together, the leader had to help a junior colleague who had missed his footing on the rock face. But Whitman knew that the comment in *The Times*' leading article that morning was just. Russell had gambled on Whitman in the reasonable hope that he would have time to work himself into the job before he was severely tested. The gamble had failed. The working-in time had been denied. In four hours, no three-and-a-half hours, he would be on his feet in the Blackpool Winter Gardens talking about a crisis on a subject the audience had never understood well, and had now largely forgotten.

Whitman ordered sandwiches on the telephone – and a half-bottle of white wine – or a full bottle? It turned out to be his most important decision of the day.

In Suite VII of the Colosseum Hotel Joan Freetown was trying to do several things at once, an exercise that she enjoyed. The television was broadcasting James Whitman's speech. He looked solid and settled, but she could not judge the success of his speech because she had turned down the sound. The mixture of a plummy voice and unexciting civil service prose did not appeal to her.

On arriving the night before she had condemned the regulation hotel desk as too small and finicky for proper work. After much telephoning, the manager of the local Social Services office had yielded up a reasonable desk, which filled one side of the room, under anaemic watercolours of fishing boats in Morecambe Bay. She had been hard at work all morning, having sent Guy out for a walk – 'a good long walk' she had specified. On a side table flanked by the piles of reference books sat her speech for the financial debate tomorrow. She knew it was as good as could be achieved in the circumstances. Her Conference speech came a few weeks before the completion of the two main exercises of the Chancellor of the Exchequer's year, the Budget and the public spending round. Then there were the markets to watch. The markets knew in theory that the Chancellor of the Exchequer was a politician but took fright if she began to behave like one. This meant restraint, even dullness, in her speech to the Conference, though Joan Freetown knew in her heart that she could never really be dull.

Her eye was caught by a commotion on the TV screen. She clicked the monitor by her side to get the sound.

'. . . nothing but a pompous fool and traitor to the Union.' Then a small scattering of applause. The bellow had come from a middle-aged man ten rows from the back of the hall, who had somehow concealed a megaphone about his ample person and was using it to good effect. Red-faced with passion and exertion, he was hustled out into the aisle and then out of the hall by two young stewards. The cameras switched back to Whitman who stood at the podium irresolute, his mouth open. He took half a decision, looked down at the script on the rostrum in front of him, and resumed reading his speech.

'Despite its obvious attractions the dangers of internment without trial were well established by the experience of . . .' He paused. The full bottle of Chablis in his brain was breaking loose.

The bronzed masterful lady in the Chair made a mistake. 'Please carry on, Secretary of State.'

The wine took charge. 'No, Madam Chairman. I'm damned if I will carry on. I want this Conference to know something. I never wanted this job. I knew it would be difficult, even dangerous, dealing with a lot of politicians who are hopeless bigots living in the seventeenth century. At least they had stopped killing each other. Now they've started again . . . and you lot.' The Secretary of State turned his attention to his audience. 'That was a piffling debate and you know it. The opener, I forget his name, gave us a load of platitudes. Which of you has ever been elected to anything or run anything? You're just gathered together to listen to the sound of your own voices and make life impossible for ministers. I've heard a lot of silly suggestions in the last half-hour, which I have no intention of adopting. And now that red-faced oaf with the megaphone . . .' He tailed off. The wine ebbed. He grabbed a glass of water. 'And that, Madam Chairman, is my reply to the debate.' The Secretary of State for Northern Ireland hiccuped.

There was a rustle of pleased excitement in front of him. That was the sort of thing the delegates came for – well worth the train fare. The lady chairman, schooled by three decades of annual general meetings, thanked Whitman in a high voice, apologised for the interruption to his speech, and passed quickly to the debate on transport. Whitman was got off the platform somehow, and led flushed and silent through the crowd of microphones that had instantaneously gathered at the foot of the platform steps.

Joan Freetown disliked any histrionics except her own, of which she was not conscious. So that was the end of Whitman. A Secretary of State for Northern Ireland should have either ideas or rock-like calm. Whitman had just shown that he had neither. The event would grab the headlines tomorrow, Wednesday. Could she grab them back for Thursday with her speech tomorrow afternoon? It was a challenge of the kind she relished.

The telephone interrupted her train of thought.

'Yes.'

'I'm sorry to disturb you, my lady. It's Inspector Harbottle, Senior Protection Officer, Lancashire Police.' It was odd how many people thought she had a title.

'Are you expecting your husband?'

'What do you mean?'

'There is a gentleman here who claims he's Mr Guy Freetown. Says he's been on a walk. But he's got no pass, no papers, not even a credit card.'

'It's my husband. Send him up.'

Guy was quite unknown to the world in general. She doubted if he would ever cope with the regime of security passes and courteously insistent police officers that had suddenly been clamped on them all since Newry.

When he appeared, he had something else on his mind.

'I've asked him. He'll come. Louise too, he thinks.'

'What on earth are you talking about?'

'The PM. I bumped into him on the seafront. In the middle of twenty-five detectives. I asked him if they'd come to Little Stourton the last weekend in November. You remember, Joan, we discussed it at breakfast the other morning.'

'But I never . . .' Then she stopped. She had neither agreed nor disagreed when Guy had surprised her with this idea one morning at breakfast at 11 Downing Street. She had wanted time to think about it. It was highly unusual, and certainly contrary to the Treaty between them, for Guy to act without her agreement on something that concerned them both.

Her instinct was therefore to override him. At Little Stourton she softened a little, turned half away from politics, almost relaxed. She would certainly not relax if the Prime Minister was there. On the other hand she did not want an argument with Guy the afternoon before her Conference speech. She was in her heart somewhat scared of Simon Russell, who saw deeper into her than she liked. She disliked Louise, with whom she shared no interest. Nevertheless there was something to be said for two days at Little Stourton during which the Prime Minister would in effect be at her mercy, exposed to no political influence except her own.

'All right, Guy, you win. Provided you cope with Louise.'

'There'll be young Julia as well.'

'Now I understand why you're so keen.'

And so the conversation petered out, as conversations between married people usually do. Joan turned to sharpen her mind on her next problem. She intended to use the Conference week to clinch the public spending round. The updated state of play was at her elbow, holding pride of place even over the Conference speech. There were still some skirmishes ahead with smaller ministers, but she could quickly win these once she had stormed the two big fortresses which still held out. Her calculation was simple. She was mistress of the facts and figures of both Foreign Office and Home Office spending. Makewell and Courtauld were not. Budgets bored both of them. They relied on the officials in their Finance Departments to protect them. But these official servants of the State could not under the rules attend a party conference. So the two rebel chieftains had been forced for these four days to leave their fortification and sally out unprotected on to the plain of Blackpool. Now was the time to pounce, cut them up, storm their redoubts.

She pressed a button on her telephone and spoke to her Private Secretary.

'Could you please arrange for me to see the Foreign Secretary? Yes, before my speech and his. I will go and see him in his suite. Tell him it's rather urgent.'

Peter Makewell knew what had happened before the telephone rang. He had been brooding over a telegram from the British Trade Commissioner in Hong Kong, who had been secretly warned that British firms might find themselves in trouble over the Zhou affair. Yet M16 swore that Zhou had never worked for Britain. Suddenly his attention shifted. There in the corner of his bedroom flickered Anatoly Dobrinsky in St Petersburg, smiling, orating, first on a warship with the thin slender spire of St Peter and St Paul behind him, then in an armoured car driven slowly through cheering streets, now on the balcony of the Winter Palace, a huge crowd gathered below. Makewell hated broadcast noise in his bedroom and anyway was changing for dinner, so the sound was down. The text of what Dobrinsky was saying would reach the Foreign Secretary soon enough. He was interested in the look of events and of people whom he did not know but who were now entering his life. Dobrinsky had glamour, that was the first point. Makewell, having no glamour himself, serving in the unglamorous government of an unglamorous country, disliked the quality but knew its power. The autumn sunshine in St Petersburg must be quite brisk. The television showed almost everyone wearing a coat. But in the armoured car, now on the balcony, Dobrinsky wore no coat and his open white shirt was unbuttoned halfway down his chest. Not right to his navel like a film star, but far enough to tell Makewell that the man was trouble.

'The Russian President on the telephone.'

Hardly a surprise. Makewell could imagine Andreyev, where he had indeed once seen him. He would be sitting in his small office in the heart of the Kremlin, decent, pedantic and today tetchy because scared. He would be ringing round the world to tell them the bad news, which everyone he talked to already knew. Remarkably there was no hint of power in his office, no suggestion of the white and gold splendour, the battlements, the cupolas and the cannon a few yards away – just a portrait of President Yeltsin staring from the bare plasterboard wall on the hardware and software, the spindly desk and angular chairs. Andreyev was President by a narrow popular vote. A margin of two hundred thousand votes had made him master of Russia. As such he disposed of millions of whatever commodity, human or material, you cared to name. Yet, by choice or inability, he never projected himself as a man of power. You would have supposed a professor of international law in a provincial university, and you would not have been wrong.

'Ah, Foreign Secretary, thank you.' Andreyev spoke good, slightly accented English, with a thin voice. 'The

Prime Minister was engaged, so as the matter is urgent, I asked to speak with you.'

Entirely lacking personal grandeur, Andreyev did not mind that he was not talking to someone at his own level. There was something about Andreyev that led even well-mannered men like Peter Makewell to interrupt him.

'I have heard your news, Mr President.'

'Ah. You have heard that Dobrinsky has taken Petersburg.'

'I have.'

'He has already named himself Governor of the Northern Region, you know.'

'Indeed?'

'Indeed. I am advised that this is a breach of Article 202 of the Russian Constitution, which deals with the titles of public officers. I am seeking a clear ruling of the Constitutional Court on this point without delay.'

'Indeed, Mr President.'

'But you will see at once that there is also a political point.'

'Of course.'

'The man wants to go back, back, back in time, heaven knows how far. The Northern Fleet are already flying the imperial eagle. I have heard, though I have not been able to confirm this, that the sailors sing the Czarist anthem each morning. This too is illegal, a breach of the military code, which has the force of law. I do not have the exact article with me—'

'Mr President, if you will forgive me, what is the military situation?'

He could almost hear Andreyev forcing his mind into an unwelcome groove.

'I can summarise. Resistance of loyal troops in St Petersburg has ceased. There is trouble in Belarus. We have lost touch with Minsk after a report of a meeting in the central barracks there. The rest of Russia is quiet. The Speaker of the Duma has called for a special parliamentary session tomorrow. In my speech I will—'

'Excuse me, Mr President. I know that the Northern Fleet helped Dobrinsky. The rest of your armed forces?'

'Sound, so far, sound. Brassev thinks they will stay sound.' Brassev was Minister of Defence. 'He is of course mobilising to retake Len— St Petersburg. The Estonian Government is siding with Dobrinsky. But that is secondary. Mr Foreign Secretary, the purpose of this telephone call . . .' he became formal, 'is to signify my intention to come myself to the G8 Summit at Halifax next week and request the support of the United Kingdom and the other governments represented there in denouncing and suppressing this dangerous rebellion. I am sending you a memorandum of which the main points are the following . . .'

Makewell let him prose away. His own mind raced through the procedural implications. There would be time for substance later. Procedure always came first.

'You have been in touch with the Canadian Government, Mr President? They are of course the hosts for that meeting.'

'Yes, indeed, and they are willing if all the others are willing. My purpose will be . . .'

Peter Makewell felt a pang of sympathy for his own Prime Minister. He knew that Simon Russell had hoped to excuse himself from the Halifax Summit on medical grounds. Consulted informally, he himself had said that, though the Canadians would be disappointed, the agenda was so thin that no one at home or abroad could reasonably complain if the Prime Minister thought of his own health first. He had even begun, though mildly because he was no longer ambitious, to look forward to the idea of sitting in the British chair in Russell's place. Now Russell would have to go.

Andreyev eventually brought the call to a close. Makewell knew that it would have been monitored by the single Private Secretary who had accompanied him to Blackpool, and that the young man would soon knock on the door to compare notes and receive instructions. The rule in the Foreign Office that juniors did not knock on doors did not apply in Blackpool.

Peter Makewell finished tying his black tie and put on a maroon velvet smoking jacket, which he had brought down from the attic in Scotland after his wife's death. It was by three decades the oldest piece of dress worn in Blackpool that night. In his early days as a minister he would by now have been fretting over his speech, for the day after tomorrow. As it was, he was looking forward to the mild pleasure of a good dinner. In a few minutes, as he passed through the hotel foyer, delegates would greet him respectfully, smile behind his back at his antique garb, and suppose he was on his way to one of the myriad of political dinners or dances being held in Blackpool that evening. In fact he was dining with an elderly and entirely unpolitical couple, in a big house on a spur of the Ribble Valley, old friends with good pheasants.

'Ah, there you are, Francis.'

'Yes, Secretary of State.'

'You'd better pass all that on to Vaughan. I'll have to have a word with the PM tomorrow about Halifax . . .'

The young man was new and looked strained.

'Vaughan *is* here, isn't he?'

'Yes, Secretary of State. It's not that. The Chancellor of—'

Joan Freetown had overtaken her own message. She would undoubtedly be going out to a political or press dinner but had not yet changed. Her severe well-cut blue suit intimidated young men. She clasped a file.

'Ah, Peter. I'm sorry to disturb you as you're going out. This won't take long.'

She inserted herself into the room, causing the Private Secretary to flatten himself against the door.

Peter Makewell could see a letter in her file on Foreign Office paper topped and tailed by himself. He looked at his watch.

'I'm sorry . . .'

'These figures from your Office simply won't do, Peter.

You're busy, you won't have had time to look at them yourself. What I suggest is that you and I meet for breakfast tomorrow and work out what has to be done. Just the two of us. I know your diary is clear. There's been far too much shillying and shallying.'

'Joan. I'm late. I have to go now. More than that, I am simply not going to sidestep the usual channels for settling these matters. There is machinery—'

She ignited first. Maybe it was the velvet smoking jacket that did it.

'You're damned right there's machinery. It doesn't work. It acts simply as a cover for laziness and extravagance. I won't—'

He sparked second. The Private Secretary gaped.

'Joan, I'm sorry. I'm going out now. I have never in my life attended a working breakfast and don't intend to start tomorrow.' He looked for a clincher. 'What is more, there is a crisis in Russia. Andreyev has just been on the line. I shall probably need to bid for a substantial supplementary sum so that we can play our part. A hundred million perhaps. You can easily find that.'

Nonsense, of course, he thought as he walked quickly down the stairs, for he hated hotel lifts. He would try to keep Britain out of any commitments. But the woman had provoked him.

All life was a holiday for Roger Courtauld, or at least that was how he treated it. The clothes were different, but there was no difference in the Home Secretary's approach to a Party Conference or a family holiday in Devon. Overcrowding in the prisons received the same genial loud-voiced leadership as a disagreeable day of pouring rain on Dartmoor. That evening he surfed from hotel to hotel in Blackpool, attending the Wessex Area reception, the Northern Area, ditto his own East Midlands, the left-wing Tory Reform Group, the right-wing Monday Club, the Conservatives for Europe. Always he was offered a choice of red or white wine. Always he declined, obtaining and often paying for half a pint of real ale.

He began to glisten, his voice becoming louder, but he kept the political content of each discussion as low as possible. He moved on to another group whenever he saw real argument looming. His real worry at the Home Office was prisons, but no one in these rooms was interested in prisons except as a receptacle for those whom they disliked. This attitude over the years had made worse the problems he now faced. But it was no good trying to thrash it out at cocktail parties. There might come a time . . .

'Got a good speech for us then, Roger?'

A stout unknown from the Potteries, also with a tankard.

'A very good speech indeed.' He moved on.

'My car radio was nicked three times last year. Police caught the last young bugger, set him painting the lavatories in the comprehensive. Powerful poor job he made of it too. I went to pee just to have a look.'

They would all be the same. He had already heard the early morning news. The only political event yesterday had been Whitman's asinine performance in his Conference speech. 'Whitman must go', they all said. So Whitman must stay. That was one of the first rules. A minister attacked by the press was a minister preserved, at least for the time being. In fact Simon Russell thought James Whitman would settle well in Northern Ireland. He would have learned his lesson from the Chablis. What he had uttered when half-tight would harm him with the Northern Ireland politicians, but not for long. Almost as a matter of routine they said worse things about him. But today Whitman would need reassurance. The Prime Minister pressed the buzzer by his bed. Get on with life. For a moment he was surprised to see Jeff Scott, his Political Secretary, appear in the doorway. Then he remembered that for this week only Scott was in the ascendant. Normally he ranked well behind Patrick Vaughan in his claims on the Prime Minister's time. But in Party Conference week it was Vaughan who lurked in the background, a civil servant uneasy at a party political occasion. Vaughan was there in case he was needed, but behind the arras, speaking only when spoken to, conscious of invisible frontiers he must not cross. Scott by contrast, a round, pleasant young man with spectacles, came into his element this week. Sadly, even in his element he failed to shine. Jeff Scott made few mistakes and everybody liked him. He had achieved a creditable second in politics, philosophy and economics at Oxford. There was no possible reason to be rid of him. But he lacked that imaginative sparkle, that saltiness Russell knew he needed in a political adviser because they were the qualities he lacked himself.

'Good morning, Jeff.'

The Prime Minister scribbled a quick note.

> James,
> Don't worry about yesterday. You are doing a good job.
> Simon.

'Show that to the Chief Whip, will you, Jeff, and unless he throws a fit, put it in an envelope and send it to the Secretary of State for Northern Ireland.' A pause. Simon wanted to shave, take a bath and dress. He needed privacy. He had once in his youth worked for a minister who had done all this in public like a mediaeval monarch, shouting instructions even from the lavatory. That minister had not ended well.

'Come back, Jeff, in half an hour with Patrick. There's a lot to talk about.'

'Yes, Prime Minister. The Speech . . .'

He spoke as if in capitals. It was Wednesday morning. The Prime Minister had to make the final speech of the Conference on Friday morning. On his way in, Jeff had glanced at the desk in the sitting room on which lay his draft of the speech. It was pretty clear that the Prime Minister had not looked at it. The thirty pages of typescript lay tidy, virgin. There was time enough yet . . . but he was beginning to worry.

The waiter who cleared away the breakfast tray brought a small batch of telephone messages. Good wishes, last-minute invitations to party receptions, a man ringing from Scarborough about the end of the world, which was due on Friday – the usual screening machinery at 10 Downing Street did not work perfectly in Blackpool. The only important message was from Julia's headmistress. She apologised for intruding at a busy time but would be grateful if he could ring her, Sunningdale 846197. Louise would have to do that. He left the folded slip on her dressing table and put on the tie with the grey tigers.

Ireland, Russia, prisons, the public spending round – what else? In what order? And of course the Conference speech. And a message for the South Sussex by-election. It was in theory a safe seat, but in by-elections there was no such thing as safety. And the draft of the Queen's speech for the State Banquet next week for the Gulf Ruler of Qatar. And a dozen other smallish tasks in the big red box. Lurking there would be traps, temptations, dangers, hidden somewhere in the ordered prose and reasoned argument of each submission.

'The Foreign Secretary would like a word. About Russia.' This was Patrick Vaughan, diminished in authority at Blackpool, but never neglecting necessary business.

Here was Peter Makewell. He did not raise substance – what could the two of them decide about the future of Russia in a tawdry bedroom in Blackpool? Nevertheless, Russell allowed himself for a moment to think of substance. The newspapers had reported the sailors of the Northern Fleet singing the Czarist anthem. Russell supposed this was the thunderous tune at the end of the 1812 overture, emphasised with salvoes of cannon. Perhaps that tune and Dobrinsky, the young man with the open shirt, could do for Russia what Gorbachev, Yeltsin, privatisation and the International Monetary Fund had not yet managed. This was not a line of thought, more a line of dreaming, not likely, for example, to be corroborated by the next report of the Joint Intelligence Committee. Here was the Foreign Secretary, tweeded as usual, to discuss procedure.

'It's up to you, Simon. You were going to let it be known quietly in the next day or so that you were cutting back on foreign travel and that I would represent you at Halifax. We could still do that. It's just that a humdrum meeting will become more important now that Andreyev is coming. He will weep all over the place.'

'The Canadians have agreed?'

'They can't refuse.'

Simon had promised Louise that he would *not* go to Halifax. More or less promised, soon after they got back from Italy. But circumstances had changed. What was unimportant had become important. Moreover he felt fine.

The Airbus they had hired from British Airways was well kitted out, with a comfortable bed. Louise was clearly in an understanding mood. She would probably come too. He hated the thought of declining into the role of semi-invalid.

'I'd better go, Peter. But you'll come too.'

'Of course. And the Chancellor usually makes the third.'

For a moment the two men considered separately how much more agreeable the journey there – the hotel, the conference, the journey back – would be without Joan Freetown. Each knew the other was thinking the same.

Patrick was hovering, and the Prime Minister conveyed the unspoken thought to him.

'The Chancellor of the Exchequer may be preoccupied with the public spending round, don't you think, Patrick?'

'On the other hand, Prime Minister, she might welcome the chance of private conversation on that subject with the Foreign Secretary and indeed yourself.'

From time to time Patrick Vaughan entered effortlessly into the role of Jeeves, purveying unwelcome but correct advice.

Suddenly Louise was with them, flinging open the meagre white door between bedroom and sitting room as if it were huge, gilded, a prop on a theatre stage. There was a hint of Lady Bracknell in her tone.

'I am sorry to interrupt you, gentlemen. But your daughter has run away from school, Prime Minister. With an Argentine drug addict. Twice her age.'

Louise had earlier slipped down to the hotel hairdresser in her dressing gown. Her magnificently smooth grey hair seemed a sign not of age but of fighting strength. The gown was rich with chrysanthemums.

It turned out to be a less vivid story. Julia's bed at school had not been slept in. She had left on the pillow a note from a man called Jervis Read inviting her to a late-night party at his flat in Windsor. When telephoned, Jervis Read had confirmed that Julia was asleep on his sofa. The headmistress had insisted that he wake her up. Read had rung back saying Julia did not wish to speak on the telephone but was all right. End of story.

'Jervis Read?'

'Jervis Read. You remember. Julia met him at that party at Cliveden. Tall, looks like a Latin American. He trains polo ponies. The police once found amphetamines in his stables. Too many women in the jury. They acquitted.'

Louise looked round the room. Vaughan and Scott and Makewell were people she knew well and within limits trusted. That was why she had gone so far. She changed tone, down to the practical.

'Obviously I must go there. To the school, to the flat, and sort her out, the stupid girl. If, Patrick, you could look up the trains and arrange a car. I'll be off as soon as I'm dressed.'

Later, as they parted, she was still matter of fact.

'There's no point in talking about it any more till I've seen her. I don't know when I'll be back, if I'll be back.

With luck we can keep it out of the papers. I'll ring you this evening.'

A kiss and she was in the lift. Privately and a bit shamefacedly he thanked God that he had a wife who could rise so competently to a family crisis, and let him return to easy things like Ireland, Russia, the prisons and the Speech. He thanked God too soon.

*

Of course they had given Dobrinsky the principal suite of the hotel. It had been christened and re-christened over recent decades, and was now called the Grand Duke Nicholas. The Mayor of St Petersburg, the General in command of the Northern Region and Admiral Volkarov had agreed to meet and confer for five minutes in an adjoining sitting room before rejoining their new leader. They had spent the day with him. For Russians it was hard to call an end to a day of triumph. However, these three were professionals. In a few hours dawn would creep in through the window and count the empty vodka bottles. They must think of tomorrow.

'News from Moscow?'

The General grunted. 'I tried to talk to Brassev. They wouldn't connect me. I couldn't put our proposition. I wasn't willing to put it to his assistant.'

The proposition, which Dobrinsky had approved, was that if Brassev would get rid of President Andreyev and rally the rest of the Russian army to their northern brethren, he could remain as Minister of Defence under Dobrinsky and be promoted to the rank of Marshal, which would be reinvented solely for him.

'Doesn't sound too good.'

'It may take months. We shall have to dig in here.'

They had all known that the next step, the sweep forward to Moscow, would be the hardest.

'If Brassev and the General Staff turn against us they won't just sit in Moscow. They'll try to destroy us.'

'They'll be angry about our agreement with Estonia.'

'Damn Estonia.'

Admiral Volkarov in particular was vexed that this cheeky little country perched on the Baltic coast just west of St Petersburg had recognised Dobrinsky as Governor of the Northern Region. Estonia had made a shrewd move. The Admiral would have preferred to gobble them up. In a just world they belonged to Russia. By jumping the right way they had forestalled him.

'Black Sea Fleet?'

'Nothing stirring.'

'Belarus?'

'Our friends in Minsk are lying low after one demonstration in the street. Won't commit themselves.'

So they rambled anxiously, forgetting their leader, the young man waiting for them next door.

Finally the only politician spoke.

'A lot will depend on *his* stamina,' said the Mayor of St

Petersburg, a grey fat man who had for years administered the city's gas supplies. He hardly knew Dobrinsky and was twice his age.

'He'll stick it out,' said the Admiral.

'Remember the crowds will stop cheering after a day or two. Winter is not good here.' The Mayor paused. But he had to trust these men. From now on their lives and deaths were intertwined. 'There's one story going the rounds, which could destroy him.' He paused again. 'Boys.'

Admiral Volkarov, because he watched these things enviously, had indeed seen Dobrinsky's hand linger on the forearm of the handsome Georgian waiter at their first dinner in the hotel the night before. The Admiral had already acted, being at heart a better politician than the Mayor.

'Don't worry about that.'

'It's not true?'

'I said don't worry. Nothing to worry about.'

The Mayor dropped the subject.

'We'd better go in.'

But Dobrinsky was asleep in the huge room, curled up at an awkward angle in a huge armchair of pink velvet with an elaborate lace antimacassar. The walls were bare except for a range of large hooks, waiting for the next batch of politically correct photographs. The three men looked at their leader in silence. Each of them in that moment re-cast their relationship with him. Gone was the magician from the far north, dominating the crowds, a stranger to failure, drawing men and women irresistibly to him. This was an exhausted boy, whose future lay in their hands.

There was no question of further discussion. It was past one. Volkarov shook Dobrinsky by the shoulder.

'Time for bed. You've done well.'

Dobrinsky sprang to his feet. In that motion he became ten years less youthful, and again a leader.

'We have much to discuss. Moscow . . .'

'Tomorrow.'

He did not demur. The Admiral propelled him towards the bedroom door, then through it. The conspirators dispersed.

Dobrinsky took off his shirt and lay on the right-hand bed in the dark room. There were chinks of light from the bathroom door ahead of him, and from the sitting room which he had just left. He enjoyed the sense of luxury around him, the knowledge that there was Georgian champagne in a humming refrigerator, big bars of soap, aftershave lotion, even a Jacuzzi in the bathroom.

It was instinct rather than sight that told him he was not alone.

'I have a few more questions for the Governor of the Northern Region.'

He turned on the bedside light and saw her, sitting businesslike on the left-hand bed, tape recorder in hand, just as she had sat at his press conference three hours earlier. She wore a cream-coloured suit. Her abundant fair hair fell loosely over the collar.

'The English girl from . . .'

'Sky Television. Half English. My father was Russian.'

Dobrinsky thought for a second, then thought fell away.

'I can answer your questions better if you come to me here.'

She wore nothing under the suit. That having been established she seemed in no hurry. By contrast he stripped quickly and pulled her down beside him.

'You do not even know my name.'

'Tsars never asked names. Peter the Great was clear about that.'

'But you are only a Governor.'

'Your name is Tanya.' There had been several girls at the press conference.

'My name is Virginia.'

'Virginia is welcome. Who sent Virginia here?'

'What a question to ask a modern girl.'

Although she was slender she was somehow able to envelop his whole body. His neck and shoulders relaxed while the rest of him stirred. The girls in Murmansk had been large and mercenary, cabbages watered by greed. They had rushed at him, and he at them. Young men had lately seemed to offer more subtle pleasure, though Dobrinsky had been too cautious ever actually to sleep with one. Here was a girl, soft and loving, cultured; the first fruits of success, to be enjoyed only in the best suite of the best hotel in St Petersburg, like the wine and the aftershave.

He hurried, thrusting himself into her, not knowing how

to wait for her pleasure, taking himself abruptly from her as soon as he had finished his own work.

'You are a child,' she said, once she had him quiet in her arms.

'I will show you the contrary again.'

'You will prove my point again.'

'A child?'

'If not a child, then selfish. But I think a child. I can make you a man. A full man.' Silence. He began to drowse, wishing she would leave him, wishing also that she would come again and again into his life.

'Do you ever watch movies?' she asked.

'Hardly.'

'In the movies this always happens. Strange girl in the hero's room. Always a big room like this. Always a beautiful girl.'

'Bad movies.'

'Beautiful girl?'

'Beautiful girl.'

'I love you.' She spoke softly. He did not know whether to believe her. He did not know what it meant. His thoughts were already on another tack. She was beautiful, she was clever, she was English, or half English, she knew about the media. She could be very useful so long as she stayed loyal. He cupped her breast as if weighing it. She misread the gesture and moved her hands down to encourage him. But he did not respond.

'I love you,' she said again.

The Governor of the Northern Region was asleep.

Meanwhile Volkarov had left his bedroom door slightly open. He possessed six or seven paperbacks which he carried everywhere with him. That night he read *Anna Karenina*, suitable for St Petersburg. After about an hour Anna threw herself under the train. If Virginia had failed he would by now have heard her footsteps retreating down the hotel corridor. He had heard nothing. He turned off his bedside lamp, content.

Chapter Seven

Thursday October 9

Joan Freetown had written the three extra pages in her quick-flowing hand on notepaper of the Colosseum Hotel. Not that she had decided to use them. Indeed, on the whole she thought she would not. Her main adversary after all was Roger Courtauld. She held nothing personal against Peter Makewell. Even towards the Foreign Office her feeling was irritation rather than hostility. But when the time came to apply the final lipstick, take the decisive look in the mirror, bundle her papers into the slim, specially designed despatch case and descend to the Winter Gardens, she took the three extra pages with her.

There they were, twenty minutes later, as she turned from page 10 to page 11 of her typed speech. By now she knew pretty well her effect on the mass audience of the Conservative Party Conference. She had a small number of young passionate admirers before her. But most of those in front of her did not love her or understand much of what she was saying. They admired her looks, her trim scarlet suit, the bracelets, the silver wave against the abundance of black hair, her certainty, her predictability. In a few minutes they would give her a standing ovation, emphatic but not tumultuous. She would settle for that. She did not angle for applause at the end of any particular paragraph. The speech contained no striking phrases. She distrusted soundbites. It was the argument that counted, and could only be counted when complete. She followed the autocue faithfully, switching her eyes from the left-hand pane of glass in front of her to the right hand, speeding up her delivery slightly as she neared the end. She spotted Guy, half concealed behind a pillar half-right. Sometimes he came to these Conference speeches, sometimes not. He never sat on the platform, though a seat would have been provided. He never said in advance whether he would come, and she never asked. She was always glad to see him, though she never said so.

There they were, the three pages of hotel paper in her own hand, loosely inserted into the rest of the text. She did not actually take a decision to use them. She found herself well launched, and it was then too late to draw back. The autocue juddered to a halt. The texts of her main speech on the two panes of glass waited patiently for the Chancellor of the Exchequer to resume an ordered life.

'We shall have to make harsh choices, Mr Chairman.

No one should be in any doubt of that. As a Party we are committed to reduce taxation whenever it is safe to do so. That is a moral as well as a political commitment. We cannot honour that commitment, which lies at the heart of our Party's beliefs, and yet preserve intact every item of public spending of which some sections of the Party happen to be fond. I warn the Conference that it will not be enough to cut back on any unpopular spending we may find. We shall have to lean harshly on programmes that are dear to some hearts, perhaps even to some hearts on this platform or round the Cabinet table, but which are not essential. The Chief Secretary and I are still hard at work.'

The Chief Secretary, a bluff Yorkshireman called Walter Stoddart, sat up straight in his chair and began to scribble fiercely, as if slashing an excessive budget. Joan looked around to check that Peter Makewell was not on the platform.

'I cannot give you any details today. But I can give you an example. We are looking very hard at the way this country is represented abroad. If you are an Ambassador it must be pleasant to live in a handsome palace and employ an army of servants paid for by the British taxpayer. Pleasant, but is it necessary? If you are Foreign Secretary it must be pleasant to receive thousands of telegrams each day telling you what happened in each country an hour or so after the same story has been shown on television. Pleasant, but is it necessary? At the Foreign Office it must be pleasant for officials to go up a huge staircase to work in some gilded office which makes our poor Treasury look shabby. Pleasant, but is it necessary? Necessity, Mr Chairman, necessity is the test, and in every case we shall apply it rigorously.'

That was the end of the hotel notepaper. She had to pause to reconnect with the text on the autocue. In the audience two groups in particular applauded loudly – her natural fans, mostly young, and a larger group who were just delighted that something untoward had happened. Because strenuous efforts are made to plan and predict a Conservative Conference, the unpredictable when it occurs always gets a loud cheer.

When Joan Freetown finally left the platform a forest of questioning microphones moved to envelop her. But she had for the moment finished her outing. She had been guilty of a soundbite. The cat had to be put back in the bag.

'No change of policy . . . simply an illustration . . . could have used others . . . high respect for the way the Foreign Secretary runs his department . . . definitely a world statesman . . . collective responsibility . . . teamwork essential . . . no decisions yet . . . look forward to discussing the figures with him as with other colleagues.' She caught sight of Guy moving slowly towards her.

'You look gloomy, Guy.'

He waited until the microphones had dispersed.

'You should never have said that. It was mean and unfair.'

She was surprised, and snapped. 'It was perfectly fair. You don't know the facts and figures.'

They moved together towards the foyer of the Winter Garden. A small group of Young Conservatives called to her.

'Brilliant, Joan. You'll be our next PM.'

'You see, Guy?' She could not help saying.

Guy saw.

'Nothing to be done,' said Artemis.

'Nothing whatever? It was a monstrous unprovoked attack on the Foreign Secretary.'

'Nothing whatever.'

When Joe Bredon said this, as he often had, it sounded feeble. Indeed it had been feeble. When Joe Bredon said there was nothing to be done it meant that he had not thought of anything which could be done. When Artemis said it, she meant that she had thought the whole thing through and was sure it was best to do nothing.

It was the first time the Prime Minister had seen Artemis in trousers. She would never have worn them at 10 Downing Street. It was part of the subtle cultural change brought about by a Party Conference. Officials knocked hesitatingly on doors. Artemis was dressed as if on holiday, admittedly a cultural rather than a seaside holiday, as it might be a minor opera festival.

It suited her. Her office skirts were often long, to conceal thin calves. Her office coats and blouses did nothing for her figure. Her height showed to advantage once waist and hips were clearly defined. She moved easily across the Prime Minister's sitting room as if it was her own and turned up the sound on the television without asking him.

'The lobby correspondents will lap it up, just as they lapped up the Northern Ireland Secretary on Tuesday. But Sir Peter is not going to retort, I've checked with the FO. Labour will try to keep it going, but they won't succeed. It's a one-day story. It doesn't have legs to run longer unless you say something to keep it going. By the time you climb that platform tomorrow they'll be ready for something else.'

But what else? He caught Artemis looking sideways at the neat little stack of paper on the sideboard by the fruit bowl. She would guess that this was Jeff Scott's draft for the Prime Minister's big speech. She would also guess from its tidy appearance that he had not looked at it. That was not quite true. He had glanced at it. He had read enough to know that it was not something he would use. There was nothing actually wrong with it. Wedges of Central Office prose, some combative statistics, a fierce empty passage about terrorism in Ireland, some fence-sitting on public spending. Russell knew he would have to insert himself into the task, yet each time he turned his mind in that direction it receded. Sustained work was needed on that speech over the next few hours for which he had no appetite. He did not even want to begin. He found the presence of Artemis comforting. It might turn out to be stimulating.

'Help me with it,' he almost said. But that would be quite wrong. She was an impartial civil servant and this was a Conservative Party speech. He imagined that she voted Labour, but would not dream of asking. Other vaguer alarm bells also rang at the back of his mind.

On the screen Roger Courtauld was finishing his speech, coasting along with an anecdote about what a prisoner had told him recently in the Isle of Wight. In the old days the Home Office debate had been a nightmare. Delegates had loudly proclaimed their worship for a god called capital punishment which, if unveiled, would cure burglary, truancy and probably sexual immorality, as well as all violent crime. The god and its miracles were withheld from these frustrated worshippers by successive Home Secretaries. Because of these savage memories the party organisers had put the Home Office debate immediately after the debate on the economy, believing correctly that Joan Freetown would take the headlines. They need not have worried.

Roger Courtauld was a liberal Home Secretary who had inherited a tough criminal justice system, which he did not have the energy to reform. He knew that as a result the prisons were in a dangerous state, but the delegates in front of him did not. The lazy streak in him ensured that he did not tell them, though he knew he ought. The audience no doubt contained secret worshippers at the old shrine, but so long as the crime figures were on a plateau and the Home Secretary was large, bluff and reassuring, most were content.

'They don't bite like they used to,' said the Prime Minister as the audience rose to a moderate standing ovation.

'Eating out of his hand,' said Artemis.

The Prime Minister wondered how he should spend the evening. He had declined a dozen invitations and kept it free for dinner with Louise. A table had been booked at Wheelers, to be carefully placed so that all diners could see husband and wife amicable together without being able to hear their conversation. But Louise had gone to look for Julia. He knew what he ought to do instead. He should summon Jeff Scott and plenty of sandwiches and get down to the speech.

'Stay and help me,' he again almost said to Artemis. But one of his compromises formed naturally in his brain. 'Could you come back a bit later, say around ten? Bring the Halifax timetable with you. If I'm to go to the Summit, we need to make a plan for press and broadcasting.'

Alone, Simon Russell felt physically adrift, as if the switch that kept him supplied with energy had been turned off. In recent days something new had gone wrong. His back had begun to hurt, not hugely, but enough to irritate. He felt that minor pain most when he was alone. He did not want to start down another avenue of polite consultation with doctors and specialists, consuming precious time all over again. He had had enough of this after his heart attack. He went to the bathroom and swallowed two tablets of paracetamol. On his way back to his desk he paused at the window. It was a calm, chilly, characterless afternoon. The tide was far out and only faint ripples differentiated grey sand from grey sea. It was hard to imagine the ferocious storm that had once robbed two police officers of their lives a few hundred yards along that front. The egotism in Simon applied the scene to his own situation. He could hear the wind rising in his life and those distant grey ripples could soon become destructive monsters destroying his sandcastles and beating on his inner wall. Would he mind? Towards the horizon he saw the frigate that had been slowly patrolling all day between the Lancashire coast and the Isle of Man. Recalled to reality, he jotted down a query. What possible threat assessment could justify that ostentatious security measure?

The telephone rang. He knew it was Louise. Only she could produce that emphatic insistent note. And so it was.

'I need you here.'

'What's happened?'

'Nothing particular. Hardly anything of consequence. Your daughter has slept, may have slept, is going to sleep with an Argentine polo player. I can't find out which. Anyway St Clare's won't take her back. Or at least I can't persuade them. I've arranged for you to see the headmistress tomorrow.'

'If it's Jervis Read, he's not an Argentine.'

'He looks like one.'

'You know I can't leave Blackpool till Friday. My speech is at—'

This was clearly what Louise had been waiting for. He had stepped on the landmine. 'Listen, you may be Prime Minister but you're a father too. Only one child, thank God, at least so far as I know. But she's at the turning point. A stupid, obstinate, deceitful girl. But she's ours. She needs you. Which is more important, your daughter or another speech? What difference will a speech make? Julia needs you, I need you – now.'

This was clearly nonsense. Louise must be deeply stirred to lose her sense of proportion so completely. Whatever Julia had done or not done, could be as well discovered, cured or despaired of at the weekend as at mid-week. Nothing Louise had said suggested any new deterioration. Forty-eight hours could make no difference. If the Prime Minister suddenly left the Party Conference the news and the reason for it would be public at once. That could not conceivably do Julia any good.

'The press would—'

A mistake. Another landmine. 'All you think about is the bloody press. I've had enough of all this, Simon. I've lived this absurd life long enough, believing that if it ever came to the point you would side with me, not politics. Now you've chosen politics. Even though you're ill, I'm distraught, your daughter going over a precipice. For you, politics always comes first. Well, I can't help you any more.' Slam.

To coin a phrase, nothing to be done. No point pursuing the argument with his wife in that state. He wondered if anyone had been listening in. He would ring her again in the morning, hoping to find a different mood. It never occurred to Simon to change his plans. But a leaden weight settled on his mind, and his back ached at the bottom of his spine in sympathy with his low spirits.

The telephone again, this time the Political Secretary Jeff Scott, tentatively wondering whether he could be of any help with the Speech. Growing anxiety lurked behind the suggestion.

'No, thank you, Jeff. You've worked hard at it already. Now it's my turn. Could you order me some smoked salmon sandwiches and a bottle of hock? Right, that's it – and make sure it's Auslese. Even here they'll have it if you ask the right man. I've got plenty of fruit already. I've got a couple of boxes of Government work. After that I'll just sit and work on the speech myself.'

But even as he spoke another intention formed in his mind. An hour later he came back into his suite, swaying slightly. He had dropped in on the party given by Lord Cross in the penthouse suite of the hotel. There was no longer any particular purpose to this annual event, since Lord Cross had achieved a fortune and a peerage and his newspapers as high a circulation as was feasible. But the champagne continued to flow each autumn. Among the political editors, the wits, the wags and gossips, for whom this was the Party of the Week of the Year, Simon Russell lifted some of the lead from his soul.

'Good to see you looking so cheerful, Prime Minister,' said Lord Cross as his guest took leave.

Artemis was there in his room, as he had hoped, having induced the waiter to admit her. She had no more news, and they did not even begin to discuss the Halifax timetable.

'Help me with this,' he said. In the evening, with the champagne still happy inside him, it no longer seemed an absurd suggestion. Indeed for a vivid second or two he thought of nudging her into the bedroom and imagined how he might undo the shirt and tackle the trousers which she still wore. But drunken kissing and fondling, let alone rape, in a Blackpool bedroom were not his style. So they settled down on hard chairs at the table and tackled Jeff Scott's white mountain of a draft speech as if it was a pudding. Page by page, they amended, improved, amplified. Artemis ordered coffee, which came tepid. She boiled the kettle in the bedroom to hot it up. He watched her move around the room as if she was in possession. Would she ever rant at him as Louise had just done?

'It's no good,' he said when the coffee was half drunk.

'What's no good? It's better than it was.'

'It's boring. The audience will go to sleep after ten minutes instead of five. I have to do better.'

Artemis paused. He could see her wondering how far she could go. She edged her chair a few inches towards him, and pushed her hand through her short curly hair as if it was abundant enough to need sweeping back from her head.

'It needs an idea, Prime Minister.' She touched his forearm with her hand, then took it away. 'I have an idea.'

He did not want to talk about Artemis' idea. He wanted to talk about his back, about Julia and Louise, about the grey ripples and the frigate, about how the hell he was going to prevent Joan Freetown wrecking his Government. He wanted to ask Artemis about her young man, and how often they made love.

Instead they talked about Artemis' idea for the Speech, and she began to put it on paper. Simon had often noticed how the handwriting of an individual contradicted their character. Patrick Vaughan, for example, wrote his sober prose with a quick dramatic hand, the ink spluttering from the pen as if in high emotion. Artemis, a girl of force and imagination, wrote tidily and without character, a hand straight from an expensive private education.

It took half an hour. It was going to work.

'We'll have to clear it with colleagues,' said the Prime Minister.

Artemis laughed out loud, began to comment, stopped herself. This time her hand came out and stroked his grey hair, lightly and only for a second. Then she was gone.

*

'The conclusion is clear,' said the Premier after they had all read the report from the Deputy Chief Executive of the Special Autonomous Region of Hong Kong. 'The confessions leave no room for doubt. The British were responsible for Zhou. As a counter-measure it is proposed that we seize the four biggest British-owned firms in the SAR. This seems reasonable. Even attractive.'

They were sitting round the swimming pool in the heart of the government complex of Zhong Nan Hai in the heart of Peking. The pool was empty. It was famous because Chairman Mao had used it long ago. It was famous again recently because it had been closed as a gesture of public economy. Photographers had been summoned from all over the world to prove by an emptying pool that the rulers of China were suffering the same austerities as the rest of the population.

'Confessions always leave room for doubt.'

In the old days it would have been inconceivable that the Secretary General of the Party, a stripling of under fifty, should have spoken in this way about confessions. But this was the new China, and the new Party.

'My own information through the local Party is that this was a matter of heroin dealing through Manila. The drug merchants bribed Zhou. The British were not involved.'

The Premier thumbed impatiently through the file.

'There is no mention of that here.'

'I would not expect such a mention.'

There was a pause. The Chinese hierarchy was not yet experienced in ways of resolving disagreement expressed in open discussion.

The autumn breeze stirred the willow at the corner of the courtyard. Its shifting shadows passed lightly over the fading scarlet pillars of the pavilion. By bending a little forward the Premier could see the golden eaves of the outer partitions of the Forbidden City, the dragons at its edge sharp against the deep blue sky. This was the best time of year in Peking. He was due to play golf in an hour, at the Summer Palace with the senior trade representative of Taiwan. He became impatient. But he could not prevent the oldest colleague present from having his say.

'In former times we used to distinguish,' said the Chairman of the Privatisation Commission, leaning back in his chair, 'between bourgeois objectivity and socialist realism. In those days we always favoured socialist realism. In this case I would say that bourgeois objectivity would lead us to re-open the case. Two confessions obtained in this way cannot objectively be conclusive. There is a lack of supporting evidence. But I would argue that socialist realism points the other way. The Secretary General of the Party is right in his analysis but wrong in his conclusions. This is realistically the right moment to take over the British-owned firms listed in these reports, and sell the shares to our own people on our own stock exchanges. It would be a great act of Chinese privatisation. There will be legal arguments, but they will drift on for years. There will be a political row, but this is the right time for it, when everyone in the world is worrying about Russia and the young man Dobrinsky. At the hour when the tiger roars, the cat catches the mice. These are fat mice, the old opium-fed Hongs of Hong Kong. We are the cat.'

Chapter Eight

Monday October 13

Back at Number 10, Julia suddenly appeared.

'Mummy said you wanted a word.'

He cursed Louise. It is not satisfactory to examine your daughter about her way of life when you are naked and have ten minutes to climb into evening dress on your way to dine with the Queen. But he realised that this was unfair on Louise. Julia lived at home but was never at home. She arrived and left Number 10 at all hours without explanation, gobbling breakfast, leaving a trail of dirty Nescafé mugs around the flat, then away for two or three days, monosyllabic, unhappy. Here at least she was, offering her father a few minutes of her own time. And his time too was almost equally hard to pin down. The good intentions about his regime that had been worked out in Tuscany had faded away. Meeting followed inexorably after meeting.

This afternoon there had been two from the top rank of difficulty – public spending (inconclusive again) and Ireland. There had been some progress on what he called Artemis' idea because she had conceived it in that Blackpool hotel room. The rest of Whitehall called it NIPMI, or Northern Ireland Prime Minister's Initiative. He had been upstairs in the flat only for a bath and shave. The two processes together had taken him ten minutes.

The Prime Minister pulled on his underpants and reached for the telephone.

'Duty Clerk, please ring the Palace and say my wife and I will be about ten minutes late for the State Banquet. I have sudden work here that won't wait. Speak to Sir Robin yourself, please, and ask him to mention it to the Queen only if he thinks it necessary. We'll be there, of course, before the company moves into dinner. Now then . . .' He sat on the bed and beckoned Julia to do the same. Louise wanted him to cross-examine her about what had happened between her and Jervis Read that night. But that was for women to discuss. His concern was for the future. He plunged into the middle of it.

'What are we to do with you, Julia? Tell me.'

'You've lost weight, Daddy. You've got no tummy.'

'Never had much of one. But you're not answering the question.'

'*He* had a ludicrous little pot belly. Tanned like the rest of him. It didn't show in those marvellous Savile Row suits but once he'd stripped for action . . . I got the giggles, I'm afraid.'

'Look, Julia, I'm not asking . . .' But he was, of course, and anyway she was determined to tell it all. In fact, if he believed her, and he did, there was remarkably little to tell. Fed up with St Clare's, beguiled by a clandestine invitation to a late-night party, there she was in Jervis Read's flat in Windsor, enticed to linger after the other guests had gone, half-full of champagne, and soon half undressed.

'But it didn't work. He collapsed and I collapsed too. I just couldn't get rid of the giggles at how ludicrous he looked. Then he got cross, I don't blame him, and he found a brocade dressing gown and stumped off into his bedroom – end of seduction.'

'End?'

'End – he won't want to see me again. Nor I him. In the morning he made coffee, black muck, not decent Nescafé. He hardly spoke a word. I thought I'd better start telephoning, and the rest you know.'

It was no good commenting on the silliness, the triviality of it all, or on the turmoil she had created at school and home. Had she learned? At least by some miracle the papers had not found the story.

Simon put on his dress shirt and black trousers and began to tie his tie. Because he refused the ready-made variety, this added a minute and a half to each dressing period. Julia was in an excellent mood. He must make the most of it. She looked enchanting, sprawled on his bed, dark eyes watching him, glad to have broken out of her laager.

'There's no point in fussing around with St Clare's any

more. That woman won't have you back, and you don't want to go. But I've arranged for you to go to France after Christmas until June, two terms. Sauvechat, it's called. An international school, lessons all in French, both sexes of course, not a bad château, beautiful countryside, a long way from the British press. You can sort yourself out. In June you can decide what next.'

'I'll think about it.' The idea had obviously reached her already through Louise.

'You'll do more than think about it—' He felt a burst of irritation as he raised his arms to finish the tie, and his back hurt suddenly. But there was no point in trying to force the issue now. 'OK, you think about it.'

She kissed him on his shirt shoulder as she left.

'Tell your mother I need her.'

He always needed Louise to put on his medal. It needed fastening with a safety pin at the back if the cross was to hang straight and immediately below the tie.

'She talked to me.'

'So I should hope. You're her father.' Louise paused, safety pin in her mouth. She had finished her hair and face, which were magnificent. She looked entirely royal, even imperial, above the shoulders. In a few minutes she would put on the shimmering silver balldress that would complete her splendour.

'You need me,' she said, operating the safety pin. 'You'd never get to the Palace in one piece without me.' She too had lived in a laager of angry solitude since Blackpool.

'And you need me. You'd never have persuaded Julia to go to that school in France.'

'You've actually persuaded her?' The decoration needed only a slight but expert tug to reach its destined position.

'Well, not actually persuaded her. But she said . . .'

They were back on married terms, and he was glad.

But in the car there was no time to think of all that. Nor was there any need to think about the State Banquet for the Ruler of Qatar. That would run smoothly and tediously on golden castor wheels. The Prime Minister and his wife were required to attend, to smile and to chat through interpreters to the assembled Arab Highnesses and Excellencies. It was also an occasion for useful pieces of business with colleagues, or the Archbishop, or a Chief of Staff who could be delayed behind a pillar for a fruitful little chat. But tonight the Prime Minister wanted to use the time to order his own priorities. Louise would be cross if he started scribbling a note in the car, so he memorised the problems and tried to assemble them in order.

1. Public spending. Dangerous deadlock. How to break it? Might need a Cabinet reshuffle afterwards?
2. Artemis' plan on NIPMI, Northern Ireland Secretary still hesitant. But must be done soon if at all. When?

3. Halifax Summit, coupled with the Russian problems. This all seemed remote. Only Makewell and the Foreign Office were in a fuss. Public opinion was not interested. But he couldn't change his mind again. He had to go to Canada, and that meant sinking himself in detailed briefs over the weekend.
4. Prisons, possibly. Roger Courtauld had gone quiet. This was unusual. It might mean the situation was better – or that the Home Secretary was planning a surprise.

As the footman opened the car door, and he followed Louise as she swept up the stairs of the Palace, he wondered how he could tell her that he would not be able to come to her charity dress show at the Savoy on Saturday.

The speeches of the Queen and the Ruler had come before the meal, under the new custom which the Queen had recently introduced. It had been followed right across London, even in the Mansion House, to the great relief of both speakers and audiences.

Simon Russell always disliked the idea of State Banquets in advance of each of them. He complained inwardly when they appeared in his forward diary, and outwardly when he had to approve the programme, the draft speeches, even sometimes the traffic arrangements. He complained most loudly of all on the actual day when the time came to change clothes and prepare for four hours in a world of long-drawn courtesy where time stood still. But once he was inside the Palace door he warmed up, admired the splendour and particularly enjoyed Louise enjoying herself. She too complained at the preliminaries, but he had never known a woman so apt for such occasions. She did not act proudly or exploit her husband's position. She was genuinely and intelligently friendly to all whom she met, moving without awkwardness from group to group, remembering names, achievements and/or predicaments with a completeness that had long escaped him. At first she had asked him to stay close to her on grand occasions, but now she preferred to sail alone, always leaving a murmur of genuine admiration in her wake. The thought that Artemis would never do it so well entered his mind and was quickly banished as irrelevant and wayward.

But now they were seated, and at the stage of profiteroles. A little heavy, Simon thought, and pushed the chocolate confection to the edge of his plate. After this State visit, indeed after the Ruler's return banquet next day, he would return strictly to the resolutions on diet taken in Tuscany. Could he fit in his visit to Northern Ireland before he went to Halifax? Was it conceivable to move Joan Freetown to the Home Office? Should he now make Julia some regular allowance? What was the name of the chiropractor whom the Archbishop had just warmly recommended for his back?

He saw Patrick Vaughan standing in the far doorway of

the State dining room. It was a white-tie occasion but Patrick wore an old-fashioned double-breasted dinner jacket, either through some muddled effort at compromise or because he himself was involved that evening in a black-tie dinner. Patrick held a folded sheet of paper.

His eyes searched the room. For a moment Simon wanted to hide behind the gold-rimmed robes of the substantial sheikh on his left. But there was no escape. Patrick began to move towards him. That paper might carry good news or, much more probably, bad. The only certainty was that it was both urgent and important. Patrick was too old a hand to interrupt a State Banquet for a trifle. With a murmur of unnecessary apology he placed a Foreign Office telegram between the Prime Minister and the profiteroles.

The Chinese Foreign Minister had summoned the British Ambassador in Peking at midnight. A serious situation had arisen, he informed the Ambassador, which unless correctly handled would seriously harm Sino-British relations. He went on to say in the stilted language of Communist bureaucracy that it had been discovered that a senior Hong Kong official by the name of Zhou Heng Feng had been illegally and corruptly suborned by British interests in Hong Kong to further their speculative ventures, some of which were concerned with the smuggling of heroin. The Ambassador was given the full text of a two-hour confession, which he sent in an immediately following telegram. The Executive of the Special

Administrative Region, which was responsible for trade matters, and the Government of the People's Republic of China, with its responsibility for foreign affairs, both took a deeply serious view of this act of criminal subversion. It was not clear to what extent the official agencies of the British Government were involved. This aspect could be the subject of confidential discussion between the two Governments. For its part, the Governor of the People's Republic had no desire to create a crisis in relationship between the two countries. But neither the Government of the People's Republic nor the competent authorities in Hong Kong could stand idly by in the face of this provocation by British commercial interests. From November 1, therefore, the British-owned shares of the following companies would be transferred to the ownership of the Special Autonomous Region under a decree to be submitted immediately to the Legislative Council in Hong Kong. These shares would then be disposed of to Chinese purchasers in accordance with the relevant legislation on privatisation. That was the end of the communication.

There followed four of the most famous names in the Eastern trade, firms that had for nearly two centuries ventured and prospered, then suffered, then prospered again mightily in Hong Kong, in the treaty ports of China, and through much of South East Asia.

The Ambassador's covering telegram said that the Minister's tone had been severe, but he drew some comfort from the reference to confidential discussions. The Foreign

Office proposed that pending further consideration a strong and public protest should be made to the Chinese Ambassador in London. The Foreign Secretary would, if the Prime Minister agreed, summon the Ambassador for this purpose tomorrow and make a short statement in the Commons. This would have to be of a holding character while the views of European partners, the United States and Japan were sought and the legal implications examined.

Simon scrawled 'Agreed. We must react firmly' at the foot of the telegram and handed it back to Patrick, who in a crouching position by his side was beginning to impede the service of coffee. 'Not good,' he said.

'No, Prime Minister. Not good.'

On the way out he found Guy Freetown waiting for his wife, who was listening raptly to a dissertation on oil prices from the Director of the Gulf Petroleum Institute.

'Bad news?' asked Guy.

'Bad news.'

'Hate those bits of paper brought in at dinner. They should be banned. Joan has them all the time. Trade figures, inflation figures, money supply figures, not a week without them. Always wrong, always corrected the next month. Not that anyone notices the corrections.

'Looking forward to seeing you both next month.' He could see that he was not carrying the Prime Minister with him. Simon had forgotten about that invitation to Little Stourton, and it showed, but only for two seconds. 'Oh, yes,

comradeship in private to relieve his own loneliness. But that was quite different from indulging her zeal as Chief Press Officer. He could see that she was longing to go through with him the points to make in the scheduled television and radio broadcasts. Fortunately, she sat out of range, diagonally across the plane. As they bumped through the skies of Wales they had to keep their seatbelts fastened, which kept Artemis literally in her place.

Opposite the Prime Minister, knees touching, mugs of coffee slurping in harmony as the plane moved into a canter, sat James Whitman, Secretary of State for Northern Ireland. James emphatically did not want to talk about NIPMI, for which he had no enthusiasm. He was constantly denounced by the professional politicians of Northern Ireland as its author. He loyally defended the idea in private and public, but he was not the sort of man who could effectively deceive anyone, certainly not the Prime Minister.

Simon was happy about NIPMI. He did not believe it had much chance, but it was the right thing to try. He had agreed the text of his speech, and knew what he would say in his broadcasts. As Prime Minister of their country he was appealing to the people of Northern Ireland over the heads of their politicians. He knew that he possessed no great eloquence. He had sketched the plan at Blackpool and harvested then the element of surprise. There would be no second crop of banner headlines. He would put the proposal effectively, as best he could. But there was no point in spending more time fidgeting with the phrases.

The public spending round was a different matter. He bent over the papers again, waving away a sticky pastry proffered by a stooping steward. Lord Downbrook, Chairman of EDX, wanted him to intervene, and Downbrook's advice was not to be lightly dismissed. EDX was the Cabinet Committee of Ministers appointed each year to resolve differences of opinion in the public spending round before final decisions came to Cabinet. Sidney Downbrook was the right person to chair it because as Leader of the House of Lords he had no departmental budget to defend and because, being sober and unambitious, he was trusted by all. But the Prime Minister did not want to intervene – as yet. His political nose sniffed danger. The main adversaries – Courtauld, Freetown, Makewell – were in their different ways too worked up about it. A false move by him could push any one of the three over the edge. He would have to move them around before long, but it should be his timing, not theirs. There were still three weeks before the matter had actually to be resolved in time for the Budget. The Treasury always argued for an earlier deadline to meet its printing schedules, but in Simon's experience these always turned out to be flexible. He judged there was a fair chance that as the Budget inexorably approached, all three of them – even the Chancellor – would feel the pressure to settle. He wrote in the margin of the submission before him: 'I will of course discuss with Lord Downbrook, but am not minded to intervene at present. He will have to continue his valiant effort.'

What need he to think of next? The South Sussex by-election, though there was little he could do about that. There had been a satisfactory strong reaction to the Chinese threat, particularly in the financial markets, but no time for that. The plane began its descent over Belfast Lough. Artemis passed him a note saying that for security reasons they were landing at the Shorts airstrip by the Lough, on the edge of the city, rather than inland at the main Belfast airport.

Simon Russell had never paid more than fleeting visits to Northern Ireland. He associated it with long speeches, overcooked vegetables, politicians suffering from an overdose of history and, of course, endless argument. He felt no wish to be rid of Northern Ireland but no emotional attachment to it either. It was just there, to be managed as a problem, to be paid for as an expense, and occasionally to be prayed for when it spilled over into bloodshed. But he knew that he was missing something. It was striking how quickly Englishmen put down emotional roots in the province. Soldiers, ministers, police officers, civil servants – they crossed the water on their assignment with the anxieties and commiserations of friends and families still fresh in their ears. But within a month or two they were in love with the place. Even solid James Whitman opposite him was beginning to talk about the Mountains of Morne, the Fermanagh lakes, and even the building projects in Belfast and Londonderry as if they were a prize he had always sought. There was an attraction, even a spell, about the place, which Simon Russell recognised but did not understand.

After landing they drove past the huge twin cranes of Harland and Wolff, which had once dominated the tidy, rainswept redbrick streets of Protestant East Belfast. The old streets were sliced now with modern roads, and the cranes belonged to history not shipbuilding. Quickly they were up into the hills, across whose sombre brown slopes sun and ragged cloud chased each other. Then the hotel, near Antrim, and the ovation as he entered the conference room. The representatives of the Churches, Cardinal, Archbishop and Moderator were already seated on the platform.

He spoke.

'Since the outrage at Newry they have been quiet. No one more has been killed. But they have not been quiet because they have been defeated. On the contrary, they have been quietly counting their gains. For they have succeeded in what I think was their main objective. They cannot hope to drive the British out of the North. They know that by now. They can hope to divide the North, to get your politicians shouting and feuding all over again, so that they by comparison seem straightforward and unselfish. That has happened again since Newry, as so often before.

'I have discussed these matters endlessly with those whom you elect, your chosen politicians. I have invited you here today because you are *not* politicians. You have chosen a different way – in business, in the professions, in the public services. I have a simple but difficult request to you.' The Prime Minister paused. The faces below him were attentive but guarded. The conference room had been built as an annex to an old village inn, and furnished to keep the rustic flavour. Opposite the dais hung the portrait of a huge ox, prize winner of the Antrim Agricultural Show 1889. They had been given coffee before he arrived. A scattered array of white cups and saucers stood on the long table at the side of the room, plain and substantial as the audience itself.

'You are not politicians – I ask you to become politicians. All my life I have heard that most people in Northern Ireland are for peace. But peace in Northern Ireland means compromise, and that means compromise between politicians. The framework within which we all have to work is clear enough, though many try to obscure it. Consent is the key.

'*First*, consent about the status of the province. No one will force Northern Ireland out of the United Kingdom. That is a huge advance since the days when most people outside the North thought that a united Ireland was the only sane outcome, and the need for consent was blurred or ignored. Now the Americans, the Irish parties, the British Labour Party accept that consent is paramount.'

He wondered whether to pause to give them time to applaud. His instinct told him it would not work. He moved steadily on.

'*Second*, consent within the Province on how it is to be run. That is for you, ladies and gentlemen. I cannot settle that, nor can the Taoiseach, let alone the President of the United States. But it won't be settled if at every turning point your politicians run back into history, finding it safer to boycott discussion, to live on old memories, to trade old insults. You cannot be content to be led continually back into darkness.

'I am not asking you to found a new party or a new movement spanning the communities. That has been tried before and failed. I ask you to join the party of your choice, Unionist or Nationalist, and transform it. Go to their conferences, stand for office. Argue morning, noon and night that peace needs compromise. Argue for the twenty-first century against the seventeenth or nineteenth. Argue for your children, not your great grandparents. It is not enough to do what you have all done – separate yourselves from politics and build peaceful, worthwhile lives without politics. In Northern Ireland that is, I must say, a form of selfishness. In Northern Ireland you may try to sweep politics out by the front door, they will return by the back. You have to make a success of politics, not shun them as if they were a disease. It is not enough to make a decent living and play a decent round of golf if you leave your children a country in which they can be mutilated or killed, as Arabella was killed at Newry.'

One or two of those in front of him shifted in their seats, and there was a subdued murmur of approval. He had resisted this last reference as tasteless, but Artemis had insisted, and won. It was going reasonably well. There were about two hundred Ulstermen and -women in front of him, mostly middle-class and middle-aged. They were listening, not enthusiastically, but he had never expected that. They were professional people, managers, farmers, teachers, accountants, small businessmen, trade union officials; Catholics and Protestants now working together in everything except football, religion and politics. They ran the place under direct rule, shared the real work and responsibilities while the politicians gestured. He would have liked to be even more forthright about their sins of omission. He thought he had struck about the right balance.

He spelled out the plan, which was simple. The audience before him, and all those to whom he would broadcast in a few minutes would be invited to join a League of Action for Peace. Unlike earlier efforts this was not to be separate from existing political parties – quite the reverse. The only qualification was that you had also to be a paid-up member of a legal Northern Ireland Party. The only commitment was to be active in that party. A presiding committee from the churches, business and professions would monitor progress.

Simon Russell moved to the necessary upbeat ending, finding new words in place of the script on the lectern before him.

'In a minute the Secretary of State will fill in the detail. I would simply say this in conclusion. My predecessors in

London have worked hard to find the right answers. Ted Heath at Sunningdale, Margaret Thatcher with the Anglo-Irish agreement, John Major, Tony Blair hour after hour, month after month of weary meetings on your behalf. We thought we had succeeded, but now the evil has begun again. I have discovered no magic answer that was concealed from earlier Prime Ministers. I am sure that the answer lies here. I am sure that you can find it for yourselves. You have much which we the other side of the water admire – even envy, because you have it in greater abundance than we do – and I don't mean just the rain. Discipline at work, a strong tradition of education, prosperous small-scale agriculture, firm religious faith – I name but a few. I am asking that you apply to politics the gifts and assets that serve you well in other fields. The key to your future is not to be found in London or Dublin or Washington. The key is here in Ulster and you, yes I mean you, present in this room, have the wit and strength to find it.'

Sipping water, from the ledge below the lectern, he measured the applause. Firm, lasting about two minutes, nothing artificial or ecstatic. He was satisfied.

He put all of himself into the broadcasts afterwards. It was a relief to have a cause, a set of arguments he could deploy without reservation. By now he had worked himself into the arguments, and felt stirred by his own words. It was dismaying that his staff remained cool, unstirred, practical.

Around him Patrick Vaughan, Artemis, the rest of the team were bustling to prepare the next move. They would drive from the hotel to the international airport, where the Government's Airbus would by now be waiting. On board were the Foreign Secretary, their team and a multitude of briefs for the G8 Summit at Halifax. They would leave at teatime and arrive in Canada at teatime. Patrick Vaughan was very conscious that the Prime Minister had not fully mastered some complicated briefs – on Russia, for example, and also the proposed changes in the statutes of the World Trade organisation.

Wednesday October 15

'Not till October twenty-third? That's impossible. You haven't pushed hard enough. I must see him before then.'

Roger Courtauld held in his office each working morning a meeting of his Home Office team; ministers and senior civil servants, a dozen in all. Ministers sat in armchairs, also the Permanent Secretary; there were hard upright chairs for the officials. The occasion lasted about twenty minutes and, like most meetings of this type across Whitehall, was called 'prayers'. But Roger's meeting more closely resembled a family gathering like, for example, the daily consultation in his holiday cottage in Devon on how the day should be spent. He boomed, roared, joked, swore, rolled in his armchair, dragged advice by brute force from even the most reticent civil servant. He had no secrets from this group. For example, most ministers would have kept to their Private Secretary any disappointment they might feel that the Prime Minister could not see them as early as they wished. But when Roger Courtauld was offended, he roared out his indignation to whoever was around, and in this way got rid of it quickly. The sun rarely went down on his wrath.

John Upchurch, he who had travelled abortively to Devon, was happier now that he had begun to realise this.

'Patrick Vaughan at Number 10 is doing his best, Home Secretary. I really think he is. I've warned him it's serious. But yesterday was Northern Ireland, now the Halifax Summit, and I've just heard a rumour about a visit to China. Only a rumour. So it goes on.'

'China, China, why the hell China? They're kicking us in the teeth. It's always the same with Prime Ministers. They start off all firm and sensible, concentrate on the economy and crime, leave foreigners to the Foreign Office. Then before you know what's happened they're bewitched. They start singing and dancing their way across the world in a sort of demented bloody ballet.'

'Northern Ireland is not exactly . . .' ventured one of the junior ministers.

'Oh yes, I know he did well there.' Roger insisted, 'It won't work, of course, but right to try. But . . .' Then he pulled out of his gallop as quickly as he had begun it. 'All right then, give me the latest figures.'

'Sixty-nine thousand, six hundred and twenty-five, Home Secretary.'

'And in police cells?'

'Two thousand three hundred last night, mostly in the north. That's extra to the first figure of course.'

'Projections for next week?'

'Up three hundred at least. ACPO wants to see you about prisoners in police cells. It's threatening not to accept any more.' ACPO is the organisation of Police Chief Constables.

'Any new prison places becoming available?'

'Not till January, when the addition to Scunthorpe opens. There are now eight local prisons packing three into a cell. The Prison Service tension index is higher than it's ever been at this time of year.'

'Thank God it's not high summer.'

They paused, trying to edge away from the possibility that haunted the whole prison service, the hideous possibility of a breakdown of control.

As sometimes happened Roger Courtauld took a reflective step backward. 'It all seemed a good idea, more and longer prison sentences, protecting the public. I was thoroughly in favour at the time. Still am, in my gut. Only two things wrong. First, once you've kicked the judges into action they'll sentence much faster than the Treasury will let you build prisons. Second, you take more criminals off the streets for a few years, clever *that* Home Secretary. But a few years later you put more criminals, the same criminals, back on to the streets, unlucky *that* Home Secretary. By then they're real professionals, trained in prison to rob and burgle, and next time not get caught.'

No one ventured into this whirlpool and Roger Courtauld returned to practicalities. His huge fist closed gently on his lap.

'So on these projections the crisis will be upon us just around Christmas. The options here are either to tell the judges to sentence more leniently.'

'Impossible,' said the Senior Minister of State.

'I agree, impossible. Second, Operation Stalag. That means jazzing up the two derelict ferries at Folkestone, plus the rotting army camps we've been offered on Salisbury Plain and in Yorkshire. They will all need a lot of money spent on them, more than £100 million, and after that security will still be lousy. If we do all this, we shall more than keep pace with convictions and so be able to free almost all the police cells. Then, unless we change the law again I will face the same problems in about a year's time. Or rather, my successor . . .'

'The Chancellor of the Exchequer . . .' John Upchurch knew that his master was being more than usually indiscreet in his speculations. He spoke to bring him back to the realities of Whitehall. He succeeded, but not in the way he wanted.

'The Chancellor of the Exchequer is planning to cut my budget by five per cent. I am planning under Operation

Stalag to increase it by about the same amount. The beauty is that the arguments don't meet. They don't clash because they're never in the same room together. She beavers away in useless EDX with bloody Downbrook and will no doubt get a good deal of what she wants. I shall present the Prime Minister *and the Cabinet* with a fait accompli. The Chancellor will be informed along with the others. I shall certainly get what I want. Nothing succeeds in public spending like a copper-bottomed crisis.'

'Perhaps we should commission a further study . . .'

'Commission nothing. Draft a minute for me to send the PM. No copies to others yet. End by saying I have to set the necessary action in hand at the end of next week if we are to avoid an emergency at Christmas.'

*

'Why am I seeing him?' Anatoly Dobrinsky had settled, perhaps too soon, into a routine. Too soon, because the extraordinary revolt over which he presided could not be carried forward by ordinary mechanisms of office, committees, diary cards, or by ordinary gifts of application and regular hard work. Admiral Volkarov, the General and the Mayor of St Petersburg were not sure whether to be glad that the messianic young figure who had swooped down from the North appeared to be dwindling into a domesticated executive. But they were in no doubt of the reason. In his office in the palace, former headquarters of the

Leningrad Communist Party, Dobrinsky was now constantly in the company of Virginia, the fair-haired girl whom the Admiral had hired for that first night in the hotel. When next day she sent back the rouble notes he had thrust into her pocket, the Admiral guessed that he had unintentionally created one problem while solving another. Dobrinsky treated her as his press spokesman the next morning and appointed her a few days later. Soon the girl was running Dobrinsky's life as well as his broadcasting, and giving countless interviews on his behalf. Oddly enough he wandered off on his own at night, trying to shake off his security guards. In this he was less successful than he supposed. Volkarov knew from their reports that Dobrinsky slept with others as well as Virginia – though not with sailors or waiters, as the Mayor had feared. He appeared to need Virginia morning, noon, but not every night, and she seemed to accept this.

'Clive Wilson is a visiting British politician, on their Foreign Affairs Select Committee, said to be close to Foreign Minister Makewell.'

'Said?'

Virginia smiled. She liked it when he caught her out. It seemed to deepen the friendship, which was her aim.

'Said by himself.'

'You've seen him?'

'He came in for five minutes yesterday, when you were at City Hall. Small head, wet handshake, intelligent, ambitious, talks too much, not pleasant.'

'An irresistible proposition.' But he let her admit him, shook the Englishman's hand pleasantly, and soon was listening, amazed, to Clive Wilson's analysis of his prospects. Green tea was served from a Thermos decorated with shapeless pink flowers.

'I will telegraph Peter Makewell as soon as I get to the confidential cipher in the British Embassy in Helsinki tomorrow. He sent you his warm personal good wishes. He is of course with the British Prime Minister at the Halifax Summit, and will welcome an update from me in St Petersburg before Andreyev comes from Moscow to appeal for help. I shoot with him on his estate in Scotland, you know.'

'Andreyev will not last long. The generals in Moscow will get him.'

Clive Wilson swept on regardless, as if giving a Chatham House lecture. By nature he was obsequious to those in higher positions than himself, but every now and then he felt compelled to display his own knowledge.

'It seems to me, Mr Dobrinsky, if you will allow me, that you face one fundamental problem. Your revolt has turned from offensive to defensive. You hoped to gain the support of the armed services, but you have only those of the Northern Region. Indeed the Chiefs of Staff in Moscow have turned decisively against you and will try to throw you out of St Petersburg before the winter becomes hard. The forces at their disposal are at least four times superior to your own. To retire to Murmansk would be a humiliation – you could go to Estonia where the government is friendly to you. This is important because of the food Estonia supplies to the city, but it is politically embarrassing because the Russian nationalists to whom you appeal despise Estonia and want to recapture it. Your political message has been deliberately blurred, and you have compensated for this by your own glamorous leadership. Objectively speaking you are now in difficulty. But it is not too late for you to reassert your authority over the situation.'

Clive Wilson finished, and there was silence. Dobrinsky simply nodded. Virginia, sitting on a hard chair behind him as if the humblest of secretaries, closed her notebook with a snap.

'You have no comment?' Clive Wilson asked eventually, somewhat disconcerted.

'No comment whatever. I am greatly in your debt, Mr Wilson.'

'No message for Sir Peter?'

'My warm personal regards. And please tell him that with God's help all will end well.'

Wilson went, smiling uncertainly.

'I do not want to see anyone like that again.'

Virginia counter-attacked. 'We cannot go on like this.'

'What do you mean?'

'The man was repellent, but he was right. Your enemies are gaining strength, you are losing it. We need to show the world again that you are a winner, a master of the dramatic.'

'You speak like a public relations officer.' But his hand moved to cover hers.

'I am your public relations officer. I speak like a realist.'

'The ceremony at the cemetery will make a big impact.'

'That is a good idea. But a small idea. Something more dramatic is needed.'

'More dramatic?'

'Perhaps more terrible.'

'You have thought of something, Virginia.'

'Anatoly, I have thought of something.'

Chapter Nine

Wednesday October 15

His snooze came first. They all recognised the need for it. The Prime Minister had had a fraught six hours in Northern Ireland. He now faced later in the same day the opening sessions of the Halifax Summit. Simon had the gift of dropping into a light sleep within five minutes of seating himself in a car, train or plane. The comfortably fitted cabin of the Airbus gave him long leg-room, a window seat with the aisle on his other side, and a table in front set for some undefined meal. After half an hour of snooze Patrick Vaughan, placed opposite to him across the table, began to cough, softly at first, then a little more distinctly. He authorised the RAF steward to serve tea, thus creating a discreet clatter. The Prime Minister woke up. Patrick Vaughan's cough disappeared.

On top of the first red box was a sealed letter marked

'Personal' from Louise. She used bright blue notepaper, thick and shiny. Simon was not worried. He knew it was contrary to the experience of others, but in his marriage the thunderbolts came by word of mouth. Letters, even faxes, were almost always peaceful, even loving.

10 Downing Street
October 12

Dear Simon, dear Prime Minister
I have tried, and in Tuscany I thought for a moment I had succeeded. But it is useless. I cannot alter your way of life. You promised me you would not go to Halifax. Peter Makewell is perfectly competent, and yet you are going there, on a ludicrous pretext, and stopping off for a little rest and recreation in Northern Ireland on the way. Since you are incorrigible and yet I belong to you, I must try to help you. How can I do this? By asking you to remember me, not often but occasionally, when you are not too busy with your innumerable staff, your uncountable boxes, and your endless journeyings. I shall help you one day when you have lost all these stimulants. Meanwhile keep calm, see that Canadian doctor we met in Harley Street, do your exercises, eat fish but not, I think, shellfish.

I worry about Julia, of course, but I was wrong to

shout at you about her. I should only worry you about her when things are desperate. You did well to get her to talk. Perhaps there will be a short pause now in her life before she boards the next rollercoaster.

Remember that I love you,

Your

Louise

Yes, that was a help, and went well with the cup of tea Simon was now sipping. He did not keep these letters that Louise sent after a quarrel. He supposed that she had written about a dozen over the years at other times, he four or five. It had become a custom of their marriage. They thus drew a clear line under an unhappiness. They made possible a fresh start. Not entirely new because their characters and circumstances had not changed, but at least in this way they gave each other the energy to keep going. Simon put the letter back in the distinctive envelope, and both in his pocket. He passed quickly to his briefs. He did not want to linger over Louise, because he did not want to acknowledge that her style, her letters, her ups and downs had recently seemed of dwindling importance to him. Politics were closing in on him again. Louise took no real interest in politics, so she was a companion for only part of his life.

As the Prime Minister worked through his brief for the Summit, he became conscious of unease in the cabin around him. Patrick Vaughan had left his seat and was conferring across the aisle with the Foreign Secretary's Private Secretary, and a senior Foreign Office official, Robert Wingfield. What was Robert Wingfield doing in the team? Simon knew him reasonably well and liked him. But his speciality was China, not Russia, and Simon was fairly sure that he had not been on the original passenger list. Meanwhile the Foreign Secretary Peter Makewell slept, almost snoring, *Country Life* open on his lap.

Patrick Vaughan returned to his seat opposite the Prime Minister and whispered, 'There are developments in Peking, Prime Minister. We may need a decision as soon as we reach Halifax.'

'Decision?'

'This telegram arrived at the Foreign Office while we were in Antrim.'

The Chinese Foreign Minister had again summoned the British Ambassador in Peking to him. A long telegram reported the interview. Its final paragraph gave the gist.

> **15.** In summary therefore the Chinese Government has amplified its earlier hint at bilateral talks with a specific invitation to the Prime Minister to visit Peking. The Minister despite my probing did not give any indication of the concessions that might be made as regards the planned seizure of British firms in Hong Kong. But he repeated several times that

if the Prime Minister came it should be possible to reach a mutually satisfactory conclusion. I conclude from this move that

- **(a)** the Chinese have been somewhat shaken by the international reaction to their announcement and are looking for a way forward;
- **(b)** the Chinese would as is their habit exploit a visit by the Prime Minister to the full for propaganda purposes;
- **(c)** they would be willing to accept or even propose substantial delays or modifications in their plan of seizure or (as they call it) patriotic privatisation.

16. I know that this is an exceptionally busy time for the Prime Minister, but I hope he will feel able to accept. The Chinese have chosen this device to get themselves off the hook. It is in the long-term interest of our bilateral relationship to do so.

17. Two full days in Peking would be sufficient for the visit, though it would flatter the Chinese if the Prime Minister were able to spend a third day visiting Shanghai. A call on the President would be included. The Prime Minister would of course be welcome to stay at the Embassy, but I am sure the Chinese will insist on accommodating him and his team at the

> Diayaoutai Guest House. The visit, if it is to take place at all, would need to be completed before the deadline for patriotic privatisation on 1 November.

The Prime Minister slowly shook his head. Before he could say anything Patrick Vaughan intervened.

'Could Robert Wingfield come and talk you through it, Prime Minister? I will change places with him.'

The Prime Minister felt a new need, and looked round for Artemis. It would be useful if she could listen to the argument. She was not in the cabin, for the rules of seniority applied. She was sitting a few yards away in a bigger length of the plane with a regiment of officials, secretaries and security officers, separated from the Prime Minister's immediate entourage by two drawn curtains. In a yet more distant section of the plane sat a group of British journalists who had paid for their seats. In the old and for them golden days they would have expected a Prime Minister to wander down the aisle and chat to them, gin in hand, pretending an intimacy that was false on both sides. Simon Russell had no intention of reviving that tradition, which for good reasons he had broken. He did think of summoning Artemis through the curtains, but could not quite frame the request.

Robert Wingfield had curly hair, and wore a tie of coloured splodges under which he had loosened the top button of his shirt. He went through the arguments soberly and professionally, repeating and backing the Ambassador's arguments. The Prime Minister toyed with an RAF scone on which sat clotted cream and strawberry jam. When Wingfield had finished, his first reaction was unguarded.

'You just don't know how much I've got on . . . Ireland, Russia, public spending, maybe prisons, Opening of Parliament, that's only the beginning . . .'

Wingfield did not answer. The Prime Minister had used an argument unanswerable by a Foreign Office official, but also a feeble one. Both of them knew that somehow there was always extra time, just as there was always extra money when it was needed. It was one of the secret truths of government.

Across the aisle in the cabin the Foreign Secretary stirred, woke up, but did not try to join in immediately.

The Prime Minister tried again.

'The Chinese have in effect announced that they plan to steal part of my property. They have now said they are ready to discuss with me how to carry out the theft. There is no suggestion that they will abandon the plan. The market and political reaction has been strong against them. They are simply trying to hoodwink the world with a process that means nothing – except probably humiliation for myself.'

'Prime Minister, I see these anxieties,' said Robert Wingfield. He was young-looking and direct of speech, whereas his predecessor had been grey and circumlocutory. Nevertheless, he spoke as the heir of their sometimes stubborn professionalism. 'But I doubt very much if the Chinese would humiliate their guest. On the contrary, it is in their interests, once the visit has been announced, that it should succeed. We British have a huge amount at stake now in China, given the build-up in investment in recent years. They are short of money at present, caught in the wrong stage of the economic cycle. But the scale of opportunity for Britain in the long term outweighs anything elsewhere in Asia, or indeed the world. If we turn down this compromise—'

'No compromise has been suggested . . .'

'If we, if you, Prime Minister, turn down this invitation, then the theft you mention will happen. They could not possibly draw back. There will be some international indignation, a few speeches and a stir against China in the markets. That will do them a little damage for three or four weeks and will then pass. The world, the whole world except Britain, will begin to buzz round the Chinese honeypot again. Only Britain will have been excluded – or will have excluded itself.'

'Elementary justice requires—'

'I'm sorry, Prime Minister, I'm really sorry to interrupt you, it's discourteous, but this will be my only chance of reaching you. We're not talking about justice, elementary or otherwise, but about the interests of Britain.'

'What do you think, Peter?' The Prime Minister thought he might bring in the Foreign Secretary and divide the two of them.

'I think Robert Wingfield's probably right. He sets it out well. So does the Ambassador. It's a nuisance, Prime Minister, but you ought to go.'

There was no point in pursuing the discussion. Simon had learned to control his temper when he began to lose an argument.

Robert Wingfield had from his point of view been right. His was skilful advocacy, not floppy, but clear and firmly argued.

'I'll think about it,' said the Prime Minister. 'Yes, yes. I know it's urgent.'

Robert Wingfield returned to his seat by the window at the other side of the cabin. The Prime Minister read his briefs.

Then, interrupting his study of the brief on world trade, he leaned forward and spoke quietly across the aisle to the Foreign Secretary.

'Peter, I shall not go to Peking. That is my instinct as a politician. Wingfield is good, he argued well. But it is our job, not his, to make the political judgement. It's nothing to do with the other commitments on my plate. I just do not think it good for the British Prime Minister to hang around in that guesthouse waiting for concessions that may never come.'

'You may be right, Simon. I don't feel strongly. But . . .'

'If you don't agree with me you must say so and it will have to go to a special Cabinet as soon as we're back from Halifax. If you do agree . . .'

'I won't try to persuade you. Your political instincts are shrewder than mine. That's why you're Prime Minister.'

'Your instincts are so shrewd that you don't want to be Prime Minister. Thank you. Tell your people I don't want to hear again of the suggestion about my going to Peking. They were right to put it forward. I am right to refuse it. You must handle it as best you can. I'll take my share of the consequences. Tell Roberts I'm sorry to make his life a misery.' Roberts was the Ambassador in Peking.

'No problem. That's what he's there for.'

Peter Makewell believed the Prime Minister should have gone to Peking. But as a connoisseur he relished the firmness and completeness of the political decision Simon Russell had taken. Nothing would have been worse than to spend the next few days worrying and re-worrying over the same points. As a Cabinet Minister he also enjoyed having a difficult job clearly delegated to him, with a promise of support in which he believed.

They crossed the harbour by boat from the airport. The ferry carrying the British delegation quite improperly flew the Union Jack and was surrounded by a flotilla of small boats, hooting and cheering. Simon Russell felt his spirits lift with the crisp sunshine. He had never been to Halifax before. It might be the capital of Nova Scotia but that evidently was not enough to turn it into one of the bored, unwelcoming capitals where the world's politicians usually met. A line of huge maple-leaf flags pulled and flapped in the stiff breeze on the dockside. The waves sparkled in welcome. No wonder Canada had chosen Halifax again when her turn to host the Summit came round.

As they trooped down the gangway the British could see that the welcoming delegation of Canadian officials was somewhat perturbed.

'Would you mind waiting for just a few minutes, Prime Minister?' said someone in tones of polite desperation.

It became clear that the Halifax traffic police and the Halifax street plan had between them been outwitted by the unprecedented number of sleek black cars in the security procession of each delegation. In short, there was gridlock.

'How far is our hotel?'

'About a mile, Prime Minister. Uphill and keep right.'

'Fine, don't worry, we'll walk.'

They demurred: he prevailed. For a few minutes he could pretend that he was free of protocol and security. The Prime Minister strode ahead of the rest up the crowd-lined street, but was conscious after a second or two that Artemis was beside him. She had a reason to justify her presence.

'There will be journalists outside the hotel, Prime Minister. We need to decide what to do. You could just march in and take no notice. Perhaps that would be best.'

He noticed the 'we'. But he assumed she spoke as his Chief Press Officer rather than as the girl who had stroked his hair in Blackpool.

'What questions will they put?'

'Ireland, I expect. Young Paisley has attacked you again as a traitor. But the League of Action has started quite well. Three hundred telephone calls already from people telling the monitoring groups that they've newly joined a Northern Ireland political party.'

'You know perfectly well, Artemis, that many were lined up beforehand.'

'The media doesn't, Prime Minister, and anyway they're genuine recruits. Three-quarters have joined the Unionist Parties.'

'Can I use these figures on the hotel doorstep?'

'Better not. They're only preliminary.'

He was pleased at her professional caution. In Joe Bredon he would have condemned it as timidity.

'What else?'

'Russia, of course. President Andreyev will arrive in an hour or two. That girl of Dobrinsky's is constantly on the BBC, Sky, CNN saying we must defend St Petersburg.'

'Having an effect?'

'Skin-deep, I'd say, literally. That is, she's very attractive, so's he, but the place is not actually under attack, and the politics are confused, so she has her work cut out.'

Then they saw, warmly wrapped up but doing a cheerful trade, the last ice-cream man of summer. Artemis found some Canadian dollars. Soon they were unable to discuss any further conceivable questions he might face because each was coping inexpertly with a double maple-nut ice-cream.

As the two licked, cameras flashed and bystanders laughed encouragingly. Patrick Vaughan, five paces behind, hesitated, then bought another himself. The security men caught up and coaxed them forward. Soon the hotel came in sight, the journalists jostling and skirmishing outside the swing doors.

They asked mostly about Ireland. He spotted and headed for the fifty-year-old woman dressed as thirty who was thrusting the BBC television microphone towards him. Her voice husky with years of summitry, she had just put him a question, which in the hubbub he had missed. Regardless, he gave as an answer the soundbite he had worked out with Artemis during the last hundred yards up to the hotel.

'It is too soon to be sure, but the first news I have from Northern Ireland is encouraging. I want to emphasise one point. I am not trying to replace the political parties. I want to breathe new life into them, new democratic life.'

It sounded good as he said it, so he said it again to some scribbling journalists. He stonewalled questions about Russia, and dismissed a complicated point about Canadian politics. Then a young Englishman thrust his way to the front of the line just where the Prime Minister had paused.

'Are you going to Peking, Prime Minister?'

Simon, pretending not to hear, moved forward into the swing doors of the hotel.

'That was fine, Prime Minister,' said Artemis, once they had passed through the obsequious greetings of the hotel manager and found themselves a lift. Patrick Vaughan and four other officials squeezed around them, but Artemis, clutching her black pouch, stood nearest to him. They were much the same height, and he felt her breath round his mouth when she spoke.

'How did that young man know about the Chinese invitation? Find out where he got it from. You must knock that story hard if it surfaces again. No invitation to Peking. No intention of going to Peking. On the seizure announcement, stick to the line you've been taking. Only the Hong Kong SAR can decide on measures affecting firms in Hong Kong. International law requires full compensation if any firms are taken over.'

'Yes, Prime Minister.'

Yes, but Artemis went pink and turned a few degrees away from him. Her black pouch held in front of her became a barrier between them. It took him a second to understand why. She had known nothing of the invitation to Peking. She was professionally vexed. Those damned curtains in the plane.

But there was no time to fuss over hurt feelings. Artemis must learn to treat small bruises as incidental.

There was commotion in the corridor of rooms on the twelfth floor of the hotel allotted to the Prime Minister's Suite. It was an orderly commotion of people long accustomed to setting up an office in a hurry in a strange place, laying lines, installing machines, unpacking reams of paper, sorting the faxes and e-mail that awaited their arrival.

Artemis left the Prime Minister's side to assert dominion over her own section of the office as it took shape from the void. The Prime Minister, guided by Patrick Vaughan, found his way to his own suite. He knew it was best to let everyone get on with their jobs for the time being. In ten or fifteen minutes his suitcases would have come, his security officers would be stationed outside his door, the Prime Ministerial machine would be operating in Halifax, and official life would begin again. There was absolutely nothing meanwhile for him to do. This was a rare and precious feeling.

For Simon the test of a hotel suite was fruit. To chocolates, nuts, drink, he was indifferent. Fruit on the other hand welcomed and stimulated. Admittedly caution was needed in North America, where hotel fruit scored more strongly on colour than taste.

But the rich red plums proved delicious. He gazed over the harbour, munched and was content.

'It was at that time the biggest man-made civilian disaster in the history of the world,' said a familiar voice behind him.

He had forgotten that Joan Freetown had flown direct from London to Halifax, and would have been in the hotel for two or three hours already. She had clearly used part of the time at the hairdresser. The silver bar across the front of her hair gleamed with metallic efficiency.

She wore the scarlet suit that had struck mingled awe and affection into the Blackpool audience. She also wore what Simon thought of as her daytime diamonds, a large brooch at her throat, saved from vulgarity by the severity of its design. In short she looked magnificent, whereas Simon, feeling tiredness and backache descend on him after the long flight, had just decided to take a shower.

'Joan – lovely to see you. How was your flight?' He was not sure whether to accompany those banalities with a peck on the cheek. He did not kiss her each morning when they lived cheek by jowl in Downing Street, but it was a week or so since they had met. He pecked.

The Chancellor of the Exchequer took no notice of any of this.

'December 1917. Out there in the harbour. A French munitions ship and a Belgian collided and blew up. The explosion devastated a fifth of the town, all that part of the harbour west of here. Nineteen hundred dead and thousands injured. Halifax was of course the harbour where most of the Atlantic convoys assembled.'

'Of course.'

Despite himself Simon found his imagination gripped by the story. Joan Freetown, a natural teacher, spelled it out in detail, using the panorama before her as a blackboard, describing the incomprehension, the blizzards hindering relief, the trains speeding up from Boston with warm clothing, then the bitter arguments about blame.

'Quite a contrast,' said Simon, thinking not only of the bustling harbour below them, but of the happy self-confident streets through which he had just walked.

'But the contrast owes nothing to us politicians. Remember that, Simon. Halifax recovered from 1917 by local and voluntary effort. And all that prosperity down there has come about despite Canadian politics, not because of them.'

This was indeed her creed. He felt like asking her a question that had often occurred to him, why she had become a politician if she thought so poorly of the usefulness of politics. But she stopped being a teacher as quickly as she had begun.

'Simon, can I sit down for a moment?'

She took an armchair with its back to the harbour view. Then, even more extraordinarily, 'Do you mind if I have one of these?'

He did mind, for he hated cigarette smoke, but she had probably seen him from time to time with a cigar, and in any case he was overcome with astonishment that Joan Freetown should confess to such a petty failing. He removed two plumstones from an ashtray, put it by her chair and took a hard chair, which suited his back, opposite.

'I want to ask you a question. Why am I here?' she asked. 'Don't say, Finance Ministers always come to G8 Summits. I know that, but why?'

He too switched tone, towards the bureaucratic.

'There are several items on the agenda that concern you. Indeed, you yourself put down the item on international debt. There are several meetings of Finance Ministers alone, which then report to the plenary.'

She drew long on the cigarette, as if deciding how far to go.

'Simon, you and I are always talking and never really talking. What you've said is true, but makes no sense. That is all secondary stuff, an agenda created to make an agenda. There is only one reason why I am justified in being here.'

'Namely?'

'Namely, as your senior colleague in Cabinet, to help Peter Makewell and yourself sort out the Russian problem. That's the big one.'

So that was it. For the Prime Minister this was a moment to say absolutely nothing. Apprentice politicians blurt out their opinions as if utterance were itself a virtue. Their wiser seniors use silence as a weapon to draw others out.

So it happened.

'Would you ever consider giving me the Foreign Office? It's a field in which I am strongly interested.'

Certainly not, was the inner answer. The thought had never occurred to him in all the juggling of different options that from time to time filled his mind. The intimacy of shared travel, shared meetings, shared problems between the Prime Minister and the Foreign Secretary was emphatically not one to which he would admit Joan Freetown. A month of it would drive him mad.

'I must say I am perfectly satisfied with Peter Makewell. And I could hardly make him Chancellor of the Exchequer.'

'Peter Makewell works by instinct, not reason. Since his wife died he tires fast. He skimps his briefs. He ought to retire to Scotland and those grouse.'

Silence was again an option, but this time she had annoyed him.

'These are matters on which I have to make my own judgement.'

'And take no advice? That is your failing, Simon. You live in your own world with your own team of officials at Number 10 and your friends. We cannot reach you.'

This from a colleague renowned for her closed circle of professors, her ambitious right-wingers whose speciality was contempt for those of her fellow ministers less intelligent than themselves.

Even from that height the two of them heard the police siren in the street below. There was something more than routine in its note, and it halted at the hotel. Standing together on the narrow balcony they could see below them the same surge of journalists as had greeted Simon. Parting a way through them, four Canadian Mounties escorted a bald head and a pair of spectacles. The President of all the Russias had come to plead his case before the world.

The interruption, the Prime Minister thought, should be made permanent. 'Joan, I don't think this conversation is getting us anywhere. I think I heard my suitcases arrive. If you'll excuse me . . .'

'Please sit down, Simon.' This was an entirely different voice. She touched her brooch with her left hand in what seemed a gesture of uncertainty. He noticed that she wore none of her warlike bracelets.

'I did not mean to go down that path. Guy will be furious

when I tell him.' Another surprise, that Guy should be admitted to this kind of discussion at all.

'But, as I said, we never talk properly. I have to ask myself what I'm in politics for. Perhaps I can ask you?'

Although Simon was an expert in getting others to undress themselves before him, he had not sought and was embarrassed by this particular offer of revelation.

He paused. 'You are an excellent Chancellor of the Exchequer. More than that, you are one of the leading spirits in our Party. I don't agree with all your philosophy, but you have a crowd of disciples.'

She wanted more, and he drew his chair closer to her.

'Look, Joan. I very nearly resigned after my heart attack. Most of the papers tipped you to succeed me. God knows how long I shall last. When I go you are as likely as anyone to take my place.' He did not add that if he was still alive at the time he would oppose her. It might happen over his dead body but not, he thought, over his living one.

'I don't want to hang about waiting for you to die.' She paused. 'Anyway those distinguished old centrists at the back of the party would dish me. The Downbrooks of this world are so experienced that they hate anything definite. You know very well that they have huge quiet power when it comes to the point. Anyway you are a better Prime Minister than I would be.'

This too was deeply surprising, but she appeared to mean it. Simon was genuinely nonplussed, and this time his silence was not tactical.

'Do you want me to stay, Simon?'

'I certainly do. We couldn't get on without you.' Realising that this sounded banal he touched her arm to reinforce the assurance. It was near enough true. It was certainly true that they could not get on with her sniping at the Cabinet from outside.

'Then you must help me. I'm in deep difficulty with this public spending round. We've only a few days left.' The Chancellor was back in departmental harness. The tone had changed again. She launched into the figures. She exposed the outstanding arguments with the Home Office and the Foreign Office. She was forceful and urgent. This was the Joan Freetown he knew almost too well. It was as if she was wearing the bracelets after all.

Later he wondered if it had been a trap from the beginning. If so, he had certainly walked into it. But on the whole he thought not. He believed that for a few minutes Joan Freetown had lifted a veil. She had quickly lowered it again, but he fed the knowledge into the invisible machine with which he computed his essential assessment of the character of others.

'I'll do what I can.'

'That's not enough.' She stubbed out her cigarette as if the ashtray were an overspent department. 'You must intervene, call us all in at once, insist on the Treasury figures. You owe me that much.'

'I'll do what I can,' he repeated. And somehow she was out of the room.

Chapter Ten

Thursday October 16

'I do not see how I can carry my remit any further. There's no point in calling any more meetings of EDX. I don't like reporting failure to the Prime Minister, but there it is.'

Lord Downbrook and Joe Bredon were walking round the lake in St James's Park, Downbrook with stick and overcoat, Bredon regretting that he had left his overcoat at home. He was not yet accustomed to these sudden summonses to walk in the middle of the afternoon, though he hoped that they were a sign of confidence from his new master.

'You've already reported your difficulties to the Prime Minister.'

'Several times and he's taken no notice.' Lord Downbrook irritably hustled a duck out of his path with the stick. 'He knows that I cannot dig those three big ministers ut of their trenches without his help. I've sorted out the mall fry, but they'll get restless soon if they see the big ninisters refusing to make the sort of compromises I've orced on the little ones.'

'There's a minute from Transport this morning trying to eopen their settlement.'

'Exactly. Out of the question, but it makes the point. One can always find technical ways of bridging a gap once t's down to a reasonable size. But this one's too big, and neither side is budging.'

'That's the Home Office.' Bredon knew the figures by eart, but he wanted to edge his master on.

'Of course. The Foreign Office budget is tiny, the gap here is tiny, though the Chancellor is stuck with that illy speech at Blackpool. The Home Office is the real roblem.'

Out in the open Lord Downbrook was willing to speak nore openly than in his office in the Lords. Perhaps that vas why he took to the Park once or twice a week. As the Prime Minister had foreseen, his new Press Officer Joe Bredon fitted him like a glove. He was willing to display his eelings, up to a point. Downbrook was vexed, partly ecause his reputation as a fixer of disputes was at risk, but nainly because his objective in life, the smooth running of he Queen's Government, was being prejudiced. Lord Downbrook had moved late into politics, from business, at he age of fifty, having made a sizeable sum in the hotel usiness. After a moderately successful career in the

Commons including a spell as a junior minister in th Home Office, he had found his niche as manager of th Upper House. Colourless himself, he disliked obstinat characters and emphatic ideas. Both the Chancellor an the Home Secretary were in his view acting self-indul gently. Compromise was the essence of soun administration. He despised ministers who so puffed them selves up that compromise became impossible for them He had thought the Prime Minister would agree with him He was disappointed.

'You worked all that time for him. How can I persuad him into action? State Visit, Ireland, Halifax, it's impossi ble to get at him, and he doesn't answer my minutes. It' not something I can raise in Cabinet without consultin him. It seems to me that office of his has become less effi cient since you left, Joe.' A dry laugh. 'Could you have word with that Private Secretary of his, Vaughan, isn't it?

Joe Bredon did not particularly like the Prime Ministe or understand him. But he understood him well enough t know that this was nothing to do with inefficiency. Simo Russell would have his own game-plan, which he might no have divulged to Patrick Vaughan, and which Patric would certainly not divulge to Joe Bredon.

'I don't think that would work.'

Lord Downbrook made no further comments. H aborted the walk, turning left across the bridge over th lake so that they had completed only a half-circuit of th park.

As soon as they were back in the cosy snugness of the House of Lords he dictated a fresh minute to Halifax.

The plenary sessions of the summit were to be held in the Maritime Museum on the harbourside. There was no question that morning of sauntering informally through the streets or sampling ice-cream. It was still called the G8 Summit but there were ten motorcades if you included, as was proper, the President of the European Commission and the President in Office of the European Council of Ministers. Each motorcade had to present itself and disgorge at the entrance to the museum in proper sequence of protocol. The last and much the longest, containing the President of the United States of America, was set to arrive at precisely ten am.

This meant that Simon Russell had to leave the Delta Hotel at nine twenty-three. It had been a pleasant enough morning up until then. He had telephoned Louise, as she took her lunch of crispbread and yoghurt at Number 10, and thanked her for her letter. She had asked how the Russian discussion would go, which was a good sign, though he knew that she would not have been interested in his reply. He had read the London press cuttings harvested by Artemis and propped against the toast rack. An opinion poll suggesting quite an easy Tory win in the South Sussex by-election, two or three speculative pieces about public spending based (he thought) on Treasury briefing, nothing new from China, some relatively subdued criticisms from

Ulster politicians of his initiative, short pieces from diplomatic correspondents on inside pages foreshadowing Andreyev's appeal for help at today's Summit.

Simon liked on these occasions to breakfast alone, and reflect. The storm clouds had indeed blown in upon him since Tuscany but they had created some balancing energy within himself. He had not yet been to the doctor about his back, and had mentioned it only lightly to Louise and to Patrick Vaughan. Maybe the ache was a bit easier today, despite the long plane journey. In any case he was willing to accept a disc pinching on a nerve if that was fate's price for keeping his heart stable. Of course there was no medical connection, but fate did not work by Harley Street rules. As was his custom he passed his main political problems quickly in review, having poured out his second cup of coffee. He had made his decision not to go to China sound very definite, but next morning was not sure that he was right. He knew himself well. One reason for being so emphatic in front of his team had been precisely to smother any second thoughts of his own before they took shape. Now there was no going back. Ireland was different, because there his proposal had no downside. Faced with the Breakaways he had nothing to lose by playing the democratic card. Time would tell if he had anything to gain.

His real problem was the public spending round at home. Had he been right to play it so long? The press were just beginning to scent trouble and from now on the tension would build rapidly. He had been relying on the tension to bring the protagonists to their senses. There was a risk that it would work the opposite way.

'We ought to be going in four minutes, Prime Minister . . .' It was the escorting officer from Canadian protocol.

'Right.' Simon Russell had noticed that those around him never referred to the fact that he might wish to go to the lavatory but sometimes allowed him just, but only just, enough time to do so. Three minutes later Patrick Vaughan was offering a bundle of papers.

'Your briefs, Prime Minister. Russia, of course, comes first this morning. Then some papers you might like to read at the table if things flag. I've put the latest correspondence about public spending together in a yellow folder. There's a minute from the Home Secretary, which you ought to see this morning. I gather you had a talk with the Chancellor yesterday evening . . .'

Patrick 'gathered' through morning, noon and night. He allowed a hint of reproach, for it was untidy of ministers, even the Prime Minister, to confer without an official present to take the record. But he was inviting the Prime Minister to say more.

'A short talk, Patrick. No conclusions. I simply said I would do my best.'

'The Chancellor seems to have taken much encouragement from what you said.'

So she had chosen to play it that way. She could equally have stuck to her original angry reaction. So be it.

'Then there's this, Prime Minister, which you really ought to read before you go. It's Top Secret Tumulus. The team there have produced something very fast.'

Tumulus was the code word for intelligence reports from Ireland.

The Canadian protocol officer was edgy, watch-bound.

'I really think—'

Patrick was firm in a way the Prime Minister rarely saw. 'This is a highly classified special report. It cannot leave this office. It has just arrived. It is urgent.'

The report, in a flaming red jacket decked with warning adjectives, was an analysis of the first reaction of the Breakaways to the Prime Minister's speech at Antrim.

> **12.** The only firm decision of the Army Council at this emergency meeting was thus to suspend all military activity including an unspecified operation on the mainland already decided on. The two Active Service Units will remain in readiness, but await further orders. The Breakaway leadership is divided. If, as they hope, the Prime Minister's initiative peters out and the democratic parties remain at loggerheads, then the Breakaways are likely to follow up the Newry attack with others around Christmas. The leadership will meet to review developments in seven days.

'Not too bad, Patrick. Indeed, as good as could possibly be expected so soon.'

'Not too bad, Prime Minister.'

The Maritime Museum, like everything belonging to the past of Halifax, had a strongly British flavour. Behind the modern chairs set round the conference table there was an abundance of red and white ensigns. Model warships defeated the Americans and French, model explosives penetrated the Far North, model Victorian oarsmen with beards competed strenuously on the lakes. Simon Russell felt comfortable. The proceedings however were not dramatic. As often happened, an event with sensational origins fell away into insignificance. When Andreyev had decided to address the Summit, it seemed that Dobrinsky was sweeping all before him, or at least that Russia would be engulfed in a ferocious civil war. Since then stalemate had descended. Dobrinsky had failed to extend his support more than a few kilometres south of St Petersburg. If anything he was the threatened party. There was no fighting and the television crews were drifting away. Andreyev did not have the temperament to turn even a high dramatic moment to best effect. He certainly could not create drama out of a problem that had become dull. He and the Canadian Chairman droned at each other for a total of about forty minutes, then the others round the table read almost identical speeches, urging all concerned to practise moderation and achieve a negotiated settlement based on respect for democratic rights and Russia's international responsibilities. The Europeans had met for ten minutes in advance to concert a line. Peter Makewell had ensured in some early telephone calls that there was no difference between the Americans and Europeans. The Japanese were by a nuance more sympathetic to Andreyev, because they did not want any nationalist commotion in the Russian Far East fleet. But there was nothing to be done except to tell the press afterwards what had been said. It was one of those private meetings that might just as well have been public.

Simon Russell, having said his unremarkable piece settled to read the prison papers. Roger Courtauld's abrupt prose style was as different as possible from the usual opaque flow of Home Office prose. There was no doubt that he personally had the bit between his teeth and was pulling hard. Simon Russell knew nothing about prisons, but a good deal about the Home Secretary. When he bothered to exert it Roger Courtauld had good judgement. He feared no man and no woman. He would not hesitate to resign if thwarted on something he cared about. Simon had never discussed the principles of penal policy with him because their dealings had always been concerned with topical matters. He suspected that if they ever did so they would both agree that they had been sold a pup by their predecessors. The public good was not best served by crowding more and more offenders into prisons that were universities of crime. But neither minister was by temperament a radical reformer, so they had to manage the system they inherited. Roger Courtauld might well have to turn those ferries and army camps into prisons over the next few weeks. But Simon Russell could not allow him to do that through a proposal made to the Prime Minister alone, without Cabinet discussion. Above all the Chancellor of the Exchequer must be involved.

Next he took up Lord Downbrook's minute. The Leader of the House of Lords wrote in as smooth running a style as any official, but below the flow of Whitehall phrases the Prime Minister sensed the man's growing impatience. Lord Downbrook would not have dreamed of saying that the Prime Minister had sent him up the creek without a paddle, but that was the gist.

The Prime Minister did not bother with the statistical tables Patrick had also included in the folder. The contest on public expenditure had reached the stage where all advocates could find statistical weapons in the armoury to suit their case. It was now a political struggle to be decided by political means. Simon pulled out a blank sheet of the hotel notepaper from the back of his briefs.

> PV
> I cannot let this drift any longer. Tell the Cabinet Secretary that we need prisons and the public expenditure review on the Cabinet agenda Thursday, October 30. Early start, 9 am. Papers to be circulated in advance. Prisons first . . .

Then he paused, crossed out 'first', put 'after public spending'. His mind was moving fast, imagining the scene round the Cabinet table. The expenditure discussion would be long and difficult. There would have been press speculation in advance. By about twelve forty-five pm everyone would be hungry, the press outside for news, and the ministers inside for their lunch appointments. The prisons discussion could then be quite short.

At the G8 Summit everyone had spoken their piece on Russia. There was a pause. A faint buzz came from a group of officials clustered round the Canadian Prime Minister at the head of the table. According to the game plan the time had come for him to sum up the discussion and send Andreyev politely on his way. This would not be difficult, for there had been no disagreement. Nor indeed had Andreyev come expecting anything in particular. He had decided to speak in different circumstances and been accepted. He could not now withdraw the agenda item nor the others their acceptance of it. The two hours had become a necessary ritual. The next discussion, on the World Trade Organisation, would be more difficult and in substance more important. Joan Freetown would sit beside him for that item, entitled to speak as a Finance Minister. He would have to bestir himself if he was to keep control of the British end of the discussion. He had had a foretaste the night before at the European preparatory meeting where she had with more justice than tact, accused the French President of protectionist tendencies.

Why was the Canadian taking so much time? The buzz of officials had if anything grown louder. Then a type-written message came on blue Foreign Office paper from Peter Makewell, who was conferring in the next room with his fellow Foreign Ministers.

> Andreyev is out. Brassev and the generals have announced that in the interests of national unity both Government and Duma are dissolved. A provisional military government will take over with the primary purpose of crushing the rebellion in the north. St Petersburg given two weeks to surrender before it is assaulted. As you know, Clive Wilson is there, sending me useful personal stuff. I am asking him to stay on for the time being. The Moscow statement goes on to announce that Estonia is to be 'peacefully reintegrated' in Russia because of bad treatment of Russian citizens. Once national unity restored in Russia the military will hold genuinely free elections and step down.
>
> No fighting in Moscow. All key points in hands of military. Surprise and success seem total. Germans, French and Italians here inclined to think we must accept coup but should warn the military in Moscow against any adventure against Estonia. Japanese actually enthusiastic for coup. Americans and Canadians more dubious. Pentagon think Brassev dodgy on nuclear understandings.

> Canadian PM is being advised to send off Andreyev politely and return to discussion later without him, giving officials time to prepare necessary passage for communiqué.

That was exactly what happened. As the meeting dissolved, Andreyev sat for a moment alone at his seat, behind the nameplate of Russia. His officials had left hurriedly. They probably did not deliberately humiliate their fallen leader. He had not even begun to put together his papers. He stared in front of him, no expression on his face, eyes impenetrable behind thick glasses. He might be planning a comeback, though his complete inertia suggested otherwise.

He might be half stunned, and sad for lost power. Or he might be contemplating his future, a quick and rewarding book of memoirs perhaps, followed by a pleasant chair at some American university.

Simon Russell did not spend much time speculating about the reaction of a man he hardly knew. He could now cross Russia off his immediate agenda. There would be no difficulty in drafting something for the communiqué. Of course, Russia would continue to be turbulent and Peter Makewell would go on trying to persuade him to worry about its twists and turns. Heaven knows who this Brassev was or what he would do. But Simon Russell had formed the habit of organising his mind on Whitehall lines. There was an outer range of matters of which he was aware but which he did not need to revisit constantly. Then there were the others. He supposed that Russia would no longer figure among the problems that had to have a place on the half-rational, half-instinctive wheel that constantly revolved inside his brain.

She was in tears. His daughter was sobbing down the telephone across the Atlantic – strong uneven sobs that tore through him as he listened in the tiny office allocated to the United Kingdom delegation. A few seconds ago with intelligent advisers the Prime Minister had been assessing the Russian drama, preparing for his talk with the American President, going over other business of the day. Now these suddenly seemed cardboard figures discussing cardboard subjects. He waved them out of the room, and they left quickly, trained in their fast-moving lives to notice at once when one reality drove out another. Simon was left alone with the telephone line and Julia.

'Bloody woman. But it's a lie. He offered me cannabis, but I never took it. I promise you that. She's a liar, out to ruin my life.' There was theatre in her voice, but also real anger and fear.

'What on earth are you talking about, Julia?' He tried to sound stern, but was deeply shaken. For a moment he imagined that she was railing against her mother, though for what offence he could not imagine.

But this fear at least was banished by Louise herself. 'Let me speak to him,' he heard her say to Julia. Then the strong definite voice of his wife, as if she was in the next room.

'The *Daily Mirror* has a story that Julia was expelled from St Clare's for taking drugs. Julia suspects that the headmistress is responsible for the story. That seems most unlikely. But I believe her when she says it's untrue. The polo-player offered her drugs when they were together in his flat in Windsor. She should have told us this before. But that is nothing to do with her leaving St Clare's. The school did not even know of that part of the story. The question is: can you kill it?'

Simon felt a wave of tiredness sweep into the little office and envelop him. In five minutes he should be seeing President Altman, the most powerful man in the world. Then a press conference to the world's media. Then the Canadian circus, for God's sake. Then a long flight home. Then . . .

But down that path lay defeat. The only technique, as he had long learned, was to concentrate hard on the immediate, and forget the rest.

'Leave it to me. We'll do all we can.'

'Thanks.' He felt relief in Louise's voice. 'Here's Julia again.'

She sounded thirteen. 'You believe me, Dad? None of it had anything to do with drugs.'

He was glad that his belief was important to her.

'I believe you, Julia. It must be late with you. Go to bed. Don't worry. Good night.'

He put down the receiver. The worry was now his. Now of course it must be passed to Artemis. He called her back into the room and explained.

'It's simple,' she said. 'We just tell them they have a story that is false, and if they print it you will sue.'

'It's only false in part. Julia was asked to leave St Clare's. I'm amazed this hasn't got out before.'

'Don't let's start being subtle. *Their* story is false in its essential details. The only way to stop it is to tell them that, but nothing else.'

He looked at her, eager, very slightly flushed. He had neither energy nor time to question her definiteness.

'You will do it? Or should I ring the Editor?'

'I will do it with the Editor. At once. Missing the Altman meeting.'

'Thanks, Artemis. That's the second time you've . . . Thanks, Artemis.'

The meeting with President Altman was held in the office of the Executive Director of the Maritime Museum, dominated by a life-size portrait of the Duke of Kent, father of Queen Victoria, a martinet in full-dress military uniform. Round the walls swam or flew in glass cases various large fishes and marine birds banished during the recent modernisation of the museum. Five Americans, the British Prime Minister and his Private Secretary squeezed into the room with some difficulty. The Duke of Kent did something to redress the balance; but physically the President was taller, broader and louder voiced than his counterpart.

'Don't like it, Simon, don't like it at all.'

The President tended to boom, even to a tiny audience. He was large but not fat. He managed at all seasons to maintain an outdoor face, which went well with his thick, slightly tousled hair and crumpled suits. Anyone who supposed that this generous informal appearance was a guide to the man within soon learned their mistake.

'Russia's a big pot, but she's not big enough for all those passions stirring inside. When they overflow, they'll scald us all.'

Donald Altman was one of the few politicians in the world to whom Simon Russell gave serious heed. This was mainly, but not entirely, because he was American President. The two men spoke often on the telephone, met less often, and got on well together. Altman could not entirely avoid that slightly patronising over-friendliness with the British (as with all other heads of government) that goes with leading the world's only superpower. He tried just a little too hard to show that the British Prime Minister was the one person in the world whom he was anxious to see. But for Simon Russell the importance of Altman went beyond the importance of America. Altman's mind was not driven by calculation along a line of reasoned argument. He jumped from one position to another under impulses in which selfishness, sentimentality and practical common sense combined. Simon Russell had hardly ever known him to jump wrong. That was why his remark about Russia was disconcerting.

'Surely we can let them fight among themselves. They're

no longer a superpower. The new military in Moscow don't want a fight with the West. They want to destroy Dobrinsky. He's nothing to us. Why worry?'

Altman paused. It took him a little time to turn his instincts into arguments. Buried somewhere in what he was about to say would be the real feeling that moved him.

'First, the Pentagon are unhappy about the nuclear. Brassev might even try some concealed testing. Second, Estonia. They're now under direct threat. Friendly inoffensive country, above all small. The great USA can't let it go under. Powerful lot of Estonians and other Balts in the Mid West. Third, it's all too dramatic. Dobrinsky is a drama in himself. That English girl of his communicates like a star. The Kremlin and the Russian Army are always good for ham theatre. I just know in my gut it's not going to stay quiet for the rest of us. Much though we'd like it that way.'

The last point, Simon Russell could see, was the feeblest but the most influential. Altman ran a country where policy came from drama on television. As its President he was saying that he could not do things otherwise. Luckily the Europeans, and particularly Britain, could be tougher minded.

'We can't get involved simply because it is a drama. We can do our share of hissing or applauding. But our place is in the stalls of the theatre, not on the stage.'

'Maybe, Simon, maybe. We papered it all over neatly in the communiqué. Neatly enough for today. I've no plans, no passion of my own in this, just . . .'

The President looked at a short list of subjects on the pad before him, and with a pencil changed the order, so that the third became second. Simon could not quite read them upside down.

'China. I gather you're resisting some blackmail from Peking.'

How did the Americans know? How much did they know? Did it matter? Probably not.

He paused only for a second before replying.

'The Chinese are trying to bully us. They have trumped up a bogus intelligence story and laid it at our door. In return they plan to seize the assets of four of the main British companies in Hong Kong. They offered privately to suspend this if I would go to Peking to negotiate with them. I refused. That's the story.'

Simon did not want to go too closely into this with the Americans, at least not yet. He had remembered that Zhou, the man arrested in Hong Kong, was supposed to have some CIA connection. American interests might be quite glad to see the British companies displaced from Hong Kong.

But Altman broke through this reserve. 'You are quite right, Simon. I asked our man in London to alert you to all this. The Chinese are behaving unreasonably – to you this time, often to us. I fully support you, and will say so. They'll lose a lot of American investment if they carry on this way. We'll join you and others in blocking the World Bank loans for the next phase of the Yangtse project. Other Europeans firm with you on this?'

'So far.'

'Then the Chinese won't get away with it.'

'That's good, Mr President.' Indeed it was a more specific assurance than he had expected.

'You can count on my total support,' said Altman. 'It's a case where Britain and America must stand together in our special relationship. Now, Ireland . . .'

So that was it. After the gift would come the request. The United States was a week away from mid-term elections. The Republicans stood to lose seats in both Houses and a handful of governorships. The President was a Republican.

'You've made a shrewd pitch there, Simon. Typical of you. I gather it's going well. Shoals of applicants to join the democratic parties . . . particularly the Unionists.'

'It was an even-handed appeal to everyone to join the democratic party of their choice.'

'Quite so. You gave it no tilt. The State Department backed what you said. But the figures up to this morning from our Consul General in Belfast are clear. The two Unionist parties have so far increased membership by 22 per cent and 18 per cent, the Nationalist SDLP by only 7 per cent.'

The Prime Minister suppressed his irritation that the Americans had more up-to-date figures than himself.

'If my plan works the Unionist leadership will not be best pleased. These new members should be keener for compromise than the leaders want.'

'That's not how it looks over here, Simon. The Boston, New York and Los Angeles papers are full of talk about Russell's subtle pro-Unionists plan, the Brits taking the poor State Department for a ride again.' A pause, then, 'You know my party has a problem next week. It would be a huge help to me, Simon, particularly in those states with a lot of Irish, if you could make it clear that you are particularly keen to see the Nationalists come stronger out of this – or at least even.'

Simon Russell considered for a moment whether he should suppress the genuine indignation rising inside him. The Irish question meant lives in Ireland and Britain, votes in America. The mismatch had always been there. It was strange that someone as acute as Altman failed to see it. He tried to be firm but not combative.

'We have to handle this from London and Belfast, Donald. We really do. With Dublin, of course, but they know the score. As you said, I didn't give my plan a tilt either way. That's why it has a chance, just a chance, of success. I'll remember your problem in anything I say over the next few days. But once this seems a plan to make one party stronger than another it's lost.'

'You're firm on that?'

Their eyes met.

'I'm firm.'

There was sometimes a moment in such conversations between two politicians when the outcome no longer turned on facts or arguments but on the respect or contempt of one participant for the other. Donald Altman had a sufficient respect for Simon Russell to accept this defeat. It would not alter his attitude on the British firms in Hong Kong.

'OK, then, that's that. Now, we've got to stick to a strong line on the WTO . . .'

Artemis paced her small hotel room, sorting out her emotions in the hope of bringing them under control. She had just presided over her first international press conference, she and Simon Russell alone side by side on a platform confronting the world. She had introduced him and poured fizzy water for him from a plastic bottle. He had used, more or less, the introductory sentences she had drafted and answered the obvious questions on Russia, the public spending round, Ireland and China in the way, more or less, she had advised. It had gone well. The British journalists had pursued the China story, scenting a disagreement between Number 10 and the Foreign Office. They implied that the Prime Minister, by refusing an invitation to Peking, was sacrificing British firms to his own idleness or convenience. Simon Russell had parried robustly, much helped by what Donald Altman had said in support of the British stance at his own press conference a few minutes earlier.

'Thank you, Artemis.' The Prime Minister had said yet again as they left the room, and held her elbow for three seconds. He would have known how nervous she had been, being that sort of man.

Before then she had spoken to the Editor of the *Daily Mirror* about Julia, a man she hardly yet knew. He had listened carefully, and said he would reflect on what she said. The paper would not carry the story tomorrow. The Prime Minister, informed of this, had simply grunted as if the matter was no longer near the front of his mind. She knew very well that this was not so, and wanted badly for a second or two to be allowed to penetrate more of the many rooms that made up the personality of this strange man.

Then Patrick Vaughan, arguing pressure of work, had given her his ticket for the circus performance. Maybe he really was busy, maybe it was his mandarin way of telling her she had done a reasonable job. For a moment she had thought naively that this would mean sitting next to Simon Russell. She quickly realised that she would be far away, somewhere at the back of the great tent. Even so it would be an experience not to miss.

She had brought only one dress that she could conceivably wear, straight and blue. It was creased from the suitcase and she had sent it quickly to be ironed. She wore only bra and pants when the telephone rang in her hotel room.

'It's me, love. How are you?'

Once she would have thrown everything out of her mind at the sound of Frank's voice.

'I've got a job, love. PR again, but this time it's a good one. The firm's called Superlative, based in Maidenhead. Twenty thousand a year straight off.'

'That's good, Frank. Sounds great. I'm glad for you.'

'I'm glad for *us*, love. It means we really can move to Fulham.'

Into her bath Artemis had emptied a small bottle of fragrance. Not the one provided by the hotel, which she thought looked cheap, but something definitely expensive that Frank had bought duty-free on a ferry six months ago. She lay on the bed conscious that she smelled good. She forgot that Frank had given it. She did not imagine Frank lying beside her, whether in Fulham, Clapham, Maida Vale or Shepherd's Bush. They all seemed distant and unexciting.

'We'll talk about that, Frank. I'll be home first thing tomorrow morning. We're flying through the night.'

'How's it going, love?'

'Really well, Frank. I've just chaired my first big press conference.'

'I'm longing to hear all about it. I'll stay home till you come.'

The doorbell rang. It would be the maid with her dress.

'I must dash, Frank. I'm going out.'

'Another press conference? A rave up with the Mounties?'

'To the circus, actually. It's the big official celebration of the Summit.'

'What a country! They won't have animals, you know, not politically correct . . . You sound a bit distant, love. Everything really all right? Boss behaving OK?'

'Fine, Frank. I've never liked circus animals. See you soon.'

'See you soon, love. Give my love to the clowns. If they still allow clowns.'

Quite.

Friday October 17

Simon Russell lay in a blur of tiredness trying to go to sleep. The RAF provided a fit of two beds on either side of the aisle of the Airbus on the homeward flight from Halifax. Since Louise was not present there was a problem about who should occupy the second. He had almost suggested, out of chivalry of course, that Artemis should have it. There were curtains screening each bed from the central aisle, the arrangement would have been entirely respectable. But he had remained silent, his team had drawn lots, and Patrick Vaughan had won. Through a gap in the curtain he had watched Patrick undress, hang up his clothes neatly one by one on the peg provided, climb into bed in his underpants, swallow a small sleeping pill and draw the curtains. Simon had taken the same pill. It was working well for the Private Secretary, who was already discreetly snoring, but not for the Prime Minister. This reversal of protocol vexed Simon. He had plenty to read, plenty to think about, but he did not want to do either of these things – he wanted to sleep. He had already been vexed by the reminder that instead of going straight to Chequers for the weekend from Heathrow he would have to go to St Adrian's School hall in Harrow for his constituency surgery, it being the third Saturday in the month. Patrick and Artemis had obviously expected him to cancel the surgery, but he stubbornly refused the idea. The constituency and its needs, however irritating, were nothing to do with civil servants. No one could take his place at the surgery. Constituents would have made appointments to see him.

The Halifax Summit had turned out as a relaxation, not a new drama. But as Simon had found before, a day or two of relaxation showed him how tired he was. With weariness came danger. The doctors had been clear about this. For a moment as Simon Russell lay back on his pillows the thought of death hung over him. The plane flew eastward, carrying the Prime Minister home to fresh draughts of the work that was keeping him alive.

Chapter Eleven

Friday October 17

'How did it go?'

'They did not meet my eyes. A month ago they cheered me. The same regiments. We were on our way to Moscow then. Today we are about to be attacked. Today the Colonel did not order a cheer. The men did not meet my eyes.'

'We are going to change that next week. Back to how you started. On to Moscow.'

'It won't be enough. I'm afraid, Virginia, I'm afraid.'

There was no one else to whom he could say that. He was glad she had stayed around. Indeed he had moved his office back into the hotel suite where they had made love. His own blown-up photograph and political posters, which she had designed, now hung from the hooks that had been empty then.

She crossed the room and put her arms round his neck as he sat slouched at his desk. He pulled her down towards him. Once they had been interrupted by one of the sentries on the fur rug, so she did not let him go far. Anyway, she knew that work, not sex, was the best cure for his lack of self-confidence.

'You still have to sign the passes for next week.'

'What passes?'

'The City Security Bureau insist that foreign guests must carry a pass personally signed by you before they can be admitted to the cemetery. We have to keep them happy. I did not insist. There are only twenty-five of them.'

Grumbling he began to sign the cards stacked in the neat pile she had prepared.

He paused at one towards the end.

'Clive Wilson, the English chatterbox? What is he still doing here?'

'He will be useful. Indeed he's useful already, you'll see. He showed me the messages he has sent to Makewell. Now he has been asked to stay on.'

She hesitated, knowing that the next suggestion was a tricky one. But the opportunity had come.

'Wilson has suggested that I go with him to London after the ceremony. Just for a few days. To broadcast, and put your case. London is much the best communications centre for this purpose. I have good contacts already. He has more. And,' she ruffled his hair, 'as you always remind me, I am English.'

'You are mostly Russian. He had designs on you. I hate the way he organises his hair. I hate to think of you stroking all that grease.'

She stopped ruffling Dobrinsky's head.

'He has a wife. He is always telling me how beautiful she is.'

'That is his trap. Anyway, I need you here. I cannot trust the others.'

She stood apart from him, and changed mood.

'Anatoly, don't joke. Wilson is a useful idiot, nothing else. Let me use him as Lenin used such men. You do not have much time. I am your Chief Information Officer. My job is to bring the world on to your side. To be honest, this is your only chance. I did not need to go with you to the regiment today to know that you have lost ground. I did not need you to tell me that you did not trust the others who work with you.'

She went to the window and turned back to him. He had never before known a woman who moved her figure as part of an argument. He did it himself, and recognised the device in others.

She spoke with force and meant what she said, surprising even herself. 'Anatoly, I don't know if you are a real leader for Russia. I shall never find out now, because I love you. I do know that these men around you are not the least bit interested in yourself or your ideas. They have respected only your success. You magnetised the north, they hoped you could magnetise Russia. Now they doubt it. They despised Andreyev, but Andreyev has gone. They are now face to face with others in Moscow like themselves – solid, unimaginative, ruthless. They are self-seeking, but inside there are *some* vestiges of patriotism. Unless you can regain your magnetic force you are irrelevant. These men will soon make a deal without you. You will be irrelevant – except as a sacrifice.'

He rested his head on his arms on the desk, and half loving, half calculating, watched her across the room.

'You are right. You can help me regain that magnetism.'

'We have made a start. Already I have taught you how to make love to an educated woman. That is a start. Lesson two is how to make love to a sentimental ill-educated world. Brassev and his crew in Moscow need the world. They are weak, not strong like the old Soviet Union. If the world were to turn suddenly to your side, then Volkarov, the Mayor and the rest of them would meet your eyes again. They would congratulate themselves once more on having found such a great leader.'

To Dobrinsky this was pleasant fencing. At heart he was tired. He did not know where to turn. The sudden bursts of political inspiration on which he had relied no longer visited him. He had for the moment lost the force behind his speeches, the magic in his wave to a crowd. Soon, he knew, he would begin to drink, and then the end would be close. So he gave way, having nothing with which to oppose.

'As you will. Desert me for England and Wilson if you will.'

'Thank you, my love. I will go the day after the ceremony. To make you strong again.'

'But come back.'

The sentry had been rebuked last time for his intrusion. This time, though he could hear enough to imagine what was happening, he stayed in the outer office, calculating his entitlement to home leave.

Saturday October 18

'Nobody takes any notice. The wind blows right through the older kids' bedroom, always coughing and sneezing they are. The council won't fix the window frames, I've told them a dozen times. Their father comes and takes the kids out, fills them with sweets, dumps them on the doorstep in the evening without so much as a word of thanks to me who has to bring them up. And his new girlfriend sitting giggling in the car all the while. I've got no money like those two for sweets or theme parks or pop concerts. Last Sunday Graham nearly clocked him when he brought them back, I had to hold him back.'

'Graham, Mrs Taylor?'

'You haven't been listening, Mr Russell. Graham's my fellow now, the father of Deirdre here. Not that he's much help.'

Deirdre was snivelling too, presumably in imitation of the older kids. Simon Russell swallowed the question that, in different forms, he felt like putting to about a quarter of those who came to his constituency surgeries. Had Mrs Taylor at any stage paused to consider the consequences of her actions? When she married Mr Taylor and bred by him, when she threw him out of the council house? When she took in Graham? When she conceived Deirdre – had she ever thought that what she did might have results, for example a chronic shortage of money, for example three children dragged into a grey confused world to carry on their shoulders a fatal load of discouragement? He knew that the question was not worth putting. No, she had not thought, she had not been educated to think in that way. Mrs Taylor believed that regardless of what she herself did she was owed happiness. Her education amounted to just that. That was her only political principle. Politicians and think-tanks and social theories came and went but they were froth on the surface of the bottomless expectations of Mrs Taylor. When Deirdre had a particularly bad cold or her ex-husband was particularly bloody, Mrs Taylor thought it natural that she should come to the Saturday surgery and ask the Prime Minister of her country to help her, since she knew he was also her Member of Parliament. Or rather she did not ask, since she had no clear idea what to ask for. The rotting window frames in the bedroom were the outward pretext. Mrs Taylor came to the surgery to let the world know that she had not received the happiness that was her due. After twenty years, Simon Russell knew that this attitude was not the prerogative of one class. Well-to-do ladies used the same tone when they came to complain about the iniquity of their neighbours who were putting up a conservatory or perhaps felling, or refusing to fell a tree.

The headmaster of St Adrian allowed Simon Russell free use of his study for his surgeries. It was a sparse room, with notices instructing visitors how to turn off the light or the radiator, a shelf full of dictionaries, and an ornate cuckoo clock derived from an exchange visit to a school in Zürich. Simon had had time to shave and put on a clean shirt in the Airbus before it landed, but he had not slept well in the plane and felt in need of a bath. There was nothing about Julia in the *Daily Mirror*, but that danger had not passed. The surgery lasted two and a half hours in theory, though in practice it took three. It was not possible to throw people out when they were still in full flow at the end of their allocation of fifteen minutes. There was usually someone who wandered in off the street without an appointment to express a forceful view about some topical matter, for example a lenient sentence passed by a magistrate in a case of which he had read three sentences in a national tabloid. Simon's constituency secretary Martha Johnson was in attendance. This was the result of a compromise. Before he became Prime Minister, Simon had seen each constituent tête-à-tête, taking the record and dictating the follow-up letters himself. Once at Number 10, he had received and rejected the work-study report recommending that he delegate the surgeries entirely to Jeff Scott, the Political Secretary. The one concession he had made was that

Martha Johnson should sit in on each interview and do the follow-up work, unless the constituent preferred to see him alone. It seemed to him an essential prop of the British constitution that Mrs Taylor should, if she wished, regard her window frames, her Graham and her Deirdre as matters so intimate that she must discuss them with the Prime Minister alone. And, of course, she did so wish.

Finally it was over. It had been a rather less strenuous surgery than usual. Simon usually reckoned that among the dozen or so constituents there would be one in tears, one mentally disturbed, one abusive. This morning no one had been abusive, though one elderly gentleman had spoken quite strongly in favour of withdrawing British troops from Ireland so that the Irish could kill each other undisturbed. That had been the only conversation on a national theme. The rest had all been personal problems. Simon Russell knew that he was good at handling these cases. He listened well, put on no side and people trusted him. With one or two he might actually be able to help, putting the constituent's case more clearly than it had been put before, helping if it was a borderline case to tilt the balance of judgement by the Inland Revenue or the Department of Social Security where the rules allowed discretion. With the rest he could at least get a clearer explanation from a public official of what was going on – clearer, that is, than the semi-literate communications which the bureaucratic computer had hitherto spewed in their direction.

At the end Simon felt as if he had been for a long, stiff walk – well exercised, reasonably satisfied with himself, even though the different stages had not been comfortable. But he did not hurry as he handed back the files to Martha Johnson, visited the headmaster's lavatory, turned off the radiator as instructed, and thanked the school porter waiting to lock up. He was free now to go to Chequers and Louise, to the last roses in the garden and the last beech leaves on the Chilterns, to half a weekend of relaxation and mild paperwork.

But he did not particularly want to go.

'Highgate, please, John, the usual,' he said.

John, his driver, was not surprised, for this had happened before. He had sandwiches in the map locker in front of him against all eventualities. But Philip, the new security officer in the other front seat, felt that he needed an explanation.

'Highgate, sir?'

'My father's house in Jackson's Lane. John knows the way.'

Simon did not feel at home in the English countryside. Its beauty transmitted its charms to him, but they made no appeal to his emotions. Moreover he knew that Chequers was not real countryside. He and Louise did not mingle with their Buckinghamshire neighbours. Occasionally he went to church, and they had once given lunch in honour of the incoming Lord Lieutenant – but that was all. Louise liked to draw and sculpt there, and had converted the

Hawtrey room beside the main hall into a studio. She invited fellow artists and writers to Sunday lunch, leaving Saturday dinner for Simon to consort with fellow politicians if he wished. This worked smoothly, but without any great enthusiasm on his part. Chequers meant nothing to Julia. She brought her dirty washing there but never her friends. Simon was born and bred in London. He felt that men and women were at their best living in the cities that they had achieved. In his experience, for most Englishmen living in the country was an artificial concept, groping backwards to a past they had superseded. He voted to retain foxhunting on libertarian grounds but would not have dreamed of attending a meet or shooting a pheasant.

His father, a prosperous city solicitor, had left him three-quarters of a million pounds and the house in Highgate. Having chosen politics as a career and quite quickly become a minister, he had seen the three-quarters of a million erode quite dramatically, and five years earlier had sold the house. It was one of the decisions he bitterly regretted. Soon afterwards Louise began to sell sculptures and when he became Prime Minister his salary had increased. But the house was gone.

The garden too had been important. Narrow cobbled paths criss-crossed a slope planted with flowering bushes, and led uphill to a small copse of hazel, holly and beech. A swing was slung on the biggest of the trees, an elderly oak beginning to die back. Louise had seen the garden, and been disappointed. Simon recognised that the special beauty of house and garden lay in the magic of his own childhood memories – the wooden feeding tray for birds on the frosty lawn, games of pursuit along the paths after children's tea parties, the crab apple tree he had pillaged each summer for unripe fruit when his mother was not looking.

The drawing room where, it was said, his grandmother had received the telegram reporting her eldest son's death on the Somme, the side door from which his mother had handed the children nuts and fruit for the animals in the Regents Park Zoo, the street lamps in Jackson's Lane which had kept him awake at night before exams, the beech under which he had moped for his first love. He had shed private tears of pleasure when his father's planning application to build three tasteful town houses in the garden had been rejected. He had kept in touch with the purchasers of the house, and they had understandingly cut for him an extra key with which he could let himself into the garden by the side door without disturbing them.

It was important that the security officer should not come into the garden with him.

'I'll go in alone,' he said.

'Right, sir,' but reluctantly. If the Government drivers knew that the Prime Minister had the bizarre habit of revisiting his childhood garden, the Breakaways might know too.

But, inside the garden, it didn't work. The memories refused to revisit. There was a new dahlia bed where the bird tray had been. The swing was still there, but had shiny new ropes. His political problems were what they were and would be what they would be. There was no point in being deceived. Thinking about them in solitude seemed to yield no extra wisdom.

The personal problems . . . even more so. There was danger even in bringing them into play. They showed every sign of proving insoluble. Unlike Mrs Taylor, Simon did not believe that he was entitled to happiness. The bright red dahlias were exaggerated, even vulgar.

'Chequers,' he said, regaining the car. The driver John had eaten his sandwiches. The security officer Philip was hungry, and thinking of a late pub lunch at Great Missenden. For the Prime Minister there would be cold ham and salad waiting on the sideboard, and several red boxes by the fire.

Chapter Twelve

Tuesday October 21

'You were wrong,' said the Secretary General of the Party. Once again, as at the previous meeting, he spoke in a way inconceivable for his predecessors.

They sat round the same swimming pool in the Forbidden City of Peking. Although ten days had passed, the breeze was now wintry and the willow in the corner of the courtyard was shedding its leaves.

The oldest minister, the Chairman of the Privatisation Commission, was for once sparing with words.

'It is too soon to revisit our decision.'

'What is the latest news on investment?' asked the Secretary General.

The Premier knew.

'Citibank and Dresdner have now joined the British banks in withdrawing from the Three Gorges project.

Altman's remarks will lead other American banks to do the same. All five main power projects are paralysed. Their lawyers argue that our privatisation decree against the four Hong Kong companies alters the legal basis on which they undertook the investment. The Japanese have signalled that they cannot remain here alone.'

They paused and gazed at the empty pool. The dead sparrow had been removed but no one had swept out the damp thin leaves as they accumulated at the deep end. Even now it was hard in the People's Republic to admit a mistake.

'The barbarian chief has refused our compromise,' said the Secretary General ironically. 'In the old days we would have issued an edict from the Imperial Palace to punish his presumption signed by the vermilion pencil of the Son of Heaven.'

Another silence. He was not funny.

The Premier stopped a discussion that had never got underway.

'We should do nothing.'

'Nothing?'

'Nothing whatever. And interpret it as appropriate. To the Chinese people the decision stands. The four companies are privatised. The People's Republic is not to be defied. But the rest of the world will see that no action is in practice taken. Gradually the investment boycott will dissolve. The banks and industrial companies will begin to chase profits in China all over again. It is their nature.'

'We could not live with that contradiction. Words and deeds would not match. In the village where the dogs bark loud, cats cannot breed.'

The Premier began to whistle a tune as if it were an argument.

'What is that?'

'It was the most popular song of my boyhood. "We will certainly liberate Taiwan". We sang it every morning in school before our lessons. It has a catchy tune.'

'So?'

'Fifty years have passed. Where is Taiwan now?'

'It will be liberated one day, of course.'

'One day, of course. Just as one day the British companies will be privatised into Chinese ownership. Of course.'

They paused again. Silence was consent. It was better not to record any actual decision.

'Now, as regards the proposal to hold the next International Rotary Conference in the Temple of Heaven . . .'

Saturday October 25

To St Petersburg, too, winter had come early. That suited Virginia and Dobrinsky quite well. It had snowed during the night and the road that ran past the cemetery gates was lightly covered. The sun was struggling to penetrate the white, heavy sky but seemed likely to fail. Snowflakes fell individually on the caps, the epaulettes, the boots, the guns and the tanks. The military parade had not been as big as Virginia had originally planned. The troops of the Fourteenth Army were moving north from Pskov and might at any time clash with Dobrinsky's outposts twenty miles south of St Petersburg. The broadcasts from Moscow had become more aggressive. A single surface-to-surface missile had landed two days before without exploding in the park of the Catherine Palace, either a mistake or a warning. Admiral Volkarov had protested against weakening his defences even for a day and the number of troops in the parade had been halved.

Dobrinsky left the dais from which he had taken the salute. He paused at the entrance to the cemetery between the two pavilions that served as museums to the Siege of Leningrad in the Great Patriotic War. Two young officers waited with a huge wreath of lilies. The professor from the university who had briefed him said that there were more people buried here than anywhere else in Europe. Ahead of him for about half a mile stretched the straight path to the stone memorial that closed the vista. There were no individual graves on either side of the path, but long mounds of turf, each marked with a year, mostly 1942 or 1943. For the soldiers of the Red Army thus heaped together there was a star on each mound, for the civilians the hammer and sickle. The rubbish collection vehicles had passed through the city each morning during the siege, loading the corpses of those who had starved in the streets during the night. To

would once again be called Leningrad. Dobrinsky had argued that this would be popular among the citizens. The Siege of Leningrad was a heroic memory for all, whereas the Czars who had earlier ruled St Petersburg were remote. His advisers had been more cautious, and he had not persisted.

'We should have changed the name,' he repeated. 'This is Russia, this is Leningrad, they fit together.'

She had come to say goodbye, since she would have to leave for the airport immediately the ceremony was over. She did not want to argue, but could not let it pass.

'We would have lost the West. For them Lenin was just a Communist.'

'Damn the West.'

She kissed him. A few alert cameras clicked.

'You look fine.'

'I'll freeze.'

'In a good cause.'

She wished the world could see his eyes, almost black, sometimes gleaming with frustration, sometimes with cunning and happiness, never empty except during that time when he had been exhausted.

Although he had been given various ranks in different services, Dobrinsky wore no uniform or medals, just a long dark coat. Virginia had insisted on simplicity. She had even forbidden a fur hat. Anatoly Dobrinsky, bareheaded, snow falling on his straight black hair, looked twenty-five. He was taller than the wreath bearers in front of him, whose youth was concealed under the long peaks of their military caps. She kissed him once more, her *jeune premier*.

The bands struck up the Dead March of Chopin. They repeated it continuously as Dobrinsky walked slow and upright behind the wreath, past the mounds, towards the waiting veterans at the Memorial. Because of the position of the bands it seemed as if the trees themselves were lamenting. The snow thickened slightly. Dobrinsky fastened his gaze, as Virginia had instructed him, on the necks of the two lieutenants goose-stepping in slow time in front of him. Both of them were closely shorn, one had a slight scar just above the shirt collar. The genuine emotion was still with him. He wanted to hang on to it. 1944, 1943, 1942 – his eyes slipped sideways to the mounds. He imagined what the cemetery must have been like then – raw frozen earth, then mud and slush, no trees, no music, shouts and manoeuvring trucks, a desperate effort each day to impose order on piles of rotting mangled corpses. Corpses of Russians who had been given dignity and were now to be honoured once more. He too was a Russian. It did not really matter a damn whether the footsteps he followed down that path were of Stalin or Lenin or Nicholas or Alexander. They were all part of the snow and the birches, the mournful music and the young men under peaked caps marching in slow time.

'Marvellous,' said Clive Wilson to his interpreter. He too was genuinely moved. Because it was rare, such sympathetic emotion pleased him. And he had been given a good place in the front line of the foreign well-wishers. With luck the BBC camera team would pick him out. He wondered if he could sit next to Virginia on the plane.

Dobrinsky paused at last at the foot of the slope leading up to the Memorial. The wreathbearers would place the wreath at the Memorial. He would move forward, tweak the lilies, adjust the card, then stand back in silence. After two minutes the military bands would play the Russian national anthem. Then he would move to talk informally to the veterans, gathered with their children and grandchildren.

He began to climb the slope. It was all straightforward. Virginia had done well.

But it did not happen quite that way.

*

Frank would normally have been at Newbury that Saturday afternoon, but in his campaign to show Artemis that he was saving money out of his new salary he was watching the racing on television instead.

'At this rate, we'll soon be able to afford the deposit,' he said, reaching into the fridge for a can of lager.

'But you always used to say you made money at Newbury.'

'But this way through Art I can still win and save on the train fare and the entrance.'

Art ran the betting shop at the corner. Frank, pleased with having won the argument, embraced Artemis with the hand not holding the beer. It all seemed a long way from Halifax, Nova Scotia. She worried that he might want to make quick love to her next door in the bedroom before the first race.

'Better get down to Art now before it starts.'

He saw through her and his hand tightened round her breast. 'Not in the mood?'

She had never repulsed him yet, and did not want to start now – or not yet. She needed to know first what would become of him at the bottom of that downward path.

'Delayed jet-lag,' she said. 'Sleepy.'

But in fact she could not sleep when she had closed the bedroom door against Frank and the television. She thought of the circus. She had half waved to the Prime Minister in the interval across the breadth of the marquee, but checked herself when he did not seem to notice. She thought of the flight home in the Prime Minister's plane, when she had slept for not more than an hour in her reclining seat. But above all she savoured that press conference, and her sense of presiding for twenty minutes over the destinies of the world. It had been the climax of her professional life.

Then she did drift to sleep. Frank had to wake her by shaking her shoulder.

'You'd better get up.'

'Telephone?' She sat up in bed, blinking, puzzled after a second that no bell was ringing.

'No, out here.'

She moved quickly, fastening her bra, then smoothing her hair.

Frank pointed at the television. He seemed in a strange state. At first she thought it was irritation that his afternoon's racing had been interrupted by an interview with an obscure MP called Clive Wilson. Wilson was on the screen talking hurriedly. Something seemed amiss with his hair. Before she could clarify this or hear what he was saying the picture switched.

An old man lay on a slab of stone, blood gurgling from his mouth in spasms. The camera shifted slightly to his shattered leg. Then again to the chest of another man, which seemed to have been shattered by two tons of medals. Then two more, then a fifth, not dead but writhing and gasping with a mass of blood and bone where the shoulder had been. A boy toddled silently among the corpses. He must have been about three. What he saw fell far outside his experience. It had not yet triggered any emotion.

Soldiers appeared with a stretcher. On to it they lifted clumsily the man with the shoulder, whose gasps turned to a continuous shout of pain. The little boy began to wail, and grasped the old man's hand. Then to a man whom Artemis half recognised, hatless, young with a great grey coat badly torn below the waist. He looked like a tramp until he moved. He snatched up the child, and the camera rose with it, closing on the man's dark straight hair, black eyes and a smear of blood on the neck. There was something theatrical about his movement and Artemis realised who it was. Dobrinsky, of course. The camera moved again to soldiers stiffly carved on a memorial and softly falling snow.

Artemis was fully tuned in now. Clive Wilson was speaking again. The know-all platitudes of his working life had momentarily deserted him.

'At first I thought it was a rocket like the one fired yesterday. But it must have been a bomb concealed here. Or a mortar fired from one of those trucks under the bushes. Excuse me, I must go.' He paused. 'Bloody fiends they are, who did this.'

For the first time in his life Clive Wilson cut short a television interview. Soon he too could be seen carrying a water can, splashing water into the mouths and on to the faces of the casualties. In the background a loud, nervous voice began to give instructions in Russian through a loudspeaker.

'Of course, it's too soon to be sure,' said the BBC reporter, 'but the finger must point at Moscow and the military forces now poised to attack St Petersburg on the orders of General Brassev. They were certainly responsible for the missile attack yesterday, which caused no casualties. This – today – what we're seeing,' he groped for a vivid phrase but failed to find one, 'this . . . monstrous outrage is in a different category. There's little I can add . . .'

He went on adding it for some time, but not on the channel to which Frank had turned.

'We'll bring you any further developments as they occur. Now we return to Newbury for the three-thirty . . .'

'About time too,' said Frank, who had money on that race. Then, sensing from the retreating back of Artemis that this might not be right, 'Horrible,' he added, 'frightening.' He went for another beer.

Artemis, back in the bedroom, dressed quickly without knowing exactly why. What she had just seen did not alter the fundamentals of what was happening in Russia. The bomb did not make Dobrinsky richer, more powerful or more admirable. It did not alter by one whit the limited nature of the British interest in the Russian civil war. And yet it altered everything. She was experienced enough in the world of the media to know that. For weeks, perhaps months ahead, when people wrote or broadcast or thought of Russia they would think of the blood bubbling from that old man's mouth – of the little boy grasping his grandfather's hand – even more of Dobrinsky with the torn coat and the blood on his neck lifting the boy against the background of the stone soldiers and the snowflakes drifting down.

She wanted to be genuinely upset, but found that her first reaction was professional. Later, analysing the day, she was dismayed by this. At the time it seemed natural. Technically she ought first to ring the duty press officer at the Foreign Office and concert an agreed line with him. There would be dozens of requests for the PM's comments. But that might mean that the Prime Minister heard the news first from Patrick Vaughan or even the Foreig Secretary. That would not do. She dialled the Number 1 switchboard and asked for Chequers.

Julia came to Chequers unexpectedly that afternoon, just a the clink of crockery in the corridor behind the Great Hal suggested tea. Simon felt uplifted at seeing her walk into hi study. A dreary day acquired some meaning. Julia in thes weeks was at a loose end. She had promised to go to th sixth-form college in France after Christmas and mean while not to see the man whom Louise always called 'th Argentine'. It had not been possible to extract furthe promises from a seventeen-year-old. Realistically, h thought (weakly, Louise maintained), he had given her small allowance, enough for her occasionally to visi friends. From one such visit she now returned, with a suit case of unwashed clothes.

Louise was using the last of the afternoon light to sculp in the Hawtrey Room.

'Say hello to your mother. Then we'll go for a walk.'

He knew that it was a bad moment to go out. He wa expecting a telephone call from William Strachan, leade of the Ulster Unionists. Things were working out quit well. NIPMI so far was justifying itself. A wing of th Unionist Party hastily formed of new recruits since th Prime Minister made his appeal at Antrim was pressing fo a special Party Conference to review policy. They were i favour of compromise with the democratic Nationalist and called themselves Constructives. Strachan now had to decide whether to compromise with the Constructives or defeat them and stick to the familiar hard line. He had asked to see the Prime Minister, but had been persuaded to settle for a telephone conversation.

James Whitman, the Secretary of State, advised that this was a hopeful sign. Strachan would probably ask what pressure the Prime Minister would be willing to put on the Nationalists to match any move Strachan might make towards them. The eternal political minuet in Northern Ireland was being resumed, as Russell and James Whitman had hoped. Like so many of their predecessors, they were playing a slightly new tune and hoped that the dancers would respond with some new steps. It was infinitely time-consuming for the orchestra.

Russell, nevertheless, preferred to seize the moment with Julia. Work would dominate eighteen hours of the day unless he sometimes took a stand. Strachan, and indeed tea, would have to wait.

It was damp outside and the two protection officers assembled gumboots and outer garments by the back door. As they started, it began to rain seriously. There had been no frost yet, but rain had begun to blotch the array of scarlet roses down the steps from the terrace. They were scentless and in Russell's opinion dull, though all visitors admired them.

He did not know how to start, or indeed whether to start. Louise believed that Julia was coming to the end of her difficult stage and would of her own accord dock alongside her parents after her first voyage out into the universe. From this point of view it would be a mistake for Simon or herself to make a further move. On the contrary, it might complicate the docking process. This was hard for Simon and his softer heart. He longed to re-establish full communication with his daughter. But how? He had no fundamental question to ask her, and there was no point in small talk. Yet silence seemed a waste of time.

'Nothing in the *Daily Mirror.*'

'Thank God.'

The *Mirror* had given no undertakings. By now their silence probably meant that they would not print the story. Another drama that petered out without a definite ending. Julia clearly did not want to revisit the scare it had given her.

'Good party?' he asked eventually. She had been staying with friends in Leicestershire. It was safe to assume there had been a party.

'Good party,' she answered. Another pause. They were out of the garden now, on the rising path which led through young trees and shrubs, mostly planted by Prime Ministers or royalty, to the natural beeches of the Chilterns.

She took his arm at a point where the path was broad enough for them to walk side by side.

'No need to chat, Dad. Let me talk when I want to. It's just good to be here. With you and Mummy. I'll sleep late tomorrow, if that's OK.' There had once been difficulties on this point, Julia having appeared, half asleep in purple pyjamas, at the start of an official lunch for the Prime Minister of Thailand.

'That's fine.'

Indeed it was.

Simon felt a charge of sheer pleasure running through him, greater than he would ever gain from anything in politics. If those were her ground rules, including the affectionate squeeze on his arm, he could live with them.

Julia had scorned a hat. The rain was bright on her dark hair, having not yet penetrated to bedraggle it. She wore a Barbour coat belonging to one of the protection officers, too big for her by far. The mismatch made her look three years less than her age. Simon wondered under the dripping beeches whether, despite the protection officers behind him, he should turn the squeeze into a hug of love in order to ratify the treaty she had just proposed. But at that moment the senior of the two escorts called just loud enough to bridge the gap of ten yards between himself and the Prime Minister. Simon detached himself from Julia and the two men came together.

'A message from the garden-room girls, sir.'

The garden-room girls were the Prime Minister's confidential secretaries, regardless of what room or indeed garden they occupied at any time.

'Artemis Palmer rang. She's anxious that you should return to the house and see something on the television.

Can't make much of it, sir, but it sounds as if something's happened in Russia.'

'Silly girl. Get her on your mobile please.' Simon was cross. He had hired Artemis for good sense, not for bureaucratic interruption of his few clear moments on a Saturday afternoon. She had that Frank boy, why couldn't she badger Frank one day a week?

But after he had spoken briefly to Artemis, he took Julia's arm with a different grip.

'Better go back in,' he said. 'The world doesn't stop for you and me.'

*

The Aeroflot jet had of course waited at St Petersburg for Virginia and Clive Wilson and the other foreigners who eventually arrived from the cemetery. None of the foreigners had been hurt. Their mood was part subdued, part excited.

Virginia invited Wilson to sit beside her. He noticed that her hands trembled slightly. They talked in an entirely matter-of-fact way, as happens after a funeral, when relatives reconstruct the surface of their lives to cover over the gap that death has made.

'I shall need your advice,' she said. 'I shall need money very quickly. Perhaps one well-paid article in an American magazine. Or possibly an advance on a book I will write. Once I have that money I do not want to argue about fees.

I will write and broadcast for free. But I am a little out of date about who to see and which programmes and papers to tackle. I have to build a campaign in the shortest possible time. International, not just British. Will you help me?'

She looked at him straight, without coquetry.

'Of course I will help you.'

He put his hand on hers on the grey plastic shelf between them. She did not respond to the pressure but waited for a few seconds before taking her hand away.

'To work,' she said, finding pen and scribble pad. '*BBC Today* is still the most influential of the radio programmes, don't you think?'

*

General Brassev had no particular desire for pomp. He occupied a simple white office of plywood partitions. A gilded Corinthian capital still visible in one corner of the ceiling reminded those present that they were in the Kremlin.

He and his colleagues hesitated for a few hours. An element that they did not understand had entered the situation. They were dimly conscious of a world working itself into uproar because a few people were dead. They decided to ignore it. Brassev summed up a brief discussion.

'Tell the Foreign Ministry they have to handle the Americans, British, Germans, French, those people in New York who may make noise. That is their profession. It should not concern us. Our problems are here in Russia. We shall implement our plan without change.'

'Including Estonia?'

'Certainly including Estonia.'

*

'Tonight I am speaking to you as your Prime Minister, Prime Minister of Estonia, and to the world outside about the danger to our country. Estonia is small but free. That has not always been our history. But it is our wish and our destiny. We have no desire to take part in a war in Russia. Dobrinsky, Brassev, what is that to us? But we need to have practical relationships with St Petersburg. Our agriculture and industry depend on it. Today I have received a threat from Moscow, I would almost say an order. They say that we must break off our trade, stop sending food to St Petersburg and allow Russian troops to cross the soil of Estonia as part of their campaign against that city.

'Always conscious of my responsibilities to the people of Estonia I cannot permit this . . .'

Monday October 27

In the Home Office the prisons paper for Thursday's Cabinet was almost ready. Officials had been unable to agree with the Treasury the estimated costs for taking over and equipping the army camps and the ferries, which were also to be converted into an emergency prison. Indeed Treasury officials had indicated that the Chancellor would strongly oppose the whole plan in Cabinet. It was therefore particularly important that the Home Secretary should pitch the central arguments in his paper right. Previous policies that he had inherited had been highly popular when introduced; they were now creating a crisis in the prisons, involving the certainty of overcrowding and the likelihood of riot. Officials were pleased with the annex to the paper, which showed in vivid graphics the rise in the prison population with a dotted line projecting disastrously into the future. By abolishing Morning Prayers his Private Office had cleared half an hour for Roger Courtauld to finalise the paper by adding the personal touches for which he was famous in Whitehall. The paper would then be circulated to other Cabinet Ministers that Monday evening, meeting the Cabinet Office rule that ministers should have forty-eight hours to brood over a paper before it was discussed.

Roger Courtauld wore a bulky overcoat too heavy for late October. He carried a thicker sheaf of daily papers than usual. His detective would bring up three red boxes of overnight work in the following lift.

Once he was settled at his desk, his Private Secretary, John Upchurch, explained with quiet professional satisfaction the state of the paperwork, but added, 'What I can't find out, Home Secretary, is the order of discussion on

Thursday – that is, whether our paper – your paper, Home Secretary – will be taken before the discussion on public expenditure. Number 10 say they don't know how the PM will handle it. We shall know, of course, when we get the Cabinet agenda on Wednesday, but I wondered . . .' He paused, but got no reaction. 'I wondered whether you might have a word on the telephone with the Prime Minister suggesting that prisons be taken first. The public expenditure discussion is bound to be prolonged and it does seem important there should be proper consideration of your paper . . .'

'That depends on whether we want what you call consideration or a decision.'

Roger Courtauld seemed grumpy.

'Home Secretary?'

'The less time for debate, the more likely we shall get our way. On these occasions, bounce is king . . . It would be better for prisons to come after public spending when ministers are hungry and looking at their watches . . . but I doubt if any of this is to the point. Look at all that.' He pointed to the pile of papers he had thrown down at the far side of his desk.

'Russia?' he ventured.

'Russia in spades. Russia, Estonia and a whole lot else. The PM might call a special Cabinet before Thursday, I suppose. If not, we'll spend Thursday morning pontificating with bogus certainty about a lot of issues most of us know nothing about . . .' He paused. His mind clicked forward.

'Get me Gerletzky on the telephone as soon as they wake up in Washington.'

'Gerletzky, Home Secretary?'

'You'll find the number in my book.'

He could be excused for forgetting the name. Only very exceptionally did the Home Secretary call Gerletzky. They had studied at the same Cambridge college, and Gerletzky was now Chief Security Adviser to President Altman.

Chapter Thirteen

Monday October 27

The Liberal Democrats in Lewes were low-spirited. Their own by-election canvass returns showed their candidate level-pegging with the Conservative. But none of them had ever heard of a by-election in which by this stage their own Liberal canvass returns had not predicted a smashing Liberal victory. Level-pegging was gloomy news. The two opinion polls recently published in the press showed the Tories ahead by six and eight points respectively, only a small swing against the Government since the General Election. The more sober of them were resigned to defeat. There would be another day, another fight. Others however blamed their candidate for a lacklustre campaign. How and for what possible reason had they come to choose a professor of international relations from Sussex University? Trevor Phelps did nothing but make speeches, long complicated speeches from the campaign van, to dwindling groups in market places and housing estates, to parents collecting children from school, even to baffled cows in fields. Take him out of the campaign van and he was tongue-tied, barely civil to individual electors. Put him back in the van and he launched without delay into another speech over the loudspeaker about the need to amend the United Nations Charter.

So there was no buzz of welcome when Trevor Phelps entered the small crowded committee room that Monday morning.

'Good morning, Trevor,' said one lady to break the embarrassed hush.

Trevor was in a condition they had never seen before. His large pale face was flushed, and he was clasping and unclasping his hands.

'That's it then,' he said.

Some of them wondered if he was about to chuck his hand in and abandon the campaign.

'We've been looking for a theme for the last few days. We've got it. Stop the Murderers. STOP THE MURDERERS. The honour of Britain is at stake.' He took a paper cup of Nescafé which had been poured for someone else.

'You mean – capital punishment?' asked the same lady, not clear that hanging people was official Liberal policy.

'No, no, no. I mean the Russian murderers. Did none of you see the pictures of that bomb last night? Did none of you hear that marvellous Virginia woman on the radio this morning? I've drafted a press release to put out at once.' He read it out.

'"Liberal candidate Trevor Phelps today gave a completely new twist to his by-election campaign.

'"'Britain's honour is at stake,' he said. 'She must show a lead to Europe and the world to stop the Moscow murderers. The appeasers at the Foreign Office and Number 10 must be given a clear message. Put principle before prudence. For once give the world a moral lead and so put the Great back in Britain. We must use all necessary means – diplomatic, financial, even military – to make sure that the gallant citizens of St Petersburg are not overrun, and that Estonia is protected. The time for action is now. The voters of South Sussex can light a beacon of freedom and justice when they vote Liberal on Thursday. Vote for Phelps and World Justice.'"'

There was a round of applause when he finished. This was the kind of talk to which Liberals had been accustomed in the golden days.

'Military means?' asked a retired colonel who had been stuffing envelopes.

'Almost certainly won't be necessary,' Phelps answered him. 'Once the message is clear in Moscow they'll hold back.'

'Well, I hope you've thought it through.'

'It's the Midlothian campaign all over again,' said a lady who ran the local borrowing library.

'Exactly. We'll start this morning outside Tesco's,' replied Gladstone's heir.

Tuesday October 28

'On Russia, we're firm but non-committal,' said President Altman. 'Firm but non-committal.'

'May I make a suggestion?' asked Gerletzky, his Security Adviser.

'Fire ahead.'

'I would suggest non-committal but firm.'

President Altman stared at him.

'What is this? A comedy backchat show?'

They were alone in the Security Adviser's office in the west wing of the White House. They knew each other well. They were able to talk at different levels of intelligence and intensity, following each other up or down the scale without explanation, guided by the instinct of friendship.

The President perched on the sofa adjoining Gerletzky's desk.

'OK, let's talk it through for a moment before the others get at it. Forget the elections on Thursday. We need a statement before then, but not a decision. I'll settle for non-committal but firm. Work out a draft for the Rose Garden this afternoon. I'll call the usual people. Today's statement is not the problem. How long have we got before we have to answer the real question?'

'Which is?'

'In or out? Stop 'em or let the tears flow?'

'The tears may flow anyway.'

'Probably. But how long?'

'A week, ten days. Dobrinsky and Estonia can hold out that long. But it's a hell of a long time to sit on the fence with this media racket building the way it is. If it weren't for the CNN and BBC and that Virginia woman in London . . .'

'If it weren't for that bomb . . .' They both gazed at the television screen, for the moment grey and empty of the pressures with which it deformed their lives.

'But it's more than that, Joe. It's the old problem all over again. We love righteousness and hate iniquity. We really do. We're Americans. Big boy beating small boy, he's got to be stopped. But we are suspicious of foreign adventures and worry ourselves silly about casualties.' He paused. 'We're a psychological mess, and the greatest people on earth. How do I sort that one out, Joe?'

'You carried thirty-eight States last time, Mr President. That's the only answer I can give. You wanted the job of chief magician and you've got it. I'm just the guy who brushes the hat and counts the rabbits. My options paper is almost ready. I have the Pentagon's comments. I'll give State another half-hour to comment.' He paused.

'Get me a coffee and talk it through now. No tape, no record.'

They talked in low voices for twenty minutes.

'It would mean rebuilding that old coalition?'

'Sure. Ring the Brits first? Ring the Brits now?'

'Not a bad idea.' The President paused again, then, 'Yes, a bad idea. I remember what Simon Russell said at Halifax. He won't be keen.'

'I've kept my contacts in London. His Interior Minister rang me – name of Courtauld. Fat and tough. Russell will be under the same pressures as we are – perhaps more so.'

'You saying he's ripe already? The Brits always think of a thousand legal and practical objections to anything of this kind.'

'And then join. And stay joined. I think Russell will ripen fast.'

'We'll shake that tree tomorrow. Put him down for a call.'

Wednesday October 29

Virginia was still concentrating on Britain but her tickets were booked for New York at the weekend. For a few days she reigned in London. Every radio and TV programme, every newspaper besought her, and quarrelled over little bits of her time.

She had at short notice invaded *Question Time*, attracted by its format. In her experience a studio audience provided the chance for a quick kill, and she had no time to waste. The BBC had told her to dress for daytime. So instead she dressed for evening by borrowing from a fashion house – simple, expensive, low cut and black, a single diamond pointing to the division of her breasts. The others were men whose suits looked crumpled by comparison, even if they were not. There was a retired but not ancient general, an academic from Loughborough, and Peter Makewell's deputy at the Foreign Office, the Minister of State who dealt daily with Russian matters. She had asked that Clive Wilson be included, but the BBC had refused, while conceding her more important request that the first fifteen minutes of the session would be devoted to the crisis in Russia. Clive had brought her in his car, had eaten sandwiches and drunk New Zealand Chardonnay in the green room with the participants. She could see him in the front row of the audience, wearing the tragic expression they had both agreed was fitting for all public occasions. She was satisfied with her relationship with Clive. He no longer kissed or tried to embrace her. Theirs was a political liaison, and since politics was more important to him than sex, he was satisfied. She was less happy with her telephone call a few hours back with Anatoly Dobrinsky. A fragment of metal from the bomb had slightly grazed his arm which was still painful. Moscow troops were concentrating thirty miles to the south, but had not yet attacked. There had been big crowds out on the streets of St Petersburg in his support, and the recruiting figures were up.

'Film the queues,' she had said.

'I'm not sure there are queues.'

'Make queues, for God's sake. Eager patriotic queues of young men and women carrying your picture.'

'I'll try.'

But he seemed flat, uninterested in the commotion that she and the bomb were raising round the world on his behalf. He harped on throughout about how much he missed her. She wondered about this. After years of virtual celibacy he was now used to frequent lovemaking. If he missed that too much there were plenty of girls in St Petersburg who would fill the gap. Did that matter? Yes it did. All in all, she felt that she did not have as much time as she had thought. She would have to accelerate. Privately she resolved to be back in St Petersburg within ten days.

The question master was replete with bogus emotion, pompously introducing the team, then explaining why exceptionally in these tragic circumstances they had decided to start with three questions on Russia. The studio audience was dimly lit, but she could see the intense look on the student's face even through the gleam of his spectacles.

'A brutal civil war is obviously about to break out in Russia. Innocent blood has just been shed in an appalling way. Does the panel think that Britain can stand aside?'

The question master looked at her, but she shook her head.

'I would rather hear first what others think,' she said. She had made her plan. The question master floundered for a moment, but soon a discussion was underway. The retired general described the range of rockets, the terrain round St Petersburg and the effect of winter on military operations. The academic talked about the tension between Woodrow Wilson's idealism and Kissingerian realism in the formation of foreign policy. The Minister of State was uneasy because Virginia was silent. He discussed the need to strike a balance and the possibility of a special meeting of the Security Council at Foreign Minister level.

He hesitated, conscious that he was on the edge of making policy for which he had no authority. He had left his Foreign Office brief in the green room. It seemed a long way away. Virginia saw her chance. As she moved her shoulders forward the diamond flashed into four million British homes, and within minutes across the world into many millions more.

'I don't understand, I don't understand,' she said, 'I was brought up here, I love Britain. I thought I knew Britain. You all saw the old men dying, you saw the blood, you saw the child. Is this to be repeated when you could stop it? Is this the world we are to bring our own children into? I spoke to Anatoly Dobrinsky an hour ago. He is hurt, you know, his arm was caught by the bomb; he is still in pain. I told him I was coming on this programme. He asked me to explain why he asked me to come here. Here to England, not to France or Germany or America. It is because, he said, the English are the first to recognise the difference between right and wrong. I have told him this, and he believes it. Now I hear all the wise words which you three gentlemen have spoken. I hear them, but I do not understand what reply you are giving to that intelligent young man in the audience. Or to St Petersburg. Or to Anatoly, whom I love and admire. Am I to tell him that what I told him was wrong?'

There was a silence on the platform. The studio audience rustled, and there were a few whispers. The Minister of State found his voice. Damn it, he had no choice, he would have to make policy.

'We certainly favour an urgent meeting of the Security Council under Chapter Seven of the Charter. It could be held at Ministerial level—'

She cut him short. Her plan involved switching her effort now away from the platform to the studio audience. The million in their sitting rooms would take the emotional cue from the sixty men and women now in front of her.

'Good,' she said, focusing on the student who had asked the question. 'You asked the right question, and in his own time and his own English way, the Minister has given the right answer. England abolished slavery. England stood alone against the Nazis. Now again England will take the lead for justice. England will rally the world to save St Petersburg, to save little Estonia, to save our old men and little children. I shall fly to New York tomorrow to pave the way. But I am just a feeble girl. Your Prime Minister will come for this meeting of the Security Council. Simon Russell is a man of courage and experience. He will persuade the world to intervene before it is too late. Will you support me? Will you support him?'

Out of the semi-darkness there was a shout of 'Yes' from many voices, then a huge roar of approval, followed by clapping. A dozen stood up, then everyone was on their feet. The applause lasted five minutes and echoed round the world. The question master at last regained control and looked round him before accepting the next question. He found that Virginia's seat was empty.

'Damn,' said the Minister of State as they prepared to discuss quarantine for dogs entering Britain.

'Brilliant,' said Clive as he and Virginia found the door out on to the street where their car was waiting.

'We shall see,' she said. But she was pleased. A small group of well-wishers had somehow tracked her down. They cheered her as she climbed into the car. In the car she had another idea.

'What's the first name of Simon Russell's daughter?'

Thursday October 30

'He lost control. That Russian woman was dressed like a tart. Your minister gabbled a lot of nonsense. He's not fit to be at the Foreign Office.'

Simon had not seen the programme. He never watched television except for an occasional snatched gobbet of news. Louise usually reserved her severity for the media or for her own family. It was unlike her to take sides on a political matter.

'I gather he was under a lot of pressure. We all are.'

Louise stared at him. 'But it's such rubbish.' She laid breakfast for three. Julia's knife, spoon and plate were untouched, though they had heard her on the telephone in the sitting room of the flat a few minutes before.

'You don't mean to say you're going to let us get involved in that Russian business?'

Simon preferred his second cup of coffee without politics, but had no choice.

'The Party Chairman rang me last night. He doesn't like the look of what's happening in South Sussex. They poll today, you know.'

'What's South Sussex to do with Russia?'

Simon felt exasperated. There were elementary gaps in Louise's knowledge of current affairs. Today ignorance was not holding her back from expressing dogmatic opinions.

'The Liberal Democrat candidate is a man called Phelps. He was trailing quite badly. Our private polling was excellent. Three days ago he changed tack. He's run amok on Russia. Stop the Murderers. Nothing but Russia morning, noon and night. And he's turned the election round. Our latest figures are terrible. It's slipping away.'

'You can't send in troops because of a by-election.'

'No indeed.' Simon had no intention of sending in troops, but being irritated with the conversation he did not want to say so. He drained his cup and scrumpled his paper napkin.

'Couldn't we really manage linen napkins for breakfast?' he asked.

It was a plea she had heard before. She sympathised, but it would involve complicated negotiation across the frontier within Number 10 between private and official eating. She had so far taken no action.

'You're trying to change the subject, Simon.'

'Yes, indeed.'

He rose, kissed his wife and left the room. He disliked starting his working day in the wake of a spat with his wife. He always tried to end their early dialogue on a peaceful note. This morning he had managed it – just.

Cabinet was in half an hour, earlier than usual, at nine thirty. He had been reluctant to agree to this because it made more difficult his private tactic for handling the morning. But Joan Freetown had pressed hard for a longer session as soon as she heard that prisons as well as public spending was on the agenda, and he found no grounds to resist. It was essential to see Peter Makewell first. The Foreign Secretary usually arrived exactly on time, neither early nor late. This morning he was pacing the landing outside the study on the first floor. Beneath his open-air face he looked weary. But, oddly, he did not start with Russia.

'Well, Prime Minister, you've won a big battle.'

'You mean?'

'China. You were right and I was wrong. They've given in.'

'You mean, withdrawn the privatisation decree?'

'No, of course not. They're Chinese. But they're letting the firms know in Hong Kong that it's on indefinite hold. No threats, no deadline, trade as usual. A big success, and your doing.'

Simon remembered the argument in the plane to Halifax and how he had overruled the Foreign Secretary and his officials.

'It's generous of you to put it like that.'

'Not generous, just. It could have done us huge harm if it had gone wrong.'

'Thanks, but no one else will think of it again. Just you and a few of your mandarins in London, real mandarins in Peking. Dangers averted are dangers forgotten. This one was never really out in the open. Some academic in twenty years time may write a thesis. The trip to Peking that never was.'

'Now, Russia.' Peter Makewell looked at the clock. He could not allow more than that small moment of self-satisfaction. There were only fifteen minutes before Cabinet. 'How much do you want me to say to the colleagues?'

'Under Foreign Affairs you will be expected to tell us what is happening.' The agenda of a Cabinet always begins with three items – Parliamentary Affairs, Home Affairs, Foreign Affairs.

'But how far should I push them?'

'Push them?'

'Prime Minister,' said Peter Makewell rather formally. 'I never expected to say this, but I am beginning to think that we and others will have to intervene in Russia or at least Estonia before long. The pressure is mounting fast. I believe it is necessary to prepare colleagues.'

Simon stared at the Foreign Secretary rather as Louise had just stared at him.

'Pressure. Because of media hype? Commotion at a by-election? A serious Government cannot respond to that sort of thing – nor a serious Foreign Office,' he added. He was not usually sharp with Peter Makewell but it was turning into a bad day.

'I am not swayed by any of those considerations,' said Makewell, even more formally, leaning forward in his armchair. 'Altman is on the move. The Security Council. The French and Germans. There's a flash flood bearing down on us.'

'Peter, this isn't like you.' The Prime Minister switched to an informal tone. 'We haven't begun to think it through. You, I, the Defence Secretary, the Chiefs of Staff haven't met to discuss possibilities. There's nothing remotely ready for Cabinet. And in any case my own view—'

Most unusually Patrick Vaughan interrupted them, standing on the threshold of the study after a faint knock on the door.

'I'm extremely sorry to interrupt, Prime Minister, Foreign Secretary, but I have had William Strachan on the telephone for, I think, the fourth time this morning. He says he has to speak to you before Cabinet, or he won't be responsible for the consequences. The Unionist Executive is meeting this morning.'

Simon Russell felt guilty, and old. In his prime he would not have forgotten Strachan. The leader of the biggest Unionist Party in Northern Ireland was never negligible. He had promised to talk to him on Saturday, but had gone for a walk with Julia instead. He did not repent of that. But since then four days had overflowed with work. If Strachan was really angry the Irish policy was at risk.

'You should have made me talk to him before.'

'I'm sorry, Prime Minister . . .'

Patrick did not defend himself, but Simon Russell knew the truth. His Private Office was trying to protect him. This showed that they were not quite first-rate. A first-rate Private Office did not protect their Minister. Even a Minister who had had a mild heart attack six months ago. They should know the limit beyond which he would cease to give his best, and in friendship, but pitilessly, they should drive him to that limit.

So the necessary conversation with Peter Makewell before Cabinet on Russia never got under way.

The Prime Minister, cursing under his breath, spent the intervening time pacifying Strachan on the telephone. He apologised profusely for the delay in getting in touch. He went a little further than he intended in promising to persuade the Nationalists to match any concession on power-sharing in Northern Ireland which Strachan and the Unionists might make, under pressure from their Constructive wing of new membership.

'It's all your doing, Prime Minister,' Strachan grumbled at the end of the conversation, having got as much as he would get. 'If it hadn't been for you none of these new nonsensical people would have come into politics at all. They're bits and pieces, odds and ends, nothing professional about them.' Strachan had been in professional Ulster politics all his life since leaving Queen's University with a law degree. He knew, in amazing detail, from the Unionist angle the facts of every conference, every statute, every initiative, every agreement or disagreement which Northern Ireland had encountered since partition in 1922. Indeed his knowledge stretched back through the centuries, regiment after marching regiment of Protestant facts. Strachan was honourable and had shown much personal courage during the Troubles. It was impossible to trip him up because he constantly brought down each discussion to the level at which he was expert, that of grinding details. It would not have occurred to him that any more imaginative equipment was necessary for the Unionist leader.

The Prime Minister was delighted that his effort to bring unprofessionals into the politics of the province was beginning to melt the Unionist position. There would need to be a similar softening on the Nationalist side before the representatives of the two communities could come within spitting distance of agreement on how the province should govern itself. Simon Russell felt in his bones that, given time, he could manage this. Like most British leaders he was suspected by the Unionists of secretly favouring Irish unity. The idea had never entered his head. It would be impracticable and wrong. The Irish Government had a role on behalf of the nationalist minority. But the essential question was how majority and minority could be brought to live together within the United Kingdom. He knew that the Ulster politicians in both communities found him knowledgeable, devious, subtle, to be feared. They liked Whitman because he was obvious and honest, but for serious transaction of Irish business they would come to Downing Street. Given time he could do it . . . but there was no time.

Simon Russell went slowly down the staircase to the Cabinet Room, past the photographs and prints of his predecessors. He had noticed over the years that at intervals the Prime Minister moved almost imperceptibly downhill into new formations, always leaving a space waiting at the top of the stairs for the photograph of the current holder of the office. He supposed that they moved spontaneously at the stroke of midnight when in conclave they judged that a change was imminent. The predecessors wore solemn and statesmanlike faces, so that he found it impossible to make a joke on that staircase. This morning he took the stairs slowly, not because his doctor had so advised, but in order to translate his mind from the difficult talk with Strachan to the difficult Cabinet ahead.

Julia bustled past him, knocking his elbow.

'Sorry, Dad.'

She looked back at him smiling as she passed the younger Pitt. She wore tight jeans and carried a plastic folder of papers. She was meant to use the lift.

'What are you doing on this staircase?' Evading her mother was almost certainly the answer, but Julia was gone before she could give it. But her two words to him had been affectionately spoken. Given time, he could keep the friendship of father and daughter in good repair. Given time . . .

The Prime Minister picked up speed at the foot of the stairs and fairly bustled into the Cabinet Room. He wanted to convey the impression that time was short.

'I'm sorry to keep you waiting.' He had a perfectly good excuse, but did not give it. If he had mentioned Strachan someone might have wanted to discuss the situation in Northern Ireland. It would be possible to take the first three routine items at high speed, though he had not had time to school Peter Makewell on minimising discussion of Russia.

He hit an expected rock before that point. The Parliamentary Affairs item was easy enough. The Queen would open the new session early next month, and the initial business of the Commons was to hear her speech setting out the Government's programme. The text of this had already been agreed between departments.

'As regards the Queen's speech, I may need to insert a sentence on prisons,' said Roger Courtauld. He seemed to overflow from his chair into the territorial space of his neighbour. Soon he would start heaving himself about, impatient at the longwindedness of others.

They would all note the 'I' and some would resent it. The Queen's speech was a collective composition.

'That will depend on the Cabinet's conclusions this morning,' said the Prime Minister.

'Quite so.'

They passed on to Home Affairs. There had been a minor ferry collision in the English Channel. Four people had been hurt. The Secretary of State for Transport began to rehearse in detail the arrangements he proposed for an inquiry. He had given the Prime Minister notice that he intended to raise the matter, but that did not gain him much space. After two minutes the Prime Minister broke in.

'The Secretary of State seems to be handling this very competently.' Turning to him down the end of the table. 'Is there any point on which you need particular guidance from colleagues?'

'Not exactly, Prime Minister . . . I just wanted to inform—'

'Exactly. Thank you very much for raising the matter. We have noted with approval how you intend to proceed. Any other points under Home Affairs?'

Whitman, also down at the end of the table, began to speak. Damn. This was a rock below the surface. Northern

Ireland of course came under Home Affairs, so he was well in order. It was perhaps natural that he should want to brief Cabinet on latest developments in the Province, though he had not given notice. Whitman was never longwinded. The problem was rather that he did not know about the conversation with Strachan fifteen minutes ago. And indeed he waded into the sensitive point within a minute.

'. . . and so it is important that in any discussion with the Unionists we should not give the impression that we can lean on the Nationalists to match their concessions.'

This was precisely what the Prime Minister had just done upstairs in the study. He glanced down the other end of the room to the chairs backing against the door that led to his Private Office. As he had suspected, the chair on which Patrick Vaughan usually sat was empty. Patrick would be in the next room tapping on to the screen of his computer the record of the conversation with Strachan, to which he had listened in. Eavesdropping by the Private Secretary of the Prime Minister's official telephone conversations was an essential technique at Number 10. Within an hour the Northern Ireland Office would have Whitman's copy of that record. Indeed they might send a messenger round with it to him before Cabinet was over. But even the rapid Whitehall machine could not work instantaneously.

'Have a word with me about the minutes on that point,' the Prime Minister whispered to the Cabinet Secretary sitting on his right.

Luckily no one took up the discussion. Since the Newry explosion Northern Ireland had relapsed into its own arcane politics, which colleagues were content to leave to the Prime Minister and Secretary of State.

Now for Russia. This time the rock was above the surface. Makewell was obviously worried at the way things were going. He had not been able to unburden himself fully to the Prime Minister upstairs, which made it more likely that he would do so now. Simon Russell sensed emotion growing all around him on the subject, emotion which he did not share and thoroughly distrusted. Cabinet had no proposal before it and could take no decision. The danger was that an unfocused, unprepared discussion now would point colleagues and the whole Government machine in the wrong direction.

Makewell began calmly and factually, recounting the rising in the North, the Halifax meeting, the coup in Moscow, the bomb in the cemetery, the Minister of State's unfortunate exposure on *Question Time*. Roger Courtauld interrupted him.

'Is the Foreign Secretary clear that the bomb was the work of the Moscow junta? Or at least one of the agencies?'

'I think it must have been.'

The Prime Minister sat upright in his chair, watching the body language of colleagues. On such occasions emotions often spoke through facial expression and hand movements from those who chose not to speak. Sometimes he counted frowns rather than voices.

Makewell went on to describe the diplomatic scene. The European Council of Ministers had met in London the previous evening under his chairmanship. The eighteen European ministers had been joined under the new Atlantic procedure by their American and Canadian colleagues. A group of senior officials of the four bigger powers (the Quad) meeting before had prepared a communiqué expressing concern, calling for restraint by all the parties in Russia and reaffirming their support for the independence of Estonia. But when the ministers themselves met in the evening after dinner the mood was different. The draft prepared by officials had been brushed aside. Opinions had varied about the nature of Western involvement. The smaller countries, notably Denmark, the Netherlands and Ireland, had pressed for the immediate despatch of a UN force to St Petersburg and Estonia. France, Germany and Britain were less sure. The American Secretary of State, intervening late, had said that President Altman was under increasing pressure and felt strongly himself that action was needed.

The congressional elections, which had run mildly against the Administration, had unexpectedly propelled into the Senate two candidates, one Democrat, one Republican, who had campaigned hard under the slogan Justice for Russia. Makewell had managed to bring the European discussion to an end before it could run away from him. The ministers had agreed to call an emergency meeting of the Security Council, initially at official then at ministerial level, and to consult urgently about measures that might be taken to preserve democracy in Russia and the integrity of Estonia.

'There is no democracy in Russia,' said Joan Freetown, looking up from the mass of her papers on public expenditure. Everyone waited for her to continue. 'The Government in Moscow is the result of a coup. The Government in St Petersburg is the result of a rebellion. The communiqué should never have been drafted in that way.' Snap.

Simon Russell's heart sank. He came in quickly before Peter Makewell could retort.

'However that may be, we are grateful for that report from the Foreign Secretary. The Cabinet has no proposal before it, and obviously we all need time to consider the implications of any action we or our allies might take. A lot of urgent work will be needed. Speaking for myself, I must say I feel reluctant to contemplate any decision that would involve the use of British troops.'

There was a pause. This was all new to the Cabinet. They genuinely needed time. But Simon Russell noted that none of his usual supporters had come in quickly to support the steer he had given. Whitman and Lord Downbrook, for example, were both doodling hard, eyes fixed downward. Whitman was composing a diagram of some old-fashioned battle, say Oudenarde or Malplaquet. Lord Downbrook sketched a beautiful mermaid reclining on the benches of the House of Lords.

The Chairman of the Party raised his hand, right at the garden end of the Cabinet table, next to the Chief Whip. Damn, another piece of bad luck. The Chairman, though not a member of the Cabinet, had been invited to attend the public expenditure discussion later in the agenda. Technically he should not have joined the table until that item was reached, but it was quite usual to see him in the room and no one had been churlish enough to ask him to leave until the business of direct concern to him was reached. He had no right to speak at this point, and Simon Russell was minded to ignore him, particularly as his intuition sensed what he was going to say. But the man persisted, raising his pencil at arm's length, as if he were a heckler at a public meeting. Sensitivity and the job of Party Chairman could not be expected to run together. Simon felt no real resentment as he sought to frustrate him.

'Chairman of the Party.'

'Prime Minister, the Liberal candidate in South Sussex—'

'I don't think Cabinet can discuss the by-election now.'

'It's relevant, Prime Minister. In the last three days the Liberal candidate, a man called Phelps, has switched his campaigning entirely to Russia. Our private poll yesterday suggested he was making substantial inroads, among both men and women, and particularly the young. Polling is of course today. I was hoping the Cabinet could make a robust statement for the one o'clock news. We would flood the constituency with it all afternoon and evening.'

It might be best to give him rope. 'You have a draft?'

'I have, but have not had time to make copies.' He read it out. It ended:

'"The Conservative Government needs no one to remind it of its duty. It is on the side of those who have suffered and those who are threatened. It will spare no effort with its allies to prevent further outrages and establish peace with justice in Russia."'

'That's quite a programme,' said the Prime Minister. There was silence. Surely thought would bring them back to reality. But he had to break it himself with the real question in his own mind.

'Can any colleague explain exactly why we and evidently the Americans and others are faced with this flash flood of emotion?' He borrowed unconsciously the phrase Peter Makewell had used upstairs.

'It's the tabloid factor. She's sexy, he's sexy. That's about the sum of it,' said the Chairman unexpectedly. 'That Virginia girl who's always on the TV and Dobrinsky out there with the torn coat and the blood on his arm.'

'It's just raw untutored emotion,' said Joan Freetown, pausing between the words, each of which for her conveyed the strongest condemnation.

The Home Secretary began to move heavily in his chair. 'There's more to it than glamour or cheap emotion,' he said. 'You must know that, Prime Minister. Every now and then something terrible happens in the world that stirs the imagination beyond the ordinary. Why? Because it reminds people that we want a decent world, that we haven't got one, and that we can't be content with the suffering and wickedness around us. So they want something done, and they insist. You can't tell in advance what event will do this. If you had described to me two weeks ago what the Foreign Secretary described to us today, I would have said that it would only touch the mind of a few freaks. I know different now it's on us. I hear the rumble in the mountains. Avalanche, flash flood, choose what phrase you like. We'd better prepare for it.'

There was a general murmur of agreement, marred by a jangle of the Chancellor of the Exchequer's bracelet. The Prime Minister, equally dismayed but with no bracelet, cut the discussion short.

'I think we have carried this as far as we can. The Foreign Secretary and I will work out instructions for our representatives at the Security Council, and he will represent us if and when the Council meets at ministerial level. We will, of course, make sure that contingency plans are in place. We will report to Cabinet again next week.'

'Two questions, Prime Minister.' It was the Home Secretary again. 'Can we see in draft the instructions to our man in New York?'

Another murmur of agreement. Another nuisance. But this was Cabinet Government.

'Very well. How many want to see the draft?' Three bold hands went up.

'Second, can we have the Chiefs of Staff at next week's

Cabinet?' The Home Secretary persisted. 'I don't want to hear their objection to any action second-hand.'

A request too far.

'You must leave that to the Secretary of State for Defence and myself.'

None of the sixteen colleagues gathered round the table was his close friend. Friendship was important to Simon Russell, but closely guarded. There were only four or five men and women in the world who had been given the key to open the inner rooms of his personality. They were in a separate category from Louise and Julia, who held a different key. Drawn from different layers of his past life, friends had selected themselves or been selected almost by accident. In the company of those who held the key he was a different person. He could then put aside the armour with which he usually protected himself. He could put aside equally the weapons of cool observation and comment with which he usually probed the intentions of those around him. The occasional company of friends was important to him, but he would not have dreamed of choosing a friend from those with whom he spent most time, namely his colleagues. Sometimes, though not often, he disliked a colleague, but he had trained himself to suppress that emotion or at least keep it strictly within bounds. More often he liked his colleagues, knowing that with all their idiosyncrasies and vanities they worked hard for the benefit of their fellow citizens as well as their own. They all belonged, as did he, to an undervalued profession, and this made a bond.

Sometimes he felt warmer towards an individual, because of his or her qualities. So it was with Roger Courtauld, whose openness and courage he liked and half envied, relishing the contrast with his own more intricate methods. Roger Courtauld was not a friend, but he was more than a colleague.

Yet this morning Roger Courtauld had been irritating. He had intervened powerfully and without notice in a sphere of policy other than his own. He had more or less led the Cabinet towards a dangerous position in favour of intervention in Russia, pleading grounds of principle. Simon Russell did not dismiss the role of principle in politics, but it was explosive material. It should be blended with other elements, namely consideration of circumstances and reality, before it could be safely used. Roger Courtauld had neglected this precaution. He had tossed principle into the discussion like a grenade. There might yet be casualties.

The Prime Minister had intended a favour to the Home Secretary. He had put prisons at the end of the agenda, thus creating a deadline for a decision at around one fifteen pm, which would certainly help Courtauld. Over the tea and sweet biscuits, served exceptionally at ten thirty because of the meeting's early start, he decided in his irritation to withdraw this favour.

'I think that, after all, we will take prisons next,' he said as soon as they resumed. 'It may take some time, and I don't want to skimp discussion.'

Roger Courtauld had no grounds on which he could publicly object. He saw exactly what had happened, and grinned. Joan Freetown looked sharply across the table at the Prime Minister, trying to fathom his motive. She knew that she lacked tactical cunning and believed that the Prime Minister had too much. But though suspicious, she too could phrase no objection in the time available.

But as Simon quickly realised, irritation was a bad guide to Cabinet tactics. He soon found himself regretting his last decision. He wondered whether before his heart attack he would have made the mistake. For Roger Courtauld changed his tone entirely. It was as if the two cups of coffee and three chocolate biscuits had created a new personality. He presented the prisons paper with the quiet authority of a senior Cabinet Minister putting forward a proposal essential to the work of his department. He was in total control of the past history, the present facts and the statistics. There were several alternatives to taking over the army camps and the ferries for use as prisons. The first was to flood the cells of police stations with convicted and remand prisoners. This was expensive and wasteful. Thousands of police officers would be diverted from catching criminals to guarding criminals already caught. The standard of security in many police cells made escapes inevitable. Another course was to urge magistrates and judges not to refuse bail or pass prison sentences except in severe cases while the emergency lasted.

The Home Secretary regarded this as politically unacceptable. A third course would be to do nothing and let the prisons overcrowd, which in many prisons would quickly mean three in a cell. This would be impossible and dangerous. There would be riots, which might spread rapidly, perhaps over the Christmas season. He spelled out particulars of the army camps in Wiltshire and Yorkshire and of the ferries off Folkestone which he proposed to take over, with the agreement of the Secretaries of State for Defence and Transport. He apologised to the Chancellor of the Exchequer for proposing extra spending at a difficult time, but emphasised that his proposal would in the end turn out less expensive than the alternatives. He spoke in strong but matter-of-fact tones, his heavy elbows firmly on the table, not wheedling or threatening his colleagues, but looking straight in front of him until he had finished. Then he looked at Simon Russell.

'We just have to do it, Prime Minister.'

The Prime Minister knew at once that this was conclusive.

'Chancellor of the Exchequer.'

As often happened, Joan Freetown had signalled that she wished to speak before she had decided her tactics. The Home Secretary had filled the room with his sense of serious purpose. She felt this, being a serious person herself. She could not mount the convincing counter-attack for which she had hoped. On the other hand it was against her temperament to remain silent. Rather desperately she plucked a statistic, almost at random, from the Treasury brief in front of her.

'There is something inefficient about the distribution of prisoners. The Home Secretary is asking us to create more prison places at great expense. But I am informed that there are at the present time five hundred and seventy-six prison cells standing empty in England and Wales.'

Roger Courtauld did not need to refer to his brief.

'The empty cells are in open prisons. For obvious reasons I do not propose to use them for prisoners charged with serious offences or convicted of such offences.'

Joan Freetown flushed. Some Treasury official would have an uncomfortable and repentant afternoon.

The only other intervention came from Lord Downbrook.

'I take it that this emergency step does not foreshadow any change in our sentencing policy? There would be strong opposition in the Lords and elsewhere to any softening of that policy – opposition which I must say I would myself share.'

There was a trap here. Downbrook had served in the Home Office when they had set in place the sentencing policy which had now clearly failed but could not safely be repudiated. Crime had started to rise again, despite the huge increase in the prison population. Simon Russell knew that Roger Courtauld felt bitter about his inheritance and would love to change it. But if he started on that argument today he would lose half the Cabinet.

Roger Courtauld saw the trap and avoided it. 'I have no proposals to change the sentencing policy,' he said, with lips tight.

And that was that. Simon Russell had expected a shindy, led by Joan Freetown. At the end he would have come in to support the Home Secretary. He would have carried the day. But by then much blood would have been spilled and Roger Courtauld would have owed him something. The less admirable part of him felt disappointed at being robbed of a cockfight and a graceful Prime Ministerial intervention.

'Very well then. The Home Secretary may implement the plan in his paper. No doubt he will keep us informed of progress.' He suppressed the words 'or the reverse'.

Meanwhile in another part of 10 Downing Street Artemis was in trouble. Not deep trouble by any real test, but maddening because she thought she had learned how to deal with it but was wrong.

She wondered afterwards if she had missed some tell-tale sign as the political correspondents filed into her room for the daily eleven o'clock briefing. Did the younger, less hardened ones look sheepish, did they move to take chairs with suspicious speed? She had certainly failed to spot any such warning. It should have been a routine day in the dull week after the Party Conferences were over, before Parliament had started the next session. She expected some snide questions about the South Sussex by-election, for commentators in the morning press had scented that something was wrong. She would sidestep that, as they knew she would, by pointing out that it was not for her as a civil servant to comment on party matters. She was heavily briefed on a change in the procedure at the Cenotaph Service for the forthcoming Remembrance Sunday. She had a ream of material on the favourable inflation figures, which the Treasury was publishing at noon. In short, it promised to be a tedious but short session, which was fine.

But no.

'Can you comment on the row in Cabinet about Russia this morning?'

Cabinet was still sitting.

'Cabinet is still sitting. I cannot possibly comment on anything that happened there.'

'Are you denying that the Prime Minister was against any action but was overruled?'

'Did the Home Secretary actually threaten to resign unless Britain intervened?'

'Is the PM going to see Virginia?'

'Can you confirm that the Prime Minister will be flying to New York for an emergency meeting of the Security Council?'

'I know nothing of any of this . . .'

Artemis was flummoxed and hated herself for being flummoxed. Cool, unflappable, that was the image she was building to protect herself from these barbarians.

'Then you can't deny there was a god-awful row?'

'I cannot deny or confirm . . . I simply don't know.'

'But you should know, dear Artemis, you should know.' The purr came from a silver-haired fraud who believed himself wronged by the Prime Minister's decision to give no honours, let alone knighthoods, to even the most sycophantic journalists.

'Do the Chiefs of Defence Staff recommend a British contribution of two battalions?'

'The CDS was not present.'

'But you said you did not know anything about the meeting. Are you sure the CDS was not present?'

'So far as I am aware . . .'

She was lost and miserable. They listened in silence as she faltered her way through the inflation figures.

Someone, presumably a Cabinet Minister, had telephoned a journalist during the break for coffee and given him a coloured version of the discussion that had just taken place. The political correspondents no longer worked as individuals, but as a pack. They had put their heads together and charged. She had totally failed to deal with them. She wrote a note of confession.

> PM,
>
> I am afraid all hell is let loose about Russia. The press are running a story of a big row in Cabinet in which you opposed intervention and were defeated. I could not head them off.
>
> I am sorry.
>
> Artemis

He unfolded the note and quickly scribbled a reply.

> Artemis,
>
> Nothing here for tears. Come and see me as soon as this is over.
>
> SR

Then he crossed out 'SR' as carefully as he had written it and wrote 'Simon'.

It was now Joan Freetown's turn to put on the mantle of a senior minister requiring Cabinet to accept the serious requirements of her department. As he scribbled his reply to Artemis, the Prime Minister listened to her prologue. The Cabinet had agreed in July to a spending total of £390 billion. The total bids of different departments amounted to £450 billion. Lord Downbrook's Committee had winnowed this down to £403 billion. The Chancellor was now arguing for a total of £370 billion so as to allow her more room for tax cuts in her Budget. But because she had been impatient and authoritarian she was playing too soon one of her strongest cards, a discussion in full Cabinet. No one was ready to argue that the July total was too low, but every colleague felt in his heart that their own claims were exceptionally well founded. If there had to be bread and water instead of cake, it should be consumed by others. Each knew that his own claim for cake was irrefutable. Peter Makewell and Roger Courtauld were still in fairly public disagreement with the Chancellor over the figures. Four others had quietly delayed signing up to the Downbrook compromise, in case there were last-minute crumbs which might fall to them from the disagreement of others.

'I am bound to say,' said Joan Freetown, 'that the situation is drifting out of hand. If we are to meet the prison spending we have just agreed and yet hold to the July total then there have to be substantial reductions in budget below what the Leader of the Lords proposed in his EDX reports. In all budgets, I would say. Certainly the bids of the Home Office for non-prison spending and of the Foreign and Commonwealth Office need to be scaled down dramatically. Both are way out of line. If Cabinet cannot agree this, then other colleagues will have to accept even higher sacrifices.'

But they would not take this attempt to divide and rule. Minister after minister reopened the arguments they had used before Downbrook's Committee. The mood was fractious. Joan Freetown was no good at tilling ground for harvest. The Prime Minister contemplated a field of policy strewn with rocks and sown with tares. It was worse than he had feared.

'Home Secretary, the Chancellor of the Exchequer referred specifically to your budget. You have said nothing.'

'I have said a great deal earlier, Prime Minister,' said Roger Courtauld. 'Colleagues have approved my prison plans. There is no question of my financing them at the xpense of police or probation or crime prevention. Extra ›risons mean extra money.'

'Foreign Secretary?'

'It's all there in the EDX paper, Prime Minister. My ›udget cannot be reduced if we are to retain the foreign ›olicy that Cabinet wants. It is far too small to affect in any erious way the Chancellor's budget calculations.'

There was deadlock. Simon Russell sympathised with he Chancellor. If only, he thought, she could develop some actical sense to match her intellectual apparatus and the orce of her conviction. It was one of those occasions where peculiar Prime Ministerial instinct had to be called into lay. The Cabinet fell silent, waiting for his summing-up. He consulted his instinct. No, he could not get away with umming-up in the Chancellor's favour. There would be a evolt and, if he persisted, resignations which he could not fford. He would have to take charge himself, and do Downbrook's work all over again.

'The Cabinet is a long way from agreement, and further iscussions today will not make things better. We clearly annot retreat from the July total, which has been pub- shed. In order to make progress I shall myself over the ext few days hold bilateral talks with the ministers con- erned. I shall report to Cabinet next Thursday and we hall then have to take the necessary decisions. They annot be delayed beyond then.'

They accepted, with relief, the delaying device.

'I should add that nothing of this must appear in the

press. We shall simply take the line that normal discussion continue on the public spending round.'

'Of course,' they all said, including the minister wh had already leaked the earlier discussion to his favourit journalist.

The Prime Minister's kind note had further upset Artemis She had hastily drafted a letter for the Prime Minister t sign to the Cabinet Secretary, instructing him to set up a enquiry into the leak on Russia. A tear had fallen on th last line of her scribble, smudging the Biro ink. Simo looked at the blot carefully, then at Artemis standing woe begone behind his Cabinet chair. Patrick Vaughan hovere by the pillars, otherwise the room was now empty.

'No good sending this,' said Simon. 'The horse is severa fields away by now. We'll never catch him. Just stir up mor trouble.'

Artemis felt another tear form. She was useless, hope less, a washout. She thought of Frank. She had made hir miserable, and not helped anyone else. She felt as guilty a if she had leaked the story herself.

'Patrick, could you see if my wife is back upstairs? I war a word with her.'

As soon as Patrick had left, Simon put his arm u around the waist of his Chief Information Officer, pulle her down to the chair beside him, carefully moved a empty coffee cup, leaned across and kissed her on the lip

'You're doing a great job,' said the Prime Minister.

Chapter Fourteen

Thursday November 6

It was not physically easy for Trevor Phelps to hug himself, but he did so now, embracing his plump chest with plump arms. The first part of the by-election count had been completed half an hour ago. The bank clerks and local government officers assembled at trestle tables had emptied the black metal ballot boxes and verified that the number of voting papers they contained corresponded to the number recorded as having voted in each polling station. The Town Hall gently rustled as they now sorted the ballot papers into piles, one pile for each of the seven candidates. There was a half-silence, as in church. Behind them stood representatives of the candidates, almost all of them Conservative and Liberal, sporting blue and yellow rosettes. Now that the arguments of the campaign were over the two sides fraternised happily in whispers, sharing reminiscences and coffee from each other's flasks. The Conservatives knew that in the last few days the election had been slipping away from them. Their candidate, a respected farmer from Alfriston, had not recovered from his failure to find St Petersburg on the map of a local school during a televised debate. His only hope was that the small traditional Labour voter in the town of Lewes would hold up strongly. But Phelps, standing behind the officials counting the Lewes boxes, could see that this was not happening. The splendid trade unionists of Lewes were voting tactically to keep the Tory out, voting Liberal for Phelps, voting whether they knew it or not to Stop the Moscow Murderers. There was not even going to be a recount. Even in the most true-blue villages the piles were evenly divided between the two front runners. Each counted bundle was taken to the end of the hall, where in municipal glory the Returning Officer held sway among his acolytes. From early on the Phelps bundles began visibly to outweigh those of the Conservative farmer.

By half-past midnight it was over. The TV camera lights shone through the November drizzle on the Town Hall steps.

'I, Maurice Jones, by virtue of the duty entrusted to me as Returning Officer for the constituency of South Sussex, hereby declare that the votes cast in the election for a parliamentary representative on Thursday, 6 November for the said constituency were as follows . . .' Four small figures for the also rans, then:

'Naylor, Andrew, Labour 4,826
Oxted, Francis, Conservative 20,308.'

A ragged cheer from one Conservative with a beer can out there in the dark who had not grasped the electoral arithmetic. He thought 20,000 was a lot of votes.

'Phelps, Trevor, Liberal 28,169.'

One other small total drowned in a salvo of Liberal cheers and the click of cameras.

'And I hereby declare Mr Trevor Phelps duly elected to serve as Member of Parliament for South Sussex.'

It was the supreme moment of Phelps's life. He had spotted the opportunity and deserved his success. He would never be heard of again. But in the small hours of that Friday morning, as the Sussex drizzle thickened into downpour, he summoned up a last reserve of energy and some recollection of ancient oratory. After thanking the Returning Officer, his own supporters, and his opponents, the new Member of Parliament, tired and triumphant, half spoke, half shouted to the cameras from his Liberal heart.

'This result will echo in the very recesses of the Kremlin. The Moscow murderers will cower when it reaches them. This truly is a vote that will be heard around the world. Wherever men and women care for justice they will thank us, thank you, for what was done today.'

Sunday November 9

By Sunday it was fine again, but cold. Simon and Louise had come up from Chequers the night before. They argued over breakfast whether or not he should wear an overcoat.

'It makes me look old.'

'You are old. And since last year you've had a heart attack.'

'That's irrelevant. The coat makes it difficult to lay the wreath properly. It gets in the way.'

'Nonsense. I'll ring Peter Makewell. If he's wearing an overcoat, so should you.'

It was not logical. But the Foreign Secretary proposed to wear a coat at the Cenotaph. The Prime Minister too wore a coat.

The notes of the Last Post died away. Big Ben chimed the eleventh hour. Yellow leaves fluttered singly, slowly and silently, from the plane trees as beside the Cenotaph Queen and country observed the two-minute silence. The gentle commotion of clicking cameras sounded like summer rain. Otherwise all was quiet. Holding the wreath of poppies tight against his chest the Prime Minister tried to lead his mind to dignified thought. His life was inevitably full of engagements that he went through mechanically, but for him Remembrance Sunday was a genuine solemnity charged with feeling. The poppies, flags, the Cenotaph, the Queen, the sunshine, the bugler sounding the Last Post combined to bring tears smarting at the back of his eyes. The day and this service commemorated an event so huge and awful that it dwarfed anything else the twentieth century had produced. That history fascinated Simon Russell.

The trenches, the mud, the machine-guns of the Great War were real to him; likewise the Blitz, the Spitfires, Dunkirk and Alamein. These events, some before his birth, others dim in his early childhood, had shaped the world in which he lived, and the profession which he had chosen. The sad happy feeling behind his eyes and in his throat reminded him how paltry were his own problems, and yet how worthwhile it was to serve where so many had served before. He tried to focus again on what it all meant, to lift his attention away from the immediate and gain some inspiration or recharged energy from the occasion. This year it was more difficult. The Bishop of London prayed. On the Prime Minister's right Turnbull, the Leader of the Opposition, a clumsy man, had handled his wreath roughly and two of his poppies were badly askew. They might fall to the ground when his turn came to move forward to the Cenotaph. But he would probably resent it if Simon pointed this out in a gesture that the cameras would notice. Did Turnbull too feel his eyes smarting? He would never know. He ought to talk to Turnbull privately about Russia, though with the Cabinet and public opinion in its present emotional state he did not relish the conversation. Turnbull, after the Sussex result, was evidently determined not to be outflanked by bloody Liberals. He had been making strong interventionist noises.

After the Reveille the ceremony began to flow easily, the peak of emotion having passed. The Queen, the Duke, the Prince moved forward in turn to lay their wreaths. The band of the Grenadier Guards played the tune Simon heard year after year at Remembrance Sunday and never any- where else. He had never discovered its name. The first part was sombre, its second part began with the glorious lilting melody of a slow march coinciding exactly with the moment when he as Prime Minister carried forward his own poppies. It was not a difficult manoeuvre, even in the black greatcoat he had bought at Cambridge thirty-five years before and resolutely defended against any threat of replacement. The figure '1' chalked on the step on the western flank of the Cenotaph showed him where he should place his wreath, leaving ample space for those who should follow. A brief pause with inclined head, a turn and he walked back to his place in line, trying to find a middle style between a march, which despite the music would have been absurd in a civilian, and the shamble practised (so Louise said) by most of his colleagues and the Commonwealth High Commissioners.

Waiting back in his place, Simon found his thought drifting back to his telephone conversation with Presiden Altman the night before. He knew, and told others repeat edly, that the world was lucky in its only superpower. In great matters the United States almost always behaved with good sense and decency. Perhaps therefore American should be excused lapses in minor matters, which usuall stemmed not from the great ones of the land but from over zealous members of their staff. For example, hotel elevator were commandeered and street sidewalks cleared long in advance of need. Common also was the failing from which Simon had just suffered, namely a reluctance to take into account changes in time zone.

When the President telephoned, the world must be ready to take the call, its lamps trimmed for the bridegroom whenever he should choose to come. Simon had been deep in his first hours of sleep at Chequers when Washington came through on the hot-line. The procedural preliminaries lasted long enough for him to stumble into the bathroom and dip his face in cold water. The conversation had not been reassuring. The President was not familiar with the details of Security Council procedure, in which the Prime Minister was by then immersed. Nor was he at all clear that the United States would contribute its own troops to the proposed international force. 'Europeans on the ground, Americans in the air. NATO organises, the UN gives its blessing. That's a canny combination, Simon, suits everyone, I guess.'

Simon had said that the Cabinet had taken no decisions, but that if, and it was a big if, they decided to participate there would, he thought, have to be American troops alongside the British 'on the ground'. In his pyjamas, with water dripping from his face because he could not find a towel, he was conscious that he was speaking stiffly, even pompously, like a lawyer, even an Attorney-General. He knew well that this was exactly the tone that Americans expected, and smiled at, from the British. Altman had thus drawn back, though he still showed no signs of realising that in England it was one o'clock in the morning.

'I won't press you any further this afternoon,' he said. 'Just wanted you to know the sea's running high here and the US of A is riding on the front surfboard.'

'Thanks, Mr President. Feeling is strong here too. We'll keep in touch.'

'Our two countries usually end up on the same square of the chessboard.'

Well, yes. The British Government also needed to work with the other Europeans. That Sunday morning Simon knew pretty well how they stood. The Scandinavians and Dutch were stirred up and hot for intervention. They had watched Virginia on the BBC. The French, normally closest to Britain in military matters, were well ahead of Simon this time, scenting excitement and a touch of glory. Only the Germans so far shared his caution. Watching Peter Makewell, in remembrance of dead killed by Germans, lay his wreath of flowers from the tiny remaining British dependencies, Simon reflected on the whirligigs of time, and thanked God for German democracy. He preferred not to imagine Hitler or the Kaiser let loose on the present situation.

The High Commissioners of the Commonwealth were laying their poppies in batches of four. The band entered for the second time on the familiar but elusive melody. Others as well as Simon became conscious of a rival noise to their left from the direction of Trafalgar Square. It grew rapidly, first for a minute or two a hum of voices, then indistinct individual shouts, then a mass of shouts amounting to a roar. In Whitehall, between the ceremony round the Cenotaph and this demonstration in Trafalgar Square, stood several hundred veterans of the Royal British Legion, waiting to parade past the Cenotaph once the Queen had returned to the old Home Office and gone up to the balcony to take their salute. They wore civilian clothes with medals, many with bowler hats, a few in wheelchairs drawn up in line as neat as any regiment. They were bent and old. Unbelievably, Simon saw these lines disintegrate as the veterans turned to face whatever was coming down Whitehall. They could see what Simon and the other dignitaries could not. So could the armed police marksmen on the roofs of Whitehall. Incredulously Simon watched them swing their attention and their automatic weapons northwards towards the trouble.

There could be only one cause of so strong a demonstration. A tall member of the choir standing three away from the Bishop of London put the question beyond doubt. From beneath his surplice he produced one of the now notorious posters, in white and scarlet, demanding, 'Stop the Murderers', and held it above his head. 'Peace with justice in Russia,' he shouted in his fine tenor before the police led him away. No one had requested permission to hold a meeting in Trafalgar Square that morning. The Metropolitan Police were taken by surprise. The front flank of demonstrators had evidently broken through a hastily mustered police cordon. They were scuffling now with the veterans, anxious not to attack them but to push past them to the Cenotaph. The soldiers lining each side of the street with fixed bayonets did not move. The crowd swirled around them, treating them as pieces of street furniture. This was Britain, and a matter for the civil power. Police reinforcements from Parliament Square were ordered to form a second cordon between the Ministry of Defence and the Cabinet office building. If it held this would keep the demonstrators nearly a hundred yards away from the Queen and the ceremony. And hold it did. Three or four stones were thrown and Simon saw police batons rise and fall round the statue of Field Marshal Lord Haig. But the mass of demonstrators, still in confused dispute with the veterans, were content to stand behind the cordon and chant, 'Stop the Murderers', 'Peace with Justice in Russia', waving scarlet and white banners. A police helicopter buzzed angrily overhead, its noise banishing all memories of the recent silence. But the riot was over.

The Queen did not turn her head. An equerry with spurs clanked over to her and whispered in her ear. She nodded but did not move. Nor did anyone else. The service moved to its natural close.

'Oh God, our help in ages past,
Our hope for years to come
Be Thou our guide while troubles last,
And our eternal home.'

Finally demonstrators, veterans, dukes and princes, ministers and the Leader of the Opposition, High Commissioners and choirboys all sang the National Anthem in unison. It was a confused and British occasion. Simon wondered what the hell it would look like on television.

One part of the answer was soon given. By the ornate gates leading into Downing Street, two dishevelled policemen were holding a girl. Blood ran from a bruise and cut on her cheek, but she was silent, hair straggling, twisting a torn banner in her hands.

'She threw a stone,' panted one of the constables. His helmet was askew on his head.

'Are you arresting her?' asked Simon, also out of breath. The constable hesitated. A sergeant appeared from nowhere and took charge. Another police officer opened the big gates and Simon pulled his daughter through them into Downing Street, but not before the alert cameraman caught the picture.

Immediately after the ceremony, by tradition the Foreign Secretary and the Home Secretary entertained the High Commissioners of the Commonwealth to a glass of wine and assorted canapés in the Locarno Room of the Foreign Office, to which they were led down a maze of corridors from the door through which they passed on leaving Whitehall and the Cenotaph. The reason for this party was not purely hospitable. In practice the High Commissioners could not re-enter their cars and drive away until the crowds had dispersed. The inevitable waiting period was pleasantly disguised as a party.

Joan Freetown plucked at Roger Courtauld's sleeve as he stood beside Peter Makewell in the receiving line. He had not worn an overcoat and was using red wine to thaw himself out. Each time a dignitary appeared to be shaken by the hand, Roger concealed his glass behind a pillar, then quickly found it again. An official with a strong voice helped the process.

'The High Commissioner of Barbados . . . The Acting High Commissioner of the Maldives Islands . . .'

'I must talk with you.'

Despite herself, Joan Freetown sounded melodramatic. Inside the bright gilded Locarno Room the guests were busy warming themselves, eating small hot sausages with their wine and gossiping about the demonstration and the calmness of the Queen.

'It's about the spending figures. The Prime Minister starts his discussions tomorrow. I have something to suggest.'

She was as ever impeccably turned out, in black, the silver streaks in her hair accentuating the pallor of her face.

He was reluctant but she pulled at his arm again. He had never seen her like this. She was half-masculine, half-feminine. She had never asked him for anything before.

Yielding, he found himself led into an anteroom full of coats, and the military capes of the Chiefs of Staff. They spent ten minutes there. She did all the talking. He listened and said he would reflect on what she said and telephone her later in the day. He did not try any of his usual bluster in argument. Afterwards he was glad that, for some reasons which he did not know, the Prime Minister had not come to the party. Simon Russell would certainly have noticed the two of them slip away. He might even, with his uncanny political antennae, have guessed what was afoot.

Chapter Fifteen

Tuesday November 11

'So I come to you from the ancient capital of my country. The citizens of St Petersburg are hemmed in tonight by evil. They cannot sleep. They linger in the streets, listening for the noise of artillery which might spell their doom. They are already short of food. Soon, as the winter closes in, they will be short of warmth, short of light. But they do not ask for your money, your food, your fuel. They ask simply for peace with justice. Peace so that no more bombs will shatter the limbs of our veterans and splash blood over our children. Justice, so that the murderers in Moscow will be checked and forced to answer for their atrocities. In the streets tonight they are waiting also for your answer. Will it be yes, for peace with justice? Or no, for cowardice and war? Mr President of the Security Council, Mr Secretary-General, Permanent Members of the Council, elected members, I appeal in the name of ancient Russia for your understanding, for your help.'

Damn the man, thought Peter Makewell, sitting behind the label of the United Kingdom. Given the time difference everyone in St Petersburg except for a few drunks would be fast asleep by now. He disliked inaccurate rhetorical flourishes. Earlier the Estonian Prime Minister had had a stronger case in international law, but on behalf of his threatened country he had spoken drearily and too long. By contrast Dobrinsky was an orator.

That girl Virginia was certainly responsible for the vulgarity. As Anatoly Dobrinsky flopped back in his chair with a theatrical gesture of exhaustion she leaned forward from her place behind him and with deliberation laid her cheek against his. The cameras, which had just left him, veered back in excitement. Virginia held the gesture until even the slowest of them had caught it. Even at this bizarre angle she knew how to smile and show just enough of her teeth. He seized her wrist and kissed it repeatedly. Peter Makewell supposed this had never been done in the Security Council chamber before. The words 'undesirable precedent' and 'slippery slope' occurred to him.

Listening to the oratory of others was always exhausting. The Foreign Secretary had read his own prosaic intervention two hours earlier. He had at the last minute crossed out the final sentence of the speech in which he had intended to announce that the United Kingdom would abstain on the draft resolution before the Council. That was what he and Simon Russell had agreed in London early that morning before he caught the Concorde, despite Roger Courtauld's strong pressure for a positive vote. But here in New York, exposed to the pressures of the debate, he doubted if abstention would be possible. Various strands of analysis and emotion tangled and untangled themselves in his mind as the Spanish Foreign Minister took the floor in harsh, masculine Castilian. Peter Makewell detested the cruelty of the terrorist bomb, the threat to little Estonia and the brutality of the thuggish generals in Moscow. He respected Dobrinsky's courage – the man had come here unexpectedly, leaving a thoroughly precarious situation at home. On the other hand he disliked the theatricality of his appeal, and everything associated with Virginia. He was conscious of the strong popular and media pressure at home. The memory of the rioters in Whitehall on Sunday stopping to sing 'God Save the Queen' was vivid to him. On the other hand he did not believe that foreign policy should be the victim of emotion. He sympathised with Simon Russell's deep caution about deploying British troops. On the other hand, he, Peter Makewell, was Foreign Secretary and he, Peter Makewell, not anyone else, would decide how Britain would vote.

As these pros and cons mobilised in his mind he looked for the clinching argument to resolve them. It came to him quickly. The clincher was what Gerletzky, the President's Security Adviser, had said to him over a cup of coffee in the US Delegation just before the meeting began. All his life

Peter Makewell had believed that when it came to a real crunch Britain should be with the Americans, even if it meant a rift with other Europeans. Here there was no rift, for the French, German and this Spaniard speaking now were strong for NATO intervention, with Security Council blessing – almost as strong as the Americans. Britain would be isolated from all her friends if she held back. He did not believe this could be in Britain's interest.

The Spaniard was the last speaker. When he finished, the Russian Ambassador bustled back into the room. He had walked out in protest early in Dobrinsky's speech, but of course he had to be back to cast a veto. In 1950 his predecessor had boycotted the session at which UN intervention in Korea had been proposed – and then carried because of his absence. In Moscow the Foreign Ministry still carried this scar on its soul.

Peter Makewell decided not to tell his staff in the seats behind him that he had changed his mind. There would be time enough for explanation later. After all he was their master. More worrying was what he would say to Simon Russell. He liked the Prime Minister and knew that the Prime Minister liked him. For a moment he wished that the relationship was closer. He had glimpsed the reluctance deep inside Simon Russell on this issue, which went beyond ordinary political caution. But he did not know the man well enough to understand the emotion, whatever its origin, and for this he was sorry. He could not say to the Prime Minister that the impending Russian veto had killed the plan for intervention, because everyone knew that it would be transferred at once to the General Assembly, which as in the Suez and Hungarian crisis of 1956 could act where the Security Council had been paralysed by the veto. He could say truthfully that the resolution before them was only tentative. After many preambular paragraphs of a virtuous nature, it authorised the Secretary General to work out with NATO a plan for intervention to protect the sovereign independence of Estonia, to safeguard the rights and freedoms of the people of St Petersburg and adjacent regions of the Russian Federation, and to report back to the Security Council within a week. He could imagine Simon Russell's expression in particular, and the look in his grey eyes when he reported this point. But he knew that it would have to be done not face to face but on the telephone. He would be expected to wake the Prime Minister up, even though it was three am in London, so that he had the news before it started buzzing in the London dawn.

Being intensely traditional Peter Makewell disliked telephone conversations on matters of importance and in particular long-distance conversations, which transformed the participants into croaking robots, bereft of intelligence or personality.

For a moment this prospect made him waver. He gazed, as he had gazed often before, at the high mural behind the President of the Security Council's chair, slightly faded by the passage of time. It depicted the human race raising itself from darkness and chains in the lower right corner through

followed by the rest of the Commons, down the long straight spine of the Palace of Westminster, to attend the Queen in the House of Lords and hear the Gracious Speech from the Throne. The pageantry had remained unchanged despite the changes in the composition of the Lords. Duchesses and Marchionesses still glittered in tiaras borrowed or extracted for the day from bank vaults. The judges and bishops still tried to look as if their robes were everyday wear. The Speech from the Throne outlining the Government's programme had of course been drafted paragraph by laborious paragraph in Whitehall. New legislation was nowadays out of fashion, and with luck the press would praise a speech that in the old days would have been denounced as thin. There had been a tussle over the paragraph on prisons, Joan Freetown fighting a rearguard action for the arguments that she had failed to put effectively in Cabinet. She had succumbed at the last minute, and there had been no need to rush an amendment to the Palace. He himself had toned down the Irish passage in order not to inflame Strachan and the Unionists, about whom he still felt slightly guilty.

Now he was back in Downing Street, worrying again about his conversation with Peter Makewell in the small hours. He looked again at the passage on Russia in the speech he would have to deliver in the Commons in just over an hour's time, after two backbenchers had opened the debate on the Gracious Speech, after Turnbull had followed them. The speech was neatly arranged, in bold type for easy reading. The Russian passage of four pages came towards the end. He had worked hard on it himself on Sunday after the Cenotaph. He had improved the Foreign Office draft and been satisfied.

It looked good and read well – sober, sound, persuasive. He tore it up and threw it viciously into the wastepaper basket. He snatched sheets of Downing Street notepaper from the rack in front of him and began to scribble. Page after rapid page – it was almost done. His back was aching again after several days without pain. God knows where he had left the black tubular cushion that fitted into his spine on a chair and brought relief. He noticed that his handwriting had begun to deteriorate. He began to thread the pages into the original text with a purple worm-like tag. He looked at the gilt clock ticking on the mantelpiece. He might just be in time. He lived with a wife who was always five minutes late, and with a daughter for whom time had no meaning. He was not himself passionately punctual. But for two types of occasion in his life, the parliamentary and the royal, the timing had to be absolute.

He heard no noise, but a physical instinct told him what had happened. Julia was with him in the room. She wore jeans, and a red shirt that had once been her mother's outside them. She carried a sheaf of papers.

'I know you're in a hurry, Dad. I just have to show you this.'

She spoke quietly. They had hardly exchanged words since the fracas on Remembrance Sunday. Louise had said that he must have it out with the girl. She must be stopped from making even more of a fool of herself. He had failed to act on this. There had been no time. There was never time. He had tried to find her once, but she had been out. The police were bringing no charges against her or anyone else. The press had gloried in the story of her involvement in the demo, but for only one day. It had blown over, as everything blew over. It had become a family matter, to be sorted out some time. The time was now, but he had no time. In five minutes precisely the House would reassemble and the debate begin. He could hear Patrick Vaughan and Artemis Palmer rustling anxiously outside the door.

The needs of the Prime Minister's life clashed again. Later, despite everything, he did not regret his decision. He was glad that he had been glad to see his daughter.

'Sit down, Julia.'

'Thank you, Dad.'

She sounded pleased. She showed him the petition she had just signed. The phrasing could hardly have been worse. It condemned the Government for craven inactivity. It urged immediate intervention to save the peoples of Estonia and St Petersburg. Despite himself he began to think professionally. He considered how the wording could be rephrased, using the drafting and redrafting skills he had brought to perfection on his way to the top. But of course this was pointless. The petition was out on the streets, gathering thousands of signatures, adding to his troubles.

She explained herself. She used arguments he had heard a hundred times on radio and television, in the newspapers for the past fortnight. Nothing was new. Julia began to work herself up, just as Louise did in other causes.

'You must see, Dad. You've got to see. You have the responsibility. You can save these people. No one else in this country can.'

He took her through it. The clock struck the half-hour. The debate would have begun. Never in history, he supposed, would the Prime Minister have been absent from his place in the Commons at that moment. The Opposition would make trouble. His colleagues would worry and be ashamed. Some would suppose he had had a fresh heart attack. In the City young men would slash the price of shares to make money for a few minutes out of the uncertainty. Others in the Commons would simply say to themselves that the Prime Minister was going downhill.

He finished defending himself to his daughter.

'And Peter Makewell voted for the UN resolution last night. What more do you want?'

She did not know this. He used the pause to gather up his papers. As he left the room, he kissed her on the forehead, feeling dishonest. He had used exceptionally harsh words to Peter Makewell on the telephone to criticise this change of vote.

'Will you sign the petition, then?'

But he was out of the door.

It would be quickest to walk to the Commons. In calm times he preferred to walk. But he knew that there would be crowds in Whitehall and Parliament Square which would heckle and jostle him on the way. So he sat patiently in the car. Patrick Vaughan was loyal and silent beside him on the back seat, the protection officer tense in front. Artemis had known better than to try to squeeze herself into the same car. Patrick had explained on an earlier occasion that the Prime Minister did not like to be squeezed. A handful of angry women with placards recognised the Prime Minister at the traffic lights and began to shout and sing. At the Sunday demonstration part of the crowd had appropriated the first phrases of the Grand March from 'Aida' and invented words for it. Verdi's catchy tune had now been equipped with a complete lyric of protest which in three days had swept the country from every radio station.

'Brassev to the gallows
Hang the murderers.'

His protection officer was about to tell the driver to ignore the lights. But red became green just in time, and he was in the safety of Palace Yard, bumping over the cobbles past Westminster Hall to the Members entrance of the House of Commons.

He sweated until he entered the air-conditioned Chamber itself. To his surprise the debate had not started. The House was in a strange state, as if subsiding from a show of emotion. There was a ragged mixture of cheers and boos as he took his place.

'Phelps,' whispered the Chief Whip.

'Phelps?'

But of course. But they should have told him. Surely it was irregular. But regular or not, the newly elected victor of South Sussex had just sworn the Oath of Allegiance on taking his parliamentary seat.

Phelps had been welcomed to the House by a noisy demonstration of Liberals, soon joined by most of Labour, and even, the Chief Whip said, by a few Tories. This had gone on for several minutes, and the Speaker had only restored order by threatening to name the ring leaders. The noise fell away. The mood changed. The debate began. Everyone would assume that the Prime Minister had deliberately absented himself from this commotion.

His back hurt like hell. The sweat turned to cold drops inside his shirt. Deliberately, physically, the Prime Minister took a grip of himself. He banished Julia, Makewell, Phelps from his mind. He concentrated on putting order into the bedraggled notes of his speech.

Patrick would normally have moved straight into the private secretaries' box, a bench for civil servants set behind a wooden barrier in the corner of the Chamber, closest to ministers – close physically but operationally out of range. Once on the bench a minister could not receive whispered advice from his officials. They could pass him a note through the backbenchers behind him, but if he faltered or made a mistake in debate that would usually arrive too late for repair. A rash or ignorant minister could destroy himself in the twenty seconds before advice reached him.

Patrick knew that Simon was neither rash nor ignorant. Nevertheless, when beckoned aside on his way to the box he hesitated. His training made him reluctant to separate himself from his master at a time like this, even if only for a couple of minutes. But the official who had intercepted him was the private secretary to 'C', the head of M16. This was a young man of thirty, with longish hair and brown shoes, who was reputed to write as yet unpublished novels in his spare time. Temperamentally Patrick was ill at ease with him, but 'C' did not send idle messages. Patrick motioned his subordinate into the box, and led the messenger without a word down a short corridor to the Prime Minister's House of Commons room. It was a mid-nineteenth century room in which Pugin had finally run riot.

Stained glass, pious Gothic texts in heavy polished wood above the doorways, crimson curtains held by gold cords, massive chairs in brown and green – to Patrick it was a horrible room, a political cavern out of his control, a place for hurried disorderly conversations, for bad, unprepared decisions late at night, after some unexpected reverse in the Chamber or sudden crisis in the world outside.

The young man from M16 took an envelope out of his despatch case and ripped it open. Inside was another envelope, which in turn contained a report of three pages. The red codeword on it signified extreme secrecy and a source based on intercepts of foreign communication. Patrick fastened on the summary.

Conclusion

These messages are not conclusive about responsibility for the bomb that exploded in the St Petersburg cemetery on 25 October. But the messages originating in Moscow indicate that after the explosion General Brassev ordered an immediate investigation, which probed thoroughly the three intelligence agencies as well as the Russian Army. The conclusion of the investigation was that none of these was involved. Brassev accepted this conclusion. The response from the Army reported rumours reaching their agents in St Petersburg that the bomb was planted on the orders of a senior member of Dobrinsky's entourage. It is understandable that the Moscow military should want to deflect enquiries in this way. But the quite independent account of an eavesdropped conversation between the Mayor of St Petersburg and Admiral Volkarov shows that these two principal lieutenants of Dobrinsky had come to the same conclusion. They believe that this was a clever propaganda ploy by others on their side. It follows that there must be serious reservations about the assumption that the regime in Moscow authorised the atrocity in the cemetery. This assumption is almost certainly untrue.

As he paused to think, Patrick could hear the chant of the small crowd that had re-formed outside in Parliament

Square. He could not at that distance distinguish the words, but there was no doubting the tune from 'Aida'.

'*Hang* the *murderers*.'

To his annoyance he found Artemis at his elbow. Joe Bredon would never have intruded into this room at this moment. But the annoyance quickly passed. He would rather discuss the immediate operational problem with Artemis than with the young, possibly novel-writing messenger from M16. He showed her the page of the report with the conclusion.

'I must send it in to him,' he said.

In the British Civil Service, unlike most others, the assumption is that information exists to be passed on. It is the communication not the possession of knowledge that represents power.

'Why?' asked Artemis, quickly. 'Will it affect his speech?'

'I don't know what he's going to say about Russia. He's just re-written it all.'

In calmer times Patrick would never have admitted this ignorance of such a crucial point. In the car he had tried without peering to read the Prime Minister's notes, but had failed.

'Don't show it till later. He's feeling strongly about all this. It would unsettle him.'

'He'll have to know.'

'Certainly. Later.'

The girl was presumptuous, almost as if she, not Patrick, was the appointed keeper of the Prime Minister's official conscience. Patrick knew that life was not straightforward. But he was deep down a believer in fair and open dealing. He knew that the same was true of Simon Russell, which was why he enjoyed working with him. In an unspoken pact, the two of them kept evasions and concealments to the minimum required for the successful handling of public business. The bond between them was integrity.

So he was vexed by Artemis for suggesting even a temporary concealment.

'But this changes the whole story. The bomb in the cemetery was responsible for all this commotion.'

Artemis liked Patrick, but at that moment felt by years his senior in worldly wisdom.

'Patrick, face reality. The world knows that the bomb was planted by the Moscow murderers.' She paused and the accusing chant in the square continued.

'You and I know now that it probably wasn't. It doesn't matter. It wouldn't matter even if we could publish that report, which we can't without revealing sources. The media are unanimous and the public are convinced. Nothing will now shake their belief. If we tried to disprove it we would be howled out of the arena. So the PM and his colleagues have to act as if it was true. It may not be true as a matter of history. We shall never be sure. But it is certainly true as a signpost for what they have to do.'

'That's too clever.' Patrick shook his head, feeling that the room in which they talked was weaving again its dishonourable spell.

Artemis searched for an argument that would persuade him.

'If you send the report into the Chamber, the PM will certainly show it to the wrong people – or lose it – or leave it behind on the bench.'

This was undoubtedly true. Simon left behind him week by week a trail of minor security indiscretions. It was an odd untidiness in his orderly way of life.

So Patrick locked the report in his own briefcase, thanked the young man from M16 and took his place in the parliamentary box.

On his way there, the Commons attendant handed him a pink slip with a message.

'Mr Freetown would like to speak to the Prime Minister urgently.'

'Mr Freetown? It must be Mrs Freetown, the Chancellor.'

'No, Mr Vaughan, I had the same thought myself. I checked. The girl took the message direct from Mr Freetown himself – Mr Guy Freetown.'

'Well, in that case it can certainly wait.' Guy Freetown had nothing to do with official life.

'Madam Speaker, I have brought the House up to date on the diplomatic situation at the United Nations. Her Majesty's Government hopes earnestly that the Moscow Government will refrain from attacking St Petersburg and from any further acts of violence within that city, and will respect fully sovereignty of Estonia. We stand ready to take part in any diplomatic effort to resolve the issues in dispute.'

An Hon Member: 'Send in the troops.'

The Prime Minister: 'I have dealt with that. Following the passage last night of Security Council Resolution 1003, we are in touch with our allies and with the Secretary Generals of the United Nations and of NATO about the possible despatch of an international force.'

The Leader of the Opposition: 'Get on with it.'

Other Hon Members: 'Order.'

The Prime Minister: 'The Leader of the Opposition tells me to get on with it. Get on with what? Get on with intensive but sober consultation with our allies and with the UN to see what realistically can be done? That we are doing. I have explained that to the House. Or does he mean that we should get on with the immediate despatch of British troops to Estonia and Russia? If that is now the policy of the Opposition, then the Right Honourable gentleman has been swept away by a flood of emotion. He is swayed not by what is happening in Russia, but what happened in the South Sussex by-election on Thursday.'

An Hon Member: 'Shame. Withdraw.'

Simon tossed aside his typescript and took up the manuscript scribbled a few minutes earlier on smaller paper. In a detached way he watched his hands tremble as they put the notes on the wooden box with brass edgings in front of him. His back pain had gone. He was out on his own. He shivered once, feeling a mix of fear and pleasure. The House, sensing a change of mood, fell silent.

The Prime Minister: 'I withdraw any personal criticism of the Leader of the Opposition. Not just the Right Honourable gentleman, but the whole House, the whole Western world is in danger of allowing its judgement to be swamped by this tide of emotion. We all feel it, we felt it on Sunday in Whitehall, we feel the angry generous emotions of a nation stirred by horror. "Hang the murderers," say some. The more sober simply say, "Something must be done." But I must tell the House that neither advice is any use to Her Majesty's Ministers. We are not men of stone. If any single action could in two or three days avert this conflict and bring peace with justice to Russia, I believe we would take it and face the risk. But what we cannot do is to send British troops into a Russian winter without a settled plan, without a clear purpose, without any idea of how they might fare or when they might return. Television programmes, by-elections, demonstrations in our streets can start an enterprise. They cannot finish it. The first holder of my office, the first Prime Minister of Britain, who was forced by public opinion into a war with Spain, said wisely, "They now ring the bells, but they will soon wring their hands." Madam Speaker, I have felt like Sir Robert Walpole in these last days. We are not sent here to impose our solutions on the troubles of the world. We are not elected ministers of universal justice. The armed services of the Crown, the Foreign Office, our aid programme are established to protect the interests of Britain. This protection of our interests includes working where we can for a more decent world. I accept that, we practise it. But this conflict in Russia, like so many conflicts in the modern world, will not be settled in the end on the battlefield. It will be settled by negotiating, by peacemaking and peacekeeping. Those who talk of negotiation and peace find their voices swamped at times of high emotion by other voices calling for dramatic acts of intervention. Those of us who propose compromises are shabby, unexciting creatures compared with those who ride on a white horse and promise drama and victory. We have to face accusations of cold heartedness and cowardice. The faces of the victims stare from the television screens in apparent reproach. But we owe this House, we owe our constituents our judgement, a judgement that must look further than tomorrow's headlines or the mood of this afternoon's crowd in Parliament Square. We have to consider the scene weeks, months, even years ahead. The Honourable Member for South Sussex, whom I welcome to the House, made much play in his campaign with Gladstone and his campaign in Midlothian against atrocities in Bulgaria. But what Bulgarian benefited from the eloquence of Mr Gladstone? What Afghan, what Armenian was saved by Mr Gladstone? Mr Gladstone gained himself a reputation, just as in his small way the Honourable Member has for a day gained himself a reputation. But the Queen's Ministers are not here to craft and polish shiny reputations for themselves. We are here to carry on her Government, energetically but soberly.

That is the test by which our success or failure must be judged. It is not part of our duty to send British troops into incalculable danger in a moment of emotion without having weighed up the risks to them against the good they might do. That at least, Madam Speaker, is my belief, and it is the belief that will guide this Government so long as I am its head.'

There was a pause when the Prime Minister sat down. More than four hundred Members of Parliament spent two seconds weighing up their own emotions and convictions. He had invited each individual to travel for an instant deep into his and her own characters, though for some that journey was a short one. As he had done often before in the Commons, though with less intensity than now, Simon waited in the silence for their reaction. He was shivering again and despite the chill of the air-conditioning he felt the sweat start up on his forehead and inside his crumpled shirt. Then the House in all parts uttered its own peculiar verdict – something between a rumble and a roar, something between applause for the man and approval for the argument.

On the front bench between the Prime Minister and the Speaker, the Chancellor of the Exchequer and the Home Secretary sat side by side. In this overfull House they were too close together for physical comfort, but they could whisper without difficulty.

'He's committed us against sending troops,' said Joan.

Roger Courtauld marvelled that this sharp intelligent

woman once again showed her lack of tactical grasp. She was brave, but not an ideal companion for tiger-shooting. For that purpose courage was not enough.

'You didn't listen. He's committed us against sending troops without a plan. That's quite different.'

'It sounded as if he might resign.'

'Nonsense. That was a flourish to end the speech.'

She paused. 'Then nothing has changed? Nothing, I mean, of what we discussed on Sunday.'

'Nothing. We must carry on. I hold you to the bargain.'

She paused again. 'He carried the House with him.'

'For the performance, Joan, for the performance, not the policy. Do you want to get your Budget through or don't you?'

Joan Freetown did not reply.

Simon met his team back in his Gothic room. Artemis held in her hand a list of bids for immediate media interviews and broadcasts. The telephone in the outer office rang constantly with fresh requests.

'What next?' asked Simon, exhausted.

She took one look at him and crumpled the list in her hand. 'What's next, Prime Minister, is bed.'

Patrick Vaughan, his authority again usurped, opened his mouth to speak, but himself looked at the Prime Minister and said nothing.

Chapter Sixteen

Thursday November 13

Louise shook the old-fashioned thermometer angrily. It refused to show that her husband had a temperature even though he looked terrible.

'You look terrible. You'd much better stay in bed.'

He was tempted. His back ached, his feet had stayed cold through the night, but above all he felt tired. It was years since he had spent a day in bed. He could read a novel, and sleep, and read, and sleep and even think . . .

He looked at the diary card, stiff and impeccably typed. For years it had been the route map of his life. Cabinet, of course, and before that separate talks with Roger Courtauld and Joan Freetown. He had a week ago cut short Cabinet discussion by promising personally to find a solution to their differences. Patrick had made manful efforts at his level with both departments, but with disappointing results. Indeed, Roger Courtauld had now fed, in at £178 million, his estimate of the extra costs arising from the Cabinet's approval of the new prison places. The Treasury thought this far too high and would only allow £98 million. So the total gap had actually widened, even though Patrick had made some progress in narrowing the differences on the police and probation services. Simon noticed an arrow and balloon on the diary card that showed that the Home Secretary and the Chancellor had for some reason swapped places. Roger Courtauld was coming in an hour's time, Joan Freetown half an hour later.

'I must do this lot,' he said. His wife took the card off the breakfast tray.

'You can see Roger here in bed. Even an extra hour will do you good. You know him well enough. Joan Freetown might be shocked by your pyjamas.'

He felt that his wife had drawn the compromise generously, and picked up her hand to kiss it. This she allowed, but at once added something to the understanding.

'You've got no PM questions in the House, and a free evening. If you look as bad at lunch as you do now, you can go back to bed and sleep it off.'

Simon knew that once he began to work he would feel better. Analysis and argument were his best medicines.

'And, by the way,' said Louise, 'I've had a strange conversation with Guy Freetown.'

'With Guy?'

'About the arrangements for the weekend after next. We're going to stay there, remember? You insisted. I can't think why. You don't like her and have nothing in common with him. But after that he said he'd tried to get in touch with you yesterday afternoon.'

'First I've heard of it.'

'At the House, apparently. He said he wasn't sure of the details, but something was afoot. Something political. Joan was all on edge, particularly when your name was mentioned. He said he was worried for you.'

How odd, but Guy was an odd man who knew nothing about politics. The last thing Simon wanted was a vague amateur political gossip with Guy Freetown.

Broadsheet and tabloid newspapers lay on the coverlet, still tidy because he had not bothered with them. Even a year ago he would have ransacked them long before to find out how his speech on the Address had been treated. He picked up one of the broadsheets. Although they no longer bothered to report in any comprehensive way what happened in Parliament or indeed the world, they continued to pontificate as proudly as ever from the leader columns. What had been compelling in papers of record had become pretentious in papers of gossip and speculation. One of the leaders caught his eye.

COLD FEET OR A COLD HEART?

The Prime Minister's speech in the Commons failed to match the wishes of the nation or the needs of the moment. It was the more disturbing because it was eloquently delivered and deeply felt. The Prime Minister is philosophically a sceptic. He is the master of the nicely calculated less or more. Enthusiasm and generous emotion sit uneasily on his lips; the suspicion must be that they rarely enter his heart. The international community is now faced with an impending catastrophe in Russia. Once a new civil war is launched in that huge disorderly country we cannot tell how long it will last or how wide it will spread. We can be certain that the savagery and the suffering will be immense. The massacre in the St Petersburg cemetery gave us a foretaste. Terrible though it was, that act of terrorism has concentrated all our minds. There has been a huge outpouring of emotion across the civilised world. And not just of sorrow and anger. Throughout Britain, throughout Europe and the United States, we are seeing an unmistakable willingness to intervene now to prevent a catastrophe. President Altman is ready, and it is no secret that he is urging us on. France and Germany, Canada and Sweden have undertaken to act if action is internationally agreed. Because of the superb professionalism of our armed services and our central role in the decision-taking of the Alliance, all eyes are on Britain. Of course there are risks and uncertainties. Inevitably they breed hesitation. But the Cabinet and above all the Prime Minister have a clear duty to resolve these hesitations, not shelter behind them. The Prime Minister's colleagues applauded his eloquence in the Commons yesterday. Today they should decide in principle on British intervention and commission the detailed planning on which the Prime Minister placed such emphasis. The absence of such a plan is a reproach to the Government, not an excuse for further inaction. If the Prime Minister continues to hesitate, then the question of his leadership will inevitably arise again. But that would be a damaging complication. If today Britain, by a decision for intervention, reaffirms its leading place among the civilised powers, then those who perished at St Petersburg will not have died in vain.

Simon looked at his coverlet, at the empty coffee cup, out of the window at a fragment of marbled London sky. The article was written in frustration of course, but millions felt like that. The decent folk who voted for him in Harrow – or voted against him – most of them felt like that this Thursday morning. Their letters were pouring in . . .

'Something must be done.' What would they write in six months' time? What would they write in reply to the message from the Ministry of Defence that their husband or brother or boyfriend had been blown up by a mine in some frozen waste outside St Petersburg? Simon Russell knew that he himself was not a coward, either physically or politically. It was right to calculate risk as carefully as possible. But was there something missing in his own make-up? Why could he not join in that flood of emotion the leaderwriter accurately described? Was it true that he suffered from a cold heart? If so, what packet could be sent for from the chemist, or what operation performed by his Harley Street surgeon? The London sky gave him no answer. The Prime Minister drifted from meditation into a snooze.

The Home Secretary was in the room.

'Are you all right, Simon? Sorry to see you out of sorts.'

Simon pinched his thigh under the bedclothes to ensure that he was fully awake.

'I'm just feeling lazy. I'll get up as soon as you've gone.'

'I don't think we need be long. That was a fine speech yesterday.'

'You don't agree with it.'

'Indeed not. But I know a real speech when I hear one. They don't come often.'

Except for a plate with one croissant, the breakfast tray

had been taken away while the Prime Minister slept and his brief placed on a table beside the bed. He found the annex with the figures.

'You're still wide apart from the Treasury, Roger. You'll have to come down quite substantially, you know. And we really have to settle it today if Joan is to make sense of her Budget next Tuesday.'

Roger took the croissant. He seemed embarrassed.

'D'you mind? I haven't had any breakfast.'

'Not at all. Let me get you some coffee.'

'No don't worry. I'll get some later.'

The bed creaked noisily as the bulk of the Home Secretary settled on it.

'I've settled already. We can save you some work.'

'Settled direct with Joan herself?'

'Yes, in principle, on Sunday. Officials finalised the figures yesterday.'

Simon was pleased but did not understand.

'What's the bottom line on prisons?'

'One hundred and one million pounds. We've compromised on the rest.'

Simon did not understand at all. If the two departments had split the difference between their two estimates, the result would have been £138 million. The Home Secretary had collapsed. The Treasury had won a famous victory. The sums were not huge but the climbdown verged on the sensational, as colleagues and soon the press would quickly see.

'Congratulations. On the agreement, I mean. You've made a big sacrifice.'

There was a pause. The room filled with embarrassment. Simon's political antennae knew there was more to come. 'I must get up,' he said, to force the pace.

'No, no, Simon. You can stay a bit longer. You don't need to see Joan now. She asked me to give you a message. That's why I switched places with her, so that I came first.'

Simon could not make sense of this. He waited. The bed creaked as Roger Courtauld shifted his buttocks. The knot of his tie had slipped below the top shirt button. He had not shaved accurately, and a tiny patch of stubble showed in the dimple of his chin. A decent man was about to confess.

'Joan asked me to tell you in advance of Cabinet that she has changed her mind about Russia. She's now in favour of British troops joining an intervention.'

Simon stared. He had been outflanked, and by a man he had thought incapable of subtle manoeuvre.

'You've done a deal.'

'We've agreed. Her Budget is now complete.'

'You've landed us in war, and sacrificed your prison budget for the privilege.' He spoke without anger, but as an analyst assessing the situation.

'We can prevent a war. It's what people want. We've got to do it, Simon, we've got to do it.'

His words were firm, but most unusually he spoke as if trying to persuade himself as well as the Prime Minister.

Simon, as ever exploring human attitudes, noticed something tentative in Roger, matching his own tentative mood a few minutes ago. They were neither of them absolutely sure that the other was wrong. Perhaps because they respected each other, perhaps because they were meeting in a bedroom rather than across a table, the uncertainties showed.

But that was that. The decisive moment had come and gone. As soon as the Home Secretary had gone the Prime Minister asked to speak to the Foreign Secretary. He was putting gold cuff-links into a new shirt when the call came through. Peter Makewell was as always brief and matter of fact. He had not changed his opinions. He was not enthusiastic about intervention, but he knew we had to join in intervening. Our place in the Alliance, particularly with the Americans, depended on it. A new and more detailed Security Council resolution was nearly complete. The Security Council would request NATO to intervene. The Supreme Allied Commander would speak to the NATO Council tomorrow morning. Peter Makewell and the Defence Secretary had held an informal meeting with the Chiefs of Staff yesterday evening.

'The chiefs are still against?' But he knew it was a show.

'Not really. They're getting quite enthusiastic. A fascinating challenge. A chance to test command and control in a mixed force. That sort of thing. They'll be ready at Cabinet with quite a detailed plan, a map with flags. You can imagine.'

Simon could indeed imagine. The Service Chiefs would

not have dreamed of proposing intervention. They had been strongly opposed when it was first proposed. They would still be grumbling about political over-excitement. But by now their own professional excitement was taking over.

'But we have decided nothing.'

'Of course not, Prime Minister.' Peter Makewell retired into formal mode. 'All this is on a contingency basis. Subject to a decision by the Cabinet that has not yet been taken.'

But that soon would be taken. Simon had thrown off his exhaustion – as he had expected. He looked at himself in the pier glass in his dressing room. He liked his shirt tails long, and this blue shirt came halfway down his thighs. It was an elegant confection with a neat collar already fastened rather high and cuffs that reached the base of his thumbs. By comparison his bare legs looked white, smooth and inadequate. Had his thighs and calves begun to shrink? He was well into the sixth age of man. The words came back to him, though he was not sure from which play:

> 'His youthful hose well sav'd, a world too wide
> For his shrunk shank.'

All in all, despite the gold cuff-links given by the Queen, he did not look to himself like a war leader. He put on his socks.

It did not occur to him to doubt the total truth of what Roger Courtauld had told him. He kicked himself for not having made sure of Joan Freetown. But it was not in his style of premiership to lobby colleagues for his own point of view. And anyway he had felt sure that Joan would stay firm. There was a strong Treasury interest against foreign adventures, and she herself liked to pour scorn on defence spending and the pretensions of generals and diplomats.

Colleagues stood in twos and threes outside the Cabinet Room, waiting for the Prime Minister. This week he was on time. Everyone, of course, knew by now that he had spent an extra hour in bed, and there was a murmur of welcome, in which pleasure mingled with concern. The Chancellor of the Exchequer stood back by the mantelpiece, for once unobtrusive. But she could not escape so easily, and he sought her out.

'You didn't come to see me, Joan.'

'Didn't Roger explain? He promised . . .' She was back on her heels.

'He explained. Congratulations on achieving your Budget.'

'I thought—'

'Just tell me one thing, Joan. How much do you think the intervention will cost? This year? Next year? The year after . . .?'

'It's hardly possible, Prime Minister, to . . .?'

But he had not stayed for an answer. It was a poor satisfaction anyway, since money was only a fraction of the argument which had gone almost by default. Simon as usual gauged the atmosphere correctly. What was unusual was that the consequences had escaped from his control. With the Chancellor he could have blocked a decision in principle in favour of intervention, even against Foreign Secretary and Home Secretary and a majority of colleagues. Without her he was a lone voice. He could fight, and if he lost, he could resign, perhaps would be forced to resign. He was not ready for that outcome.

The public spending agreements were quickly ratified. Lord Downbrook congratulated the Prime Minister on the skill with which he had personally presided over the final stages of the negotiation. The Cabinet murmured agreement. No doubt most of them thought that he, Simon, had leaned heavily on Roger Courtauld and forced him to surrender. The truth would soon be apparent.

The discussion on Russia went just as smoothly. Peter Makewell reported on the latest diplomatic moves, stressing the growing consensus within the Alliance. Roger Courtauld simply stated that the Cabinet knew his views, which had not changed since last week. Joan Freetown was almost equally brief, without fire or her usual individual phrasing. Having reflected and listened to a wide range of views she had come somewhat unwillingly to the conclusion that we should join in intervention, for a period of six months only, and on the assumption, to which the Treasury attached particular importance, that operations should at all stages be conducted with the utmost regard for economy.

They began to look at the Prime Minister wondering

how he would react to this desertion. 'Pole-axed' the evening papers would report a few hours later. In fact he did not move a muscle. Obviously he had not been surprised. He called in the Chiefs of Staff for their presentation. They were better prepared than Simon had expected, though there were still gaps in their assessment. The discussion then centred on the number of troops that should be sent. The Foreign Secretary had suggested 2,000 men only as adequate to show the necessary solidarity with our allies. The Chiefs of Staff, supported by the Defence Secretary, would have none of that. A minimum of 6,000 men and support staff was essential if they were not to rely to an inappropriate extent on the facilities of the Americans and the French. Simon always smelled a rat when the word 'inappropriate' was used, since it usually meant that some more precise objection was being concealed. This was certainly so in this case.

The Chiefs of Staff did not want to play second fiddle in the allocation of command jobs on the ground between the different countries. The extra men were rather an expensive way of keeping Britain's end up. But Simon, though seeing this clearly, had no intention of fighting on secondary issues when he had decided to abandon the main ground.

He could not resist one last flick.

'Chancellor, content with the extra cost?'

Joan Freetown nodded grimly, with just one subdued clink of her bracelets.

Simon summed up. A small War Cabinet was set up, excluding the Treasury. Intervention was agreed provided that the Americans, French, Germans and Canadians participated in a detailed plan that the War Cabinet found acceptable. A time limit of six months was established and should, if possible, be incorporated in the impending Security Council resolution. The Defence Secretary would make a statement on these lines in the House of Commons that afternoon.

'On that point,' said Lord Downbrook, 'I don't think we need worry too much about the contradiction between this and what you said in the Commons yesterday, Prime Minister. As I understand it, you were saying we could not intervene without a proper plan. We are deciding today to intervene once there is a proper plan. Some people will criticise the contradiction, but really there is no contradiction.'

'Thank you. I'm much obliged.' The Prime Minister spoke drily. He knew this was only the beginning of a long travail. There was indeed no contradiction between yesterday and today – if one left out of account impressions, emotions and personal convictions, in particular his own.

Thursday November 13 – Monday November 17

The Prime Minister passed the next three days as if under a partial anaesthetic. He sat beside the Defence Secretary as he made his statement on Thursday afternoon. When the taunts began from the Labour backbenchers, and the cautious criticism of a U-turn from behind him, he composed his features into a total lack of expression, wishing that custom permitted a tall hat which he could pull down over his face as Peel once protected himself from Disraeli.

But it passed, the House was pleased with the new policy, and when he got back to Number 10 he agreed to go to bed. He slept well, then and through the weekend at Chequers. To Louise's disappointment he developed none of the symptoms that would have enabled her to assert total control. He worked mechanically through his boxes, reaching decisions as thoroughly and sensibly as ever. He watched Louise sculpt and walked alone through the bright frosty woods, specifically requesting his protection team not to come with him. There was no sign of Julia or word from her. His mind kept itself within the channels dug by the immediate workload and the smaller decisions of the household – whether he would like a fire lit in the Hawtrey room, how many Christmas cards they would need, whether claret or Rioja would go better with the Sunday joint. His thoughts did not wander into the future. He kept his deepest worries under wraps, hoping that when he revisited them he would find them in promising convalescence.

On Monday he drove from Chequers to RAF Brize Norton in Oxfordshire to see off the advance party of the Expeditionary Office to Russia. There were only forty of them, fitting easily into a VC10. He chatted to them in the lounge over coffee, tea and sweet biscuits while their kit was loaded. There was nothing ominous about the occasion. He might have been a relative seeing off a group of youngsters on a package tour. Patrick Vaughan had provided him with a few notes for a speech wishing them Godspeed and describing the justice of their mission.

'Just in case, Prime Minister.'

But any speech would have been absurd. Simon jammed the speech notes deep into his overcoat pocket as he shook hands with each of them on the Tarmac. The cameras whirred. There was by coincidence a lad from Harrow, a constituent, to whom he had given a school prize two years earlier. He was taller than the average, blue eyes deep-set into bony sockets, a mop of black hair. James Southey – Simon made a note of the name and address so that he could drop a line of congratulations to the lad's mother.

When he reached 10 Downing Street the emphasis at the heart of government had switched to Ireland. The Ulster Leader Strachan had dined with James Whitman the night before, the two of them alone with the Lavery portraits in the dark dining-room at Hillsborough. James Whitman had expected an evening of reproaches and accusations. Instead he had been offered a deal. Strachan was prepared on one condition to go to the Party Conference of the Unionist Party at Coleraine in ten days' time and recommend that they accept a compromise for the future government of Northern Ireland.

The compromise would contain (though of course without acknowledgement) the two main British achievements in the Province of recent decades – a power-sharing executive of Unionist majority and Nationalist minority agreed at Sunningdale in 1974, but overthrown a few months later, and the right of the Dublin Government to hold a watching brief without sovereign or executive power, agreed between Britain and Ireland in 1985 and consistently rejected by the Unionists thereafter. In short Strachan, recognising the surge of public opinion behind the Prime Minister's initiative, was willing to accept the dream settlement of successive British Governments. But, of course, there was a but. Strachan's condition was that Simon Russell should stand at the lectern in the university in the Unionist stronghold of Coleraine, declare to the Unionists that he was himself a Unionist, that he would always oppose the unification of Ireland, that as leader of the Conservative Party in England, Scotland and Wales he welcomed the Unionist Party of Northern Ireland back into the old integral partnership with the Conservatives across the water.

Ireland was always a matter of fine print. Whitman had flown over. He and officials were already closeted in the Cabinet Room working on a text of what Simon might say at Coleraine. The plan was full of prickles. Neither the Americans nor the Dublin Government would be pleased. Some Conservatives at home would dislike having the Orangemen thrust back into the party fold. In Northern Ireland the leaders of the Nationalist minority were perfectly capable of registering fury against a performance at Coleraine, so failing to recognise that the deal would bring them everything they had recently been asking for, an end to discrimination, an end to the triumphalism of the majority, a place in power.

At the moment of Simon's arrival at the meeting the difficulties were speaking for themselves – rather too loudly and insistently for James Whitman. Normally happy under the nursing of his officials, he now had the experience to rebel.

'I don't follow these ifs and buts,' he said. 'All I know is that Strachan is taking risks, and we must do the same. This is fundamentally what we want, we must go for it.'

They went over the ground laboriously again for the Prime Minister, who listened in silence.

'Could you please wait a moment?' he asked them. 'You two, a word please. Something urgent to be done.'

He took Patrick and Artemis out into the room in the Private Office they shared.

'What do you two think?'

They were flattered. Simon normally took more trouble with his private secretaries and senior officials than most ministers. He didn't regard himself as a caste apart. They had worried over recent weeks that they had drifted away from him, that they were of less use than before to someone of whom they were fond. Now they were back in touch, tugs pulling a giant ocean liner.

Patrick and Artemis had not consulted together. Independently they both agreed that he should go to Coleraine.

'On balance, yes, Prime Minister.'

'Of course, of course, Prime Minister. It's a breakthrough.'

'Would you both have given the same advice to another minister in the same position?'

'Certainly,' said Artemis.

Patrick paused. 'Probably not, Prime Minister. But it's right for you.'

'You're an honest man.' And he actually put his arm round Patrick's shoulder for a second as they turned back to the Cabinet Room.

That evening was yet again free. The official machine was at last keeping official engagements to a minimum. Simon and Louise dined together upstairs in the flat. They said little to each other, for their lives had diverged. The coming together after his heart attack had been temporary. She knew and he knew that when he finally died she would be desperately sorry. But there was nothing much to be done about that meanwhile. That evening they were relatively at ease. He went to bed early after the television news and read *Madame Bovary* in translation. What hell to be married to such a restless, self-centred woman. He felt for her clumsy husband. He wondered whether Julia was turning out that way. Here again there did not seem a great deal to be done. He dozed. Louise joined him. He kissed her. It did not occur to either of them to make love.

Chapter Seventeen

Tuesday November 18

Next morning there was an extra Cabinet so that Joan Freetown could inform her colleagues of her Budget before she presented it to the Commons in the afternoon. Tradition was observed in that all Cabinet colleagues congratulated the Chancellor on her ingenuity and imagination. Those who had been bludgeoned in the public spending round joined in the general good cheer. In fact Joan had recovered her pose. She was on home ground, assertive yet stopping just short of the intolerable. Simon, though still angry with her for letting him down over Russia, was too professional not to admire her skill.

There was little real discussion, and he was able to wind up Cabinet at eleven forty-five. In the cloakroom he put on a black tie.

'Are you really going to that memorial service? There's so much to do,' said Artemis.

The girl must learn to be less blunt. He felt less affection for her than the day before.

'I am, Rupert Cranleigh was an old friend.'

It was not strictly true. Sir Rupert Cranleigh, the recently deceased member for South Sussex, had not been a continuous friend. Indeed for the last twenty years they had hardly done more than exchange greetings and pass on when they met in the Commons. He had been a man of great promise, which had gradually ebbed. It was not drink, and Simon refused to believe it was women. But somehow an intelligent man had become obvious and stupid, while remaining perfectly agreeable. There had been little time in Simon's life for agreeable stupid people, and he had never been fond of the obvious. He needed friends with salt in them. Sir Rupert's salt had lost its savour many years back.

But Simon's memory was beginning to focus vividly on certain episodes of his past. Rupert Cranleigh's death brought them back to him. One evening, when both in their early thirties, they had shared a train on the way back from a Conservative Selection Committee in Lancashire. They had both put themselves forward as candidates and both been rejected. In their gloom they had drunk two whiskies and then dined together, finding a good claret while the still-nationalised train trundled very slowly through middle England in high summer. They had never talked before, and were never to talk like that again. School and university, money, girls, even religion – but overwhelmingly politics, what it was about, why it fascinated, whether they should abandon the search for a seat, gossip and speculation mixed up together with a search for purpose. The conversation had lasted three hours and they had shared a taxi from Euston, making a promise to keep in touch which neither had respected.

So it must be right to go to Rupert Cranleigh's memorial service, particularly as it was only five minutes away. It was extremely cold in St Margaret's, Westminster, even in an overcoat. The church was reasonably full, and contained a number of people who Simon thought had died some time ago. He sat in a reserved seat in the front row, next to the Speaker, across the aisle from the Cranleigh family. He had declined an invitation to give the address himself; it was competently done by the Lord Lieutenant of Sussex. Understandably he found it impossible to find anything very dramatic to say about Rupert Cranleigh. What was remarkable about the man was his ordinariness, his persistence in decency as his ambition faded.

Simon looked across the aisle at the three rows of Cranleighs. Fair hair, sharp noses, a chin – the grandsons seemed to have inherited the family equipment without mishap. This was the England in which at heart Simon believed, though he did not belong to it. For decades its decay and disappearance had been gleefully predicted; yet here it still was, maintaining country houses, marrying skilfully, producing children, members of Parliament, magistrates and memorial services. Theirs were the names in memorials on brass from the Boer War and the Great

War, on memorials of stone after that, crowded together in the cloisters of ancient schools. Such places with their history had for Simon a complicated appeal. He sometimes proclaimed proudly in public that his own education was at a grammar school. It had gone independent in the seventies but in character was a far cry from Eton or Winchester. But privately he felt an affectionate envy for the ease, breadth and extraordinary persistence he associated with the ancient schools. These were the faces in portraits with foxes, or lots and lots of dogs and dead birds. What were Rupert's grandsons doing? He did not suppose that he would have advised any of them to go into politics. That might be a loss for politics rather than for the Cranleighs.

The elegant yellow and green shards of the Piper windows on the south aisle accentuated the cold of the church. Simon refused to think of Ireland or of Russia, of Roger Courtauld, or of Joan Freetown now fidgeting with the final phrases of her Budget speech. He tried to think of mortality and eternity. He tried then to pray, but that art had long escaped him. He doubted anyway if Sir Rupert Cranleigh, though a regular churchgoer, would have approved of spiritual exercises at his memorial service.

When the service ended with a triumphant blast on the organ, an usher proposed to lead him out of the church by a side exit, following the Speaker, in order to avoid the bottle-neck of elderly people leaving slowly down the nave to the west door. Simon instinctively disliked being told what to do by ushers, toastmasters, protection officers and

'Why are we going to the Home Office?'

'The Home Secretary has set up a crisis room. He is in charge and feels he cannot leave. He is particularly anxious to brief you in person.'

Simon had not talked to Roger Courtauld since Cabinet last week. He had avoided him at the Budget Cabinet that morning. This was not a considered snub. Simon was not sure how to handle a colleague who had inflicted on him in Cabinet a defeat from which he was still sore. It was better to avoid contact until he had made up his mind.

But there was Roger, waiting for him in the vestibule of the Home Office. The Home Secretary was massive in purple cloth braces in spite of the chill of the building.

'Thanks, Prime Minister. Good of you to come.'

In the crisis room on the ninth floor the Home Secretary resumed direct charge. Briefly, he introduced the officials on duty to the Prime Minister, without taking them away from their screens and telephones. Then he took Simon into a tiny side office. The desk was covered with an array of white-bread sandwiches and two tankards of ale.

'Help yourself, Simon. Can't control prison riots on an empty stomach.'

Through his own munching he revealed what Simon knew must exist, his real reason for virtually hijacking the Prime Minister to the Home Office.

'The whole system is shaky. There's nothing so infectious as a prison riot. I've warned all Chief Constables to prepare for an emergency, but the police are always reluctant to go inside a prison. Gloucester is the key. If we can defuse Gloucester, the whole thing may subside. The prisoners are holding the Governor – you know that already. He's in the hands of a particularly dangerous group, led by a man called Evans, with a terrible record.'

'A murderer?'

'No, of course not.' Roger let the surprise show in his voice. Then he remembered that no Prime Minister had ever visited a prison. This was the hidden service. 'But I forgot, you wouldn't know. Murderers behave impeccably in prison. This man came in as a forger, never hit a man in his life. Until he got to Gloucester, that is. His record of violence is in prisons, not out. It sometimes takes them that way.'

'So?' Simon disliked being ignorant.

'The man Evans says he has a high regard for you. He says he will let the Governor go if you will promise him personally on the telephone to visit Gloucester and hear their grievances.'

'What are their grievances, for God's sake?'

'Not enough work, not enough training, overcrowding. Usual story. Gloucester, they say, is hell. But they're dead scared they might get transferred to one of the army camps I'm taking over.'

The Prime Minister couldn't resist a jab. 'You'll have even less money for prison work and training after your deal with Joan.'

But the moment it was out of his mouth the remark seemed remote. It came from an artificial politician's world. They were living with reality and a prison service that might go up in smoke.

'That's my look-out,' said Roger. 'That's my sense of priorities. Not easy. Not easy at all.'

'*Should* I talk to Evans? My instinct is against.'

'I think we should tell him you will talk to him after he's freed the Governor unharmed, not before.'

'Still giving in to blackmail.'

'He's a good Governor.'

'All right, tell him. I'll do that.'

Simon stayed in the small office while Roger went into action. Then he remembered something. He sought out Patrick and Artemis in the main operation room.

'You said Moscow was up in smoke too.'

'Figuratively, Prime Minister.'

In his worry about the prisons Patrick, too, had forgotten, most unusually, to pass on essential information.

'Brassev has announced that his attack on St Petersburg will begin next week, before the intervention force can get there in anything like full strength.'

A cold stone formed in Simon's stomach. Anything to do with Russia was now affecting him with a particular emotional charge. He would rejoice, he would weep, he would worry about Russia and the intervention force with special intensity. Privately, because that was his nature. But those closest to him needed to understand.

'Listen, you two. From now on, anything about Russia has priority. Automatic and immediate. I need to know.'

'Understood, Prime Minister.' But they didn't. How could they? Even they did not understand how hard it was to keep intact his reputation for serenity, how thin was the membrane that separated his work from his feelings.

'I'm afraid we can't locate Evans. We're still trying.'

So back to Number 10.

'Nice quiet day,' said the policeman at the door. It was his usual greeting.

'Nice and quiet indeed,' said the Prime Minister. 'A bit colder, though.'

He took the lift upstairs to scribble a note of apology to Joan for missing her Budget Speech.

Patrick and his wife had asked Artemis to dinner to celebrate his forty-first birthday.

'Subject to the exigencies of the Services, of course.'

'Of course.'

That morning she had assumed that as usual those exigencies had prevailed. The small festivity would, like so many others, be crushed by the juggernaut of work. But Patrick, or in the background his wife, had decided otherwise, and after a quick word with the Prime Minister he told Artemis that they still expected her at the restaurant about seven thirty pm. The fashion for later dinners had not yet reached Patrick.

Artemis, made bold by his boldness, snatched another

hour to go home for a bath and change. Since her promotion she had bought off the peg at Harrods a dress in bright red with silk cuffs also in red. There had been no occasion yet to wear it. It might be a shade too colourful for Patrick's restaurant, or indeed Patrick's wife. But Artemis felt tired and needed the fresh energy she knew the new dress would give her.

She let herself into the flat and moved straight to the bedroom. She sensed disaster as she paused at the threshold. The room was a little warmer than she had expected and slightly scented.

Frank lay on their bed in a position she knew well – naked, coverlet thrown off, on his side with his back to the centre, sated, fast asleep. Facing him in the bed was an unknown girl, young and blond, wearing a pair of cheap pyjamas from Indonesia that Frank had given Artemis last Christmas. They were considerably too large for the girl, who was awake. She started up at the sight of Artemis in the doorway and screamed softly. As she leaned forward to shake Frank out of sleep she knocked over a glass of red wine, half-full, which spilled on the carpet loaned to Artemis by her mother.

'What the bloody hell is going on?' Artemis shouted at the pair. It was, she realised, a trite beginning, but then the scene itself was unbearably trite.

Frank woke and stared. His thinning hair was dishevelled and two folds appeared in his stomach as he sat up in bed. An old desire swept through her, stronger than her resistance. Then Frank laughed. She had expected confusion and shame. Something terrible was happening.

'You haven't met Laura, I think? Department of Transport. You have a lot in common.' He laughed again. She could have forgiven the unfaithfulness. The laugh was lethal.

Artemis stumbled from the flat, down the lift and out into the early darkness of Hammersmith.

*

The snow would stay now till spring. But where would they be by spring?

Virginia travelled now with Dobrinsky on his visits to the outposts. The climax might come at any time. She did not want to find them separated, he on the front line, she useless in their hotel suite. They sat side by side in the armoured car, seeing nothing except the lower half of the corporal who manned the gun mounted in the turret. A puddle of thawed snow had formed round each of his boots. When he stamped his feet for warmth, icy water splashed on to Dobrinsky's own boots, dimming their polish.

'You must decide today.' It was just possible to talk over the noise. They would have no other opportunity for private talk until they got back to the city.

'Decide? We must fight. Brassev will find us hard to attack.'

'Certainly. But by spring he will have cracked us.' She put her gloved hand and quilted forearm on his thigh.

'I can't surrender.'

He spoke without fire. Indeed, she thought, the spirit, the wit, the fun had gone out of him.

'You must use the international force.'

He laughed without humour. 'Those fools. You worked hard to get them, but it won't work. Too few, and they haven't come here to fight. I'll do better by myself when the fighting comes.'

'All by yourself?'

That was the point. Men were deserting every night, creeping through the woods to Brassev's outposts. A colonel with a dozen from his unit had disappeared yesterday. Only five days till Brassev's ultimatum expired.

Suddenly he put his head in his hands. 'It's without hope. It's over.'

'Stop behaving like a Russian.'

'I am a Russian. It's hopeless, but I'll fight.'

'That is exactly being a Russian. Brave but fatalistic. And because fatalistic, verging on the stupid. Listen, Anatoly, of course this international force will be small, and confused. I talked to the British reconnaissance team this morning. But if you let them in, they can deploy in between your party. Brassev will hesitate, maybe turn back.'

'No. They will always be too few. He can sweep through them.'

'Anatoly, your horizon has shrunk. The world is not confined to this city you have made your own. Does Brassev want sanctions, hardship. Even bombs on Moscow?'

'It wouldn't come to that. Why should the West fight for me?'

She must prevent him putting his head in his hands again. With her gloved hand she took his flesh through the thick cloth above the elbow, and pinched him hard.

It hurt. 'Stop it.'

The corporal shifted his feet as if about to come down into the interior of the armoured car and investigate the noise. But he thought better of it. The car slowed as it approached the next post.

'You'll give the order to let them in, Anatoly? Trust me, trust me. It's your best hope.'

'I have no hope. I have only courage.'

But to her great relief she saw that this time he was parodying himself. She took off his fur hat and kissed him on the forehead as she had often done. There was a ghost of a smile in his eyes and tears in hers. For a moment he was as he had been. She prayed that the spark would not go out again.

*

He bundled into a red box the neat heap of work that he had to do, and took it up to the flat. Patrick and Artemis were of course out, eating at a restaurant. He wished that he had invited himself to join them. Had it occurred to either of them to ask him? Was there something in the British Constitution or (more likely) in his own nature that prevented his staff from treating him as a friend?

> Don't forget that I'm at Chequers tonight opening that exhibition of portraits. Milk and eggs in the fridge.
>
> Louise.

There was a second note on the small breakfast table.

> Daddy,
> Bomb Moscow NOW.
> Love Julia.

He sat down at the table and took the first paper from his box. An afternoon and early evening solid with meetings had left him drained. The memorial service for Sir Rupert Cranleigh and the session with Roger Courtauld at the Home Office seemed distant. He remembered Gloucester prison and lifted the telephone.

'Any success yet with Evans?'

'Evans, Prime Minister?' The Duty Clerk was bemused.

'Evans, Evans, Evans.' Unusually he snapped, then recovered. 'Evans is the ringleader in Gloucester jail. The Home Office are trying to get him to speak to me.'

'Ah, Evans . . . I'll check with them, Prime Minister. I'm sure they'd have told us if—'

He had put down the receiver.

'I take the opportunity to emphasise to this gathering that in my best judgement there is no likelihood in my lifetime of a change in the status of Northern Ireland as part of the United Kingdom, given the paramount importance in this question of the principle of consent.'

That was how civil servants drafted speeches. It was unbelievable. They made no distinction between the written and the spoken word. He thumbed quickly through this draft of his speech to the Unionists at Coleraine next week. As usual he would have to re-write it all. Was there no one in his office capable of drafting a speech he could actually deliver? In time he might be able to train Artemis. He thought of Artemis for two seconds, then took up his pen.

'The Union will remain in my lifetime. That is because you, the majority, wish it. I have come here today simply to say that I wish it too. I believe in the Union not as it has been but as with your help it can be . . . tolerant, embracing all its citizens . . .'

It was flowing well. The telephone rang.

The Duty Clerk had been startled out of his Whitehall style by the small drama of which he was part.

'It's the convict Evans. He'll come through direct . . .'

'Is that Russell?'

'It is.'

'You're the Prime Minister?'

'I am the Prime Minister.'

'Tell the bloody BBC to lay off me.'

'What do you mean?'

'They're calling me an armed robber. It's a black lie. Seven years for forgery, that's me.'

'Is the Governor safe?'

'Safe and eating his supper. Baked beans and bacon, with a gun in his back.'

'You are to release him at once.'

'That depends.'

Then a silence. The Prime Minister judged that he must not be eager. He was trying to weigh the vowels. West Midlands, perhaps a touch of Welsh to go with the name. A dangerous man, but a man who was going to do a deal.

'Will you come here? We don't trust that big bluff bugger of a Home Secretary.'

He had rehearsed the answer to that at the Home Office that morning. 'I'll come to Gloucester prison next week provided you release the Governor at once and return with all your confederates to your cells.'

'No disciplinary action against us?'

That was the hard question. To yield would be indefensible in the House of Commons – and also wrong.

'I cannot undertake that. You have committed a further serious offence.'

'At least listen to us first.'

Simon Russell paused. Occasionally, only occasionally,

say once a month, a Prime Minister had to use his judgement alone, without benefit of colleagues, on something important.

'No disciplinary action will be taken until I have visited the prison. I can give no undertaking on what will happen after that.'

Another pause.

'You're a hard man. I accept.'

'Tell the Governor to ring the Home Secretary direct as soon as you've set him free.'

He sat back in his chair. The Duty Clerk would have been listening in, and would without any instruction pass the good news to the Home Office. Good news? Bad news? How would the press react? The Commons? Were these reactions relevant to whether he had done right or wrong? He was tired, more tired than at any time since the summer holiday.

His mind stuck in a groove, and would not answer its own question. He ought to ring Roger Courtauld, even though it was not strictly necessary. But that would mean putting through the call, finding phrases, choosing a tone of voice, redefining a relationship that had become confused. He could not summon the small energy needed for the task. He returned to his papers.

Staring up at him from the middle of the box was a chart of command and control for the proposed British Force in Russia, showing how the units would relate to each other and to the French, German and US contingents. Someone had enjoyed complicating the pattern of the organogram.

There were squares, there were oblongs, linked by continuous lines, by dotted lines, as if tracing the family tree of some particularly incestuous dynasty. On top was a scribbled note from Patrick: 'Prime Minister. This is obviously of high political sensitivity. PV.' Which being interpreted meant 'Don't just tick it off'. He had told his staff to show him at once everything to do with Russia. He ought to read it before going to bed – but he could not.

He told himself that this was because he was tired, but he knew the real reason. Inside him a psychological block had formed on the proposal for the force in Russia. Was it resentment because he had been outmanoeuvred, virtually in public, by two senior colleagues? Or was it cussedness because he disliked policy being swept forward by ill-informed emotion? Or was some accurate political instinct warning him of catastrophe? These squares and oblongs were not conceptual playthings of the defence planners. They were servicemen and women, with cases packed, waiting for orders, half excited, half anxious, holding farewell meals with friends and family, asking questions to which there were no answers, learning a phrase or two of Russian, their lives entrusted into the hands of the Prime Minister.

He slammed shut the box and thought of Henry V before Agincourt, prowling through the darkness among the men who would die next day. His fatigue was laced with loneliness. The familiar cigar and the Glenfiddich were within reach, but this time the rest and companionship they offered was not enough. Almost invariably Simon finished his work, or at least broke its back, before going to bed. But tonight sleep must be his medicine and his ally. Without bothering to wash or even find his pyjamas in the bathroom, he undressed and took refuge in the bedclothes. He had taken no pills but to his great relief he felt sleep coming down upon him in friendly waves.

He did not know who had turned on the television in the bedroom. It conceivably might have been Julia, he supposed, wandering round the flat after a party, perhaps mistaking rooms. There was no sign of her or anyone else. He had little time to speculate. The special news bulletin had already begun. The digital watch by Simon's bedside showed 1.58.

'As it happens our correspondent was on the spot when the disaster occurred. He had been invited with others to a press briefing by the British reconnaissance team, and was filming the team's arrival.'

Three Warrior armoured cars were moving fast along a country road towards the camera, churning up mud and slush from its ruts. The Union Jack on the pennant of the leading car continued to flutter for a second or two after it hit the mine, and was then enveloped in a mixture of flame and black smoke. There was a single cry of human pain, just audible to the microphone of the television team after the sound of the explosion. The two following armoured cars stopped and discharged their crews on to the roadside. Evidently following a well-rehearsed drill, they moved towards the first Warrior, which was wholly engulfed in fire. Within a few seconds they had extricated two human beings and carried them, gently but fast, towards the cameras. The nearest passed close enough for Simon to recognise the casualty. It was James Southey, the lad from Harrow with deep-set eyes to whom he had said goodbye at Brize Norton. On Simon's desk, among constituency letters awaiting signature was one to James' mother, saying how smart and eager her son had looked. She must be proud of him, he had dictated. She might still be proud of his face, which she would recognise even in death. The rest of him was a charred, twisted mess. He must have caught the full charge of the explosion.

Simon groped for the telephone.

'Duty Clerk – Duty Clerk, there's been a disaster in Russia. Please come up at once.'

He hoped that his voice had been composed. Normally in a crisis he had no difficulty in keeping composure by moving to the future, assembling in his mind what had to be done and who should do it. This time this drill did not work. Next of kin, statement in the House, reinforce or withdraw, talk to Altman – the pieces jostled in his mind, but incoherently. He had never felt so astray.

There, in the door, was an astonishing sight. Artemis was herself weary and dishevelled. If asked, she would have said that she had spent two hours since she left the restaurant wrestling with the draft speech for Antrim. For much of the time she had instead tormented herself with Frank's smile, stupid and wounding, as he roused himself beside his new girl from the Department of Transport. She still wore her blazing red dress, but inside she felt like a heap of ashes. It had been a relief to take over from the Duty Clerk the response to the Prime Minister's summons.

'Thank God, Artemis.' His recent irritation at her bluntness was long forgotten. He needed her. 'You've heard the news?' He saw that she had not. 'A disaster outside Petersburg. A Warrior blown up, several killed, perhaps more to come . . . but, watch it yourself.' He turned away from her into the bedroom towards the television.

The grey square looked at him, mocking and empty. It took him a second to realise what had happened, and another to grasp that he stood before Artemis trembling and naked, a white forked nothing. He stepped towards her and collapsed into her arms.

There were stages in what followed, but neither of them felt afterwards that either had been in control. It was Artemis who took off the blazing dress. They lay quietly side by side for some minutes, neither thinking of the other. It was he who began to kiss her breasts, and it was he who put a hand between her thighs. It was she who encouraged him to move on top of her. After that their movements became inevitable, bringing fulfilment rather than excitement. She felt Frank's power fade as Simon entered her, and was glad. He felt that by sealing this new companionship he could bring himself some peace. But his last thoughts before he slept in her arms were for the crews of those Warriors, for the time being still alive, their lives at risk.

Chapter Eighteen

Saturday November 22

Guy Freetown, wearing a sweater with holes at the elbows, was raking the leaves shed on the lawn by the walnut and the cherry that flanked the grey Cotswold farmhouse. More surprising, the Chancellor of the Exchequer was herself making tea in the kitchen. She had not, however, lost her desire to score first.

'I asked the police to ring in once you had passed Northleach,' she said. 'In that way I could make sure that the kettle boiled just as you came into the drive.'

Simon did not know what to expect from the next forty-eight hours. He had been surprised when the Freetowns had invited them to spend the last weekend of November at their farmhouse at Little Stourton. Louise could find no reason either for the invitation or for refusing it. Neither of them relished the combination of the Freetowns and the

English countryside in winter. Guy they knew distantly as a humdrum consort, Joan they knew too well. Until their talk at the Halifax Summit, Simon Russell had found her capable of striking one note only. She was a thoroughgoing politician of not quite the first class, her exceptional determination balanced by tactical ineptitude.

As for the English countryside, both Simon and Louise were city dwellers. The upper-middle-class English summer, with orderly herbaceous borders, marquees, chilled white wine and distant views of sunlit downs, was benign, particularly to visitors who did not have to worry about moles, the stable roof or the inheritance tax. But nothing in their upbringing reconciled them to bare woods, grey fields, rooms either too hot or too cold, and puddles under foot from October to April.

When they came to pack cases on Saturday morning they still expected that some compulsion of state, either for the Prime Minister or the Chancellor, would abort a weekend that did not fit into the pattern of their lives. But by now Simon wanted a break, somewhere that was neither Chequers nor 10 Downing Street, somewhere where neither Russia, Ireland, Her Majesty's prisons had been discussed, somewhere where Artemis had never been. Physically the tiredness and anxiety had for the moment receded. He remembered from his youth that making love could have this effect. He felt neither guilt nor any special happiness over what had happened in his bedroom on Tuesday night. Artemis had left him silently before it was light. Louise had returned a few hours later in good humour from her exhibition at Chequers.

They had heard nothing from Julia for more than a week, apart from the short note about Russia he had found in the flat the night before. It emerged that a young man had handed this to the policeman at the front door. In the car, speaking too low for the protection officer to hear, they worried together about her waywardness and whether she would in the end go to France after Christmas as she had agreed.

In short, life had resumed its usual pattern. If by making love to Artemis he had intended to break one relationship and form another, something more was clearly needed. The act itself was no more than haphazard, the coming together of an overwrought man and an overwrought girl – unless they now turned it into something else. But how? Or to be more precise, did he want to? Did Artemis? She had not been in the office since Tuesday, having rung to plead 'flu. Patrick had said that she had indeed seemed not quite herself at the restaurant on Tuesday evening. The Duty Clerk must have known more, but said nothing.

After a quick supper a fire burned erratically in the sitting room – real logs, spitting from time to time, unlike the decorous dance of the artificial flames in Downing Street.

'Bring your box down, if you like,' his hostess had said. So there they sat, short of conversation, in upright chairs on either side of the fire, Prime Minister and Chancellor of the Exchequer, each dipping into the red box, balancing a paper on their lap, annotating it in silence and setting it down on the opposite side of the chair.

'You're like two Victorian ladies at their knitting,' said Louise. She had finished the weekend sections of the Saturday papers. Guy was nowhere to be seen, busy no doubt with some household chore.

Joan Freetown, as if on cue, put back unread the bulky Treasury file she had just taken on to her lap. She cleared her throat, thus signalling that whatever might be the purpose of the weekend, it was about to be revealed.

'Perhaps we might have a little political chat?' She paused, but Louise made no move to leave the room. If that had indeed been Joan's hope, it was forlorn.

'Things are going quite well, it seems to me.' Joan got up and fiddled with the white-painted wooden shutters in the Victorian bow window. She wore a rather heavy Norwegian sweater in black and white wool, offsetting the black and silver of her own hair. She looked elegant but uneasy.

'The Budget was a triumph if that's what you mean,' said Simon.

'We got there in the end.'

'You got there by an immoral pact with Roger.' He spoke in banter, concealing his scar.

'You were refusing to help. I had to get those figures tied up.'

This was a gross misreading of recent history but Simon had no appetite to refute it. Where was this leading?

'You're looking well, Simon.'

'Thank you. I have my ups and downs.'

'What do the doctors say, Louise?'

Louise had put down her magazine. Joan Freetown was talking like a relative or close friend. She was neither.

'I think we are perfectly satisfied with what the doctors say.'

Simon, embarrassed but not surprised by his wife's tone, could see exactly what was happening. Joan Freetown had something important that she wanted to unload. It was weighing on her mind to such an extent that she was willing to speak even in the presence of Louise. She was searching for a way into the subject, whatever it was, but not finding it. Once again he marvelled that her formidable intelligence was hampered by a failure to handle human conversation. Supper had been a silent affair. The hours were moving slowly this weekend.

In the end she decided simply to spit it out. Her body language relaxed. She stopped fidgeting, the words came fast, like a stream that has found its way through a dam.

'I'm glad you're better. I know you worry yourself sick about Russia. I'm sorry about that. Maybe I was wrong, maybe I was right. It's not a huge matter, we can pull the force back if the cost becomes unmanageable. I had to get my Budget in order. You can see now that I was right.'

The Prime Minister saw nothing of the kind. Realising this she plunged into her main theme.

'You'll have to retire some time. We all have to choose the moment. I'm sure you'll choose it right. It's better to go when some people, many people, are still pressing you to stay.'

She paused. Simon said nothing. He saw no reason to make this easy. She plunged on.

'I'm not saying that you should go now. You'll want to choose a moment when things are going quite well. This is one of them, but of course there will be others. And anyway it is certainly not for me to advise you or press you.'

Another pause, more silence.

'Because – and this is what I wanted to say, Simon – when the time comes, whenever the time comes, I will want to take your place. I think I'll be the best qualified to lead the Party and Government.' She ended almost defiantly, as if expecting disagreement.

'You would certainly be well qualified,' said Simon.

'Would you support me?'

'I expect I'll be in my grave by then.'

'Then you're going on?' But she did not finish, worried that he was teasing her.

He did not know if he was teasing her or not. The weariness he had shaken off returned to envelop him. He tried to think of a way to bring the conversation to an end. But Louise cut in sharply.

'Did you invite us here, Joan, to ask Simon that question?'

'Of course not. Guy and I are delighted . . . after all . . .'

At that moment Guy pushed open the door, carrying a basket of logs. Whether or not he sensed tension in the room, he broke into the conversation at once.

'Have you told them our guilty secret for tomorrow night?' he asked his wife.

'I have not.'

'Julia, your Julia, is coming to supper. Not a party, just Julia. I hope that's all right.'

Louise let pleasure follow surprise across her face, before it returned to its usual expression of handsome crossness.

'Of course it's all right. How on earth did that happen?' asked Simon, also pleased but less concerned to hide it.

'Oh, I met her one evening. A few nights ago, in fact. By accident. We got talking. I told her you'd be here, invited her, she accepted.'

'But where did you meet her?'

'At a rally – one of those rallies for Russia, in fact.'

'What on earth were you doing at a Russia rally?'

Guy placed a log carefully on the fire.

'Curiosity, just curiosity.'

The spare room, at the top of the house, contained several uncertain buzzing flies, roused by the onset of central heating. Simon bumped his head on the lintel leading down two steps to the bathroom. He liked old houses only when they were large. The Freetown house was not large. Lying on his bed after washing in tepid water, Simon watched Louise undress with a sense of unease. He wondered whether he any longer had the right to see his wife with no clothes on. He pushed the doubt aside as unworldly. He had made love to his Press Secretary. He probably would never again make love to his wife, or indeed to his Press Secretary.

Louise was and would continue to be his wife. The woman who worried about him and cared for him, whose habits and expressions he knew intimately, even if he no longer noticed them. To her surprise he roused himself from his bed, crossed the narrow divide between them and kissed her on the forehead.

Back between his own sheets he thought about retirement. Three hours later he woke from a deep sleep and thought again about retirement. An owl sounded in the old yew outside their window.

Night in the countryside was particularly lonely.

Joan had been right, damn her. There was never a tidy close to the work of a Prime Minister. It was a ragged job, with loose ends at the close of each week, each month, each year. He did not believe that either Joan or Roger would be as good at the job as himself, but this was probably the prejudice of the old against their successors. Simon had learned never to take important decisions in the small hours, when the darkness increased fears and diminished judgement.

'Lighten our darkness, we beseech thee, O Lord.' The fragment of the liturgy for evensong came back to him. In the days of Cranmer's Collect they would have crept about this house with candles. They would lie awake listening to mice in the wainscoting, worrying about the devil and damnation, about weak lungs and blood on the handkerchief, about the rent due on Lady Day. He remembered

Russia, but turned his mind away from it and from the rest of the heap of worries that he carried through daylight hours as the invisible burden of a Prime Minister. There was no doubt that nowadays his shoulders carried that weight with greater difficulty. Inside himself he was becoming bent and stooped. Set it all aside till the morning, but in the morning he must think again about resignation.

The Lord was not in the earthquake, nor in the fire, but in the still small voice. Or at least that was what Guy read from the brass eagle on the lectern. The vicar, slightly flustered at the unexpected presence of the Prime Minister, preached on the same text. He had previously prayed with pessimistic emphasis for the spiritual well-being of those set in authority under the Crown. Simon deduced that the man probably voted Liberal. Simon did not listen to the sermon. He was not quite sure why he had come to church at all. The still small voice eluded him, even here where 'the kneeling hamlet drains the chalice of the grapes of God'.

He felt humble not in the presence of God but before this simple past, so different from the bustling Victorian church in Hampstead to which his father had taken him in distant childhood. He set himself to think about resignation, but the arguments did not organise themselves in his mind. He needed a pen and paper to set them down in neat pros and cons. Instead he counted the twelve children, praying in stone, of Jas Trinder, gent of Little Stourton in the county of Gloucester, departed this life in the year of Our Lord 1695. Eight of the children died before their parents. Guy had whispered that at Easter they put a posy in each small pair of praying hands, primroses for the boys, violets for the girls.

'His disconsolate widow erected this monument to his memory, but his virtue and pyety hath raised him one more rich and durable in the hearts of all that knew him.'

A sort of peace came to the Prime Minister. It was good to find time to notice small things. 'Rich and durable'. Durable was a sound honest word. The monument was too big for the space on the wall into which it had been crammed – no doubt by Victorian restorers. The chancel stood at a slightly different angle from the nave, presumably because one medieval generation had despised the effort of its predecessor to find the true east.

Back at the house the two women were happily bustling, Louise restored to good humour by the domestic tasks Joan had asked her to share. A cook had been hired to prepare lunch for ten, but he needed constant supervision. Joan had long ago mastered the political content of the Sunday newspapers, piled high by the renewed fire in the drawing room. Louise was busy polishing already bright glasses. Guy disposed of his prayerbook and went down to the cellar to choose claret.

There were, of course, telephone calls to answer. From Roger Courtauld, who was amused to discover that the Prime Minister was spending the weekend with the Chancellor.

'Hatching the next Budget, I suppose?' he began. There was a lull in the prisons following the release of the Governor of Gloucester. But the situation was still tense, and Roger was working to resolve a dangerous argument between Chief Constables and the Prison Service about the rules for police intervention inside a prison gate. 'I may need you to knock their heads together.'

Next from Peter Makewell:

'I would not have rung, but I had a message that you wanted to hear everything about Russia.'

'What's happening then?' Simon could not prevent the tension forming in his voice.

'The news is that nothing has happened. Some sporadic firing ten miles south of Petersburg, nothing serious.'

'None of our people hurt?'

'That's for the MOD to answer. But as I understand it, the Finnish advance party handled the incident. They persuaded the local Brassev commander to pull out a couple of snipers. Our group was not involved.'

'Their ultimatum expires on Tuesday.'

'At midnight. Jenkins in Moscow reports that Brassev may be having second thoughts.'

'But how can he get himself off the hook?'

'Jenkins hears he may propose talks with Dobrinsky. Probably in Minsk.'

Simon suppressed a surge of relief. The Foreign Secretary stepped into territory that he usually avoided. 'Don't worry about it, Prime Minister. It'll work out all right.'

'I don't worry.' Not true, of course, as they both knew. A pause. 'Thank you, Peter.' A decent man. He had chosen well to put him there.

Last, from Artemis. She started the conversation in a voice just a shade higher than normal. It was her only concession to the recent past. Simon, who had not known what to expect, felt a quite different sense of relief.

'I'm sorry to bother you, Prime Minister, but *Panorama* have come up with a request for tomorrow night. An extended programme, forty-five minutes, an interview with you alone.'

'Amazing, what's come over them, Artemis?'

'They say they want to take stock of the whole political scene. You've had a particularly active time, they say, the country would like to hear from you before Christmas.'

'The real reason?'

'Falling audiences, ambitious new producer, football on the other channel.'

Simon chuckled. This was the real Artemis, professional to her fingertips. He banished a thought of her, long and shadowy, stretched beside him in his moment of despair.

That was the past. They would both bury it. That was suddenly clear.

'Your recommendation?'

'I think you should do it.'

He could use the broadcast to announce his resignation. One of the pleasures of the job was the occasional power to surprise the world. This could be his last surprise.

But of course he had not yet decided.

'The interviewer?'

'Paxman. He's getting on now, of course, but still good.'

'I'll do it.'

Lunch passed smoothly. The wife of the High Sheriff and the wife of the property developer from Cheltenham on either side of him found the Prime Minister courteous but somewhat silent. They gossiped across him, and he occasionally threw in a comment. They assumed he was distracted by Russia or the prisons or Ireland or the coming *Panorama* interview of which he had told them. Being married themselves to busy men they knew the signs, and were not offended.

Then the whole lunch party walked round the village, briskly because of the cold. Simon fell a little behind the others, thinking now of what he should say to Julia when she joined them that evening. But once again his thoughts refused to coalesce into a coherent decision. Was he getting old? Or just tired? He felt physically well, his back hadn't ached for several days, the Sunday papers were not too bad, Russia was quiet, he would soon see his daughter again.

Guy slowed down to join him.

'Did Joan talk to you last night?'

'You mean . . .'

'About wanting to take your place when the time comes?'

'She did.'

'I'm sorry.' Guy slashed a thistle with his walking stick.

'No need to be sorry. She put it well. It's entirely legitimate.'

'It won't happen.'

'Won't?'

'Two reasons. It's a leap too high for her. She can run the Treasury, not the country.'

Simon did not want to comment. He agreed, but it was not a matter for him. 'The second reason?'

'You have to go on.'

Simon looked around him, relishing the power to notice small things which had come back to him in the church. The windless afternoon was without character, as if there was no weather. The heavy grey sky seemed permanent, pregnant with neither rain nor snow nor frost. It hung low over the trees, which were almost bare now, except where an oak clung tenaciously to curling brown leaves. The only colour came from the hips and occasional holly in the hedgerow down which they walked. Sometimes a wren or sparrow dipped silently through the thick hawthorn. The only noise came from a pheasant clucking itself to roost. This was, Simon supposed, the true England which he hardly knew, any more than he knew Guy.

'Why do you say that?'

'You bring humanity to politics. You are not a machine. You understand.'

Simon was genuinely surprised. 'Most people say the opposite. Most people think of me as scheming, even devious, without principle, a politician through and through.'

Guy said nothing.

'Anyway I am getting old, and have been ill. I need time before age and illness catch me.'

'You have no right to that time.' Guy spoke sharply in a way Simon had never heard. 'Priests cannot stop being priests because they are old or ill. They cannot shuffle off their vocation. Nor can you.'

'That really is nonsense, Guy. A politician is not a priest.'

'You are a servant. That is the similarity. You have chosen a despised profession and brought to it gifts that you cannot pass on. The good servant cannot lay down his burden.'

'He must carry it until it crushes him?'

'If he lays it down, he will at once be crushed. Can you imagine yourself snoozing in an armchair, lecturing on cruise ships, following Louise round picture galleries, tottering up the aisle week after week at memorial services?'

Simon could imagine all this easily, even pleasantly. 'The old find that their horizons shrink quite naturally. I shall not fret for telegrams, summit meetings, Cabinet disputes, all the rest of it.'

'You do not know yourself. Work is your life, your food, your purpose.'

It was an extraordinary conversation. The two men had stepped out of their roles. Guy had always seemed deeply non-political, even anti-political. Simon realised now that Guy kept his wife sane by insisting on a private life for them both here in this remote Cotswold village. Yet he was pushing Simon back into politics, trying to bolt the door of escape for a man whom he hardly knew.

'Time to go back, I think.' Guy became again the solicitous host. The dusk thickened around them. Within fifteen minutes they were back at the house. The lunch guests declined tea, made farewells, climbed into cars. Julia would be there within an hour, or perhaps a little more. Simon took a cup of tea and a toasted muffin. Then, having climbed the stairs to their bedroom, he opened one of his weekend boxes. He admired again the skill with which Patrick had arranged the contents. Artemis would send down some briefing for the *Panorama* interview by special messenger. All was in order. Next week would follow this week, just as Guy had decreed. Louise would preside over Christmas at Chequers. Service would continue. The important thing now was to think about Julia and her future. He could do that lying on his bed, and perhaps snoozing a little. He drew the curtain and shut out the last grey glimmer of daylight.

They found him an hour later, his expression surprised but serene, as if he had done nothing to resist the final attack. The red box of unfinished work lay open beside him on the bed.